TO: VIC...

C. Lymari *(signature)*

A TWISTED TALES NOVEL

GILDED CAGE

C. LYMARI

www.clymaribooks.com

Editors: Heart Full of Reads Editing

Cover Design: Pretty In ink Creations

Proofreading: Jennifer Mirabella, Becca

❀ Created with Vellum

ALSO BY C. LYMARI

DON'T BE AFRAID OF BREAKING
SOMEONE'S HEART IF IT MEANS
SETTING YOURS FREE.

AUTHORS NOTE

Hi guys! If you've read my books before. You know the deal.
If you are new to me, this is a dark romance that deals with
triggering content.
I ask you to be patient with these two characters and their
stories since they are broken in different ways.
Now allow me to tell you a fucked up fairytale.

ONCE UPON A TIME

THERE WAS A GIRL WITH HAIR LIKE GOLD. SHE WAS
SUBJECTED TO THE CRUEL OF THIS WORLD.

FOR SHE WAS NO PRINCESS, BUT A MERE PAWN. HER
BEAUTY SOMETHING OTHERS SOUGHT.

IN THIS WORLD SHE DIDN'T KNOW WHO TO TRUST.
BECAUSE TO THE CRUEL PRINCE SHE DIDN'T WANT TO
BELONG.

THIS MADE HER CALLOUS AND COLD. THE ONCE NICE GIRL
TURNED INTO A MONSTER ON HER OWN.

SO SHE STRUCK A DEAL WITH AN UNSUSPECTING
KNIGHT-BUT THEY SPOKE IN RIDDLES, DECEIT AND LIES.

BECAUSE NOT EVERYTHING THAT GLITTERS IS GOLD
SOMETIMES IT'S SOMETHING MUCH WORSE...

PART I

INNOCENCE

WE WERE JUST CHILDREN WRAPPED IN IGNORANCE,
WHO WERE ABUSED AND LOST THEIR INNOCENCE,
WE TRIED SO HARD TO HOLD ON, BUT THE MAKESHIFT
WORLD WE HAD COLLAPSED

PREFACE

Sooner or later, we all ended up on our knees. Whether it be to beg God for mercy or to suck the devil's dick.

My devil was as handsome as he was cruel. He was the king of the underworld, and I had been running from him since I was nineteen. I used to have it all. I was the queen of the Upper East Side. The one everyone wanted to follow.

Maybe being up so high in the sky made me forget where I came from. When I was a little girl, my family used to work for the Stiltskins. My parents were bound to them by a contract that spanned over centuries. This was modern slavery at its finest. There was an elite group of families that called themselves Orden Infinite. Or Infinite Order. It started as an elite group of wealthy families that followed what the monarch said back in the day. When they traveled to America, they rebelled against their king and became their own rulers.

They had power that spanned generations—their reach went from coast to coast—across all seven continents. You couldn't run from them. I was born to one of the working families. My fate had been decided the moment I had been born, but the families of the order did not count on the cunning ways of my parents.

They were tired of being oppressed, so they turned their daughter into gold.

I was alone in my golden castle.

A queen to an unwanted throne.

I was nothing but a liar.

A cheater.

A traitor.

A lying bitch.

And a cunt.

You got a more degrading word to call me? Say it; I've been called all that and more. My skin was forged into impenetrable steel. The words that used to cut me deep don't even scratch the surface anymore.

I once fell in love with a boy and married his enemy. I can't complain about my life; I'm simply lying on the bed I made for myself. A bed of lies and deception with my own misery keeping me company. But is a lie even a lie when you've said it for so long that you start to believe it?

The thing about lies is that they always unravel, and it's always at the last moment. You could run from anything but the truth. Sooner or later, it was bound to catch up with you.

I looked up at my reflection, and it was the first time in a while I recognized myself. One should not cast their pearls before swine.

Hair like gold.

His voice mocked me. I could feel the rough timbre in my ears, causing my body to break out in hives. The media had compared my gold hair to strands of gold. Now, after being on the run for a few days, it was all greasy and dull.

Eyes like whiskey.

Even in the worst moments of my life, he followed me.

My eyes were red from lack of sleep and the tears I refused to shed. I was not going to feel sorry for myself because I had only myself to blame for being where I was today.

My cheeks were starting to hollow; my face lacked the glow I was supposed to have, and every time I closed my eyes, I saw those stupid pink lines saying I was pregnant.

The only problem? The baby didn't belong to the man I married but to his sworn enemy.

Mason Stiltskin was going to cash out on the favor I owed him.

"I'll do this for you, Aspen." He looked at me with a mix of love and regret, and I didn't dare break under his stare because I was tired of living like the other half. I was tired of eating people's shit. His cold fingers grasped my chin, and he forced me to look up at him. "In return, you'll give me the thing you love the most."

Back then, I didn't think much about my promise because I came from nothing, and there was nothing Mason Stiltskin could take from me.

Except he did.

He took it from me on what was supposed to be the day of my wedding. He tainted what should have been the happiest day of my life.

I was now pregnant with his child, and before he came to collect me, I ran.

I came from nothing, and it was time that nothing I became.

ONE

SIXTEEN YEARS OLD

My parents were arguing again. It wasn't something out of the ordinary, though. We were birds stuck in cages set by our forefathers. I ignored them and continued to study my history book.

I always found history so funny. How people blindly believed words that were printed on a piece of paper. Words that had been sugar-coated to hide the truth about the world we lived in. No one talked about modern-day slavery —how we became chained to credit bureaus and capitalism. I mean, those people were lucky they at least had a chance to succeed.

My family would never have an opportunity like that because our forefathers signed a contract in blood, ensuring our survival. Stupid fools thinking that their lineage was more important than our freedom.

"What do you want me to do, Lisa?" my father shouted at my mother. "It's not like I can say no when she calls me over."

My mother huffed in annoyance.

My father's face was grim. He was not as tall as the master of the house, but he hovered over my mother. His hair was a shade darker than mine, and his eyes were light brown. All in all, his features were considered symmetrical.

Now, my mother was slim, and it made her look taller. Her hair was a yellowish blonde, and her eyes dark. She could have been beautiful if it wasn't for her constant frowning. She was tired of the way we lived, knowing there was a world out there that we would never get to see.

Maybe I was foolish to ignore the said world and instead chose to be content with what I had. What was the point of wishing for something that could never be yours?

I picked up my textbooks and made my way outside our living quarters toward the back yard. It was late enough that no one would be outside, and I wouldn't cause discomfort to our masters if they saw me.

The gardens in the Stiltskin house were gorgeous. Twinkling lights all around, with high bushes that cocooned the back yard, flowers that spanned from wall to wall, and a beautiful golden fountain.

It was a shame no one ever used them unless they had parties, but they have not hosted one in a long time. The fresh Vermont air hit me as soon as I stepped foot outside, and I hurried to the small round table. I could work in peace here. I was a slave to this house; a change of scenery was nice.

As soon as the table came into view, I halted. Sitting down was the young master of the house. Mason "Mase" Stiltskin. His face turned around to look at me the moment he heard me coming.

I swallowed even though my mouth had run dry.

Mr. Stiltskin was a kind man, or so he seemed. He wasn't like some of the other founding family members. He spoke to us with respect. His wife, on the other hand, was a little haughty. She screamed high class and oozed sexiness. As for their only child—well, what could I say about him?

For being born to genetically blessed parents, he wasn't much to look at. He was short, about three inches shorter than me. His hair was cropped so close to his head he might as well be bald. Maybe if he smiled, he would look better, but there was always an angry scowl on his face. Still, there was something thrilling about seeing him. Maybe because he was the only other person of my age in this place.

"I'm so sorry, Master Stiltskin," I said in a rush as I bowed to him, hoping that this incident didn't have ramifications on my parents. I didn't need to add to their troubles. They managed that all on their own.

"I'm not my father," he said in a cool tone. He was already a sophomore in high school while I was a freshman.

Not like it mattered since we didn't go to the same school. He went to the fancy private school, while I had to be homeschooled since the nearest public school was too far for the bus to pick me up, and there was no way my parents could take me. They didn't know how to drive. Only the chauffeurs of the family learned how to do so, and we had no need for that.

"Sorry..." I said again, taking a step back.

"Sit," he commanded at the same time.

I instantly stopped. Fraternizing with him was strictly forbidden.

"I said sit down," he repeated, annoyed.

Slowly I made my way to the table. I hesitantly put my book down, aware that his eyes were on me. As soon as I sat down, he got up, and I started to panic. If anyone saw this, it would be bad.

The lights behind us turned on, and that didn't ease my

worries. At least in the darkness, we were obscured from view.

Mason Stiltskin pulled out the chair and took a seat once more.

"What are you waiting for?" He tapped the table. "Study."

I took a deep breath and opened my book, although it was hard to concentrate since I felt him staring at me.

"What grade are you in now?"

"I'm a freshman," I replied, without looking up from the book.

"Do you like your school?"

I stopped pretending like I was getting any work done. I was a lonely girl deprived of friends, and he was the first person around my age I'd ever talked to.

With the new age, less and less servants had kids. It was a silent fuck you to the Orden Infinite for keeping them oppressed.

"My mother is in charge of my homeschooling," I told him while I shyly cast my eyes his way.

His hand was on the table, his fingers furiously tapping against the tiles. That's when I noticed there was blood on his hand.

When he saw that I was looking at it, he put it under the table.

"Do you hate me?" He turned his profile my way, and it was hard not to notice the magnitude of his presence.

My head shook furiously.

"If I were you, I'd hate my family, the damn Order," he went on.

It was at that moment that something inside me broke. Something that was already broken, but I repeatedly put it back together with hopes that it would just mend on its own.

Time didn't heal all wounds. Some things were beyond scarred and it was better to replace them.

"It's not your fault. You were born into this just as we were. With the only difference that you were born on the right side of the Order. You were blessed with a good last name."

He snorted.

"Would it be easier if those textbooks explained this? This lifestyle we all breathe and sleep." He leaned closer, and my gaze got caught on his jade ones. He had the prettiest eyes I had ever seen. Or maybe I was saying that because I had never been so close to anyone like him.

"You know why you can't leave?"

I didn't say a word, so he continued.

"You're oppressed by the same laws that keep the rest of us in power. Orden Infinite is something that is not talked about. That's why we can't just hire any simpletons off a newspaper ad. We risk too much exposure, and even if the press buys it or not, it doesn't matter. What does matter is the questions it would bring. It would cast doubt on all we do. We would go from socialites to terrorists in a second in the public's eyes."

I was holding my breath hearing him speak so idly of the Order. He didn't care if he was blasphemous; he kept going.

"Instead, we have all of you who know about us, our laws, and what we stand for, but don't have a dime to your name to do a thing about it. For generations, we have raised you like helpless children to make sure that you will never betray us."

And there staring right back at me was the reason why my parents were so bitter. Why they hated that we had colonized in America because the American dream would never be for us. We had been forced to live a life our ancestors wanted.

For a chance to flee the old country, they doomed us all.

"If it makes you feel any better, no one can escape their positions in this cursed Ferris wheel. Feel free to come here whenever you want."

With those parting words, Mason Stiltskin left. No matter how much I spied on the grounds to catch a glimpse of him, I didn't see him again.

I was too scared to ask my parents or the maids, but luck came when I heard the lady of the house talking about it as I got her bath ready.

He had gone abroad and wouldn't be returning for a year.

It was silly of me to be disappointed about it because Mason Stiltskin wasn't anyone to me. There was no reason to feel like I had lost something, so I just went on with my life like I always did.

Like it didn't matter that I was a slave to this society.

One Year Later

My eyes followed the movement of my parents' lips, but I wasn't comprehending what they were saying.

I was going to throw up.

"You should be grateful, Aspen. I would have killed for this opportunity at your age," my mom said in a snide tone that was full of jealousy.

"Why?" My brain was starting to hurt from all the over-thinking I was doing.

Why, after all of this time, was I being let out of the manor? Why were the Stiltskin going to let me go to school?

Nothing made sense.

"How did this happen?" I tipped my face to look at both of my parents. The thought of leaving terrified me, but I was thrilled. I couldn't breathe. To breathe air that didn't come from this place was a dream; I never had dared to dream.

Unlike my parents, I didn't like to torment myself with the what-ifs and could-bes if I wasn't chained to my masters.

"What about school? We have no money."

We had nothing to our name. The only reason why servitude families existed was that we got what we needed from our serving families.

We asked for our essentials, and they provided them for us.

Money was never given to us. The only reason I knew how money worked was because of pictures in my textbooks and basic math.

"Mr. Stiltskin has graciously agreed to help you," my mom said, sounding proud of herself.

My dad cast her a dirty look, and since being at each other's throats wasn't new, I ignored them.

"I...I need some air," I told them as I ran toward the gardens.

Why was the sudden thought of freedom terrifying me? Wasn't this something I had always wished for but never dared say it aloud?

My running came to a halt when I made it to the golden fountain. I leaned over it, breathing heavily as I clutched the golden rails and steadied myself so I wouldn't fall over. The breeze from the water cascaded on my face as a telltale sign that I was not dreaming.

"Thought you'd be happier to start school?"

That voice. It wasn't how it had been a year ago. It didn't sound as high-pitched anymore, but neither deep enough to confuse it for a man's voice.

I turned around and came face to face with jade eyes I hadn't seen in a while—Mason.

He had grown from the last time I saw him, but so had I. There were two inches of difference between us, but even though I was taller than him, there was no way I could ever look down at him. His face had more acne now than it had back then. No one would call him handsome, but there was something about him that called you to him.

"You're back," I breathed.

"I couldn't stay away longer, duty calls," he joked sarcastically.

"Did you not want to come back?" I cocked my head.

His green eyes were dull and sad, and I wondered what made him that way. He had it all; what was there to be sad about?

I didn't know much, but I did know the role each Order member played.

The Kings were at the top of the oil industry. The Astors in big pharma. The Waters family practically ruled the oceans. The Morgans had real estate worldwide, and the Archibalds had successful luxury hotel chains worldwide. As for the Stiltskins, they had old money from investing into their friend's endeavors like some of the other families, but their time to shine came in the 2000s when they became some of the new leaders in the cyber world.

So I couldn't understand why Mason looked like he didn't want anything to do with his family's money.

Instead of answering me, Mason asked me a question of his own. One that I had no business thinking about, not when my own parents refused to answer it.

"Have you ever wondered about your grandparents?"

"No," I lied.

"You're not a very good liar," he mocked.

"It's not forbidden for the lower class to have children. In fact, it's encouraged," he tacked on, and I felt sick. The way he spoke, I felt like cattle.

"Free servants," I spat through gritted teeth.

"Bingo," he said. "Then, once a pregnancy is announced, they send the grandparents elsewhere. Ensuring that no one else steps out of line or they get their loved ones killed."

I was going to throw up.

"Why are you telling me this!" I gasped.

Mason took a step toward me, and even though he didn't tower over me, I still shrunk in his presence.

He took a tendril of my hair and played with it.

"Your hair looks like strands of fine gold," he remarked as if he hadn't dropped a bomb on me.

Without thinking, I went to smack his hand away. I instantly realized my mistake. Mason didn't get mad at me; instead, he smiled.

"You're just like them," he said. "Your parents didn't care about what happened to their parents. I believe their words were: *Kill them all...*"

Unease spread through me. Bile rose up in my throat because what he said didn't surprise me.

"Back in the day, they would simply be killed, but good help is hard to find nowadays," he joked, knowing damn well that was not the case. "The only thing that would keep your parents in check is you, their darling daughter."

This confused me since my parents have never been affectionate toward me.

"For years, your parents have begged for my family to send you to school."

Something didn't add up, but I couldn't think on the why or how now.

"See you around, *Goldie*." Mason's words lingered in the air as he left, heading back to the house.

That was the moment that started my fucked-up friendship with Mason.

TWO

MASON

PAST

High school was hell on earth.

It was the first day back, and I would rather drink dirty sock water than be back here. What was the point of titles? They didn't mean dick when you died. Grabbing my leather backpack, I flung it over my shoulder, ready to get going to school.

Just as I went to grab my keys, my mother flung the door to my room open.

"Aren't you embarrassed, Hilda?" I said, looking at what she was wearing.

You'd never catch her in anything other than a designer gown with half her tits spilling out.

She glared at me.

The years were passing extremely fast for her, and she didn't like it. I was surprised she let the servant and her mother stay in our house when their beauty surpassed hers. Hilda Stiltskin didn't want anyone who was a threat to her youth on her premises.

"Your father said he's been trying to contact you all

weekend, but you haven't answered any of his calls." I gritted my teeth so I wouldn't snap at her and give anything away.

"Sorry, I've been busy catching up with my friends," I lied to her.

"Oh, yes." She waved me off as she lay in my bed. "How are Liam and Jason?"

I rolled my eyes. Figured she would remember those two phoneys. Number one and number two in the current Order standing.

"Great," I said. "I'll bring them over sometime."

She hummed her approval. I wouldn't bring them over, and she wouldn't ask again. This was just her pretending to care.

"Goodbye, Hilda," I said, trying to hide the urgent need to get away from my home.

"Honey," she said in a motherly voice that made me sick. "Don't befriend that blonde bitch."

My response was to slam the door in her face. Hilda was part of our family now, but she wasn't first in line to inherit her father's business —she wasn't my father's first choice either, but to her my father was a step up from marrying into a second branch. Being a Stiltskin made her part of the main core of Order Infinite members. She was in this relationship for power.

I was doing fine, but she had to bring it up by mentioning my father. I didn't realize what I was doing until I found myself in the bathroom. My breathing was jagged, and I felt like I was going to explode. I had so many emotions; I didn't know how to contain them, but one thing always helped.

It didn't ease the asphyxiating feeling inside me, but it gave me some room to breathe. I looked at myself in the mirror afterward, marveling at how the crazy look in my eyes had left. I quickly rinsed my hands in cold water and walked out.

My white Rubicon was waiting for me as I walked out the front door. The burning pain that I felt was the only thing that kept me grounded most days.

I was halfway to the school when I noticed a lone figure walking down the isolated road. This town was built by the rich. The only thing those entrance gates contained was scandals because no one was stupid enough to try and steal from us.

Without thinking, my jeep came to a stop.

The blonde girl that lived in my house looked at me with wide whiskey eyes as if she couldn't believe I was waiting on her. Well, that made two of us. The only reason I could think was that if I didn't stop, some *Order Infinite* asshole would stop, only to rape and discard her all before the first period. Technically, this servant girl was *my* property.

"M-m-master Stiltskin," she said as I rolled the passenger window down.

"Get in the jeep, servant girl," I told her as I moved my left hand from her view so she couldn't see the blood that had stained my wrist.

"I shouldn't," she said as she took another step.

"If you want to get raped, then go ahead, but whatever deal your parents worked out won't be hanging over their heads—not only will you wish you were dead, you will be."

Was I harsh? Maybe so, but the world was a cruel place, and she was naïve. She was safe at my house, but here in the real world, she was a lamb ready to be slaughtered.

She looked between the open road and me. I sighed, then unbuckled my belt, opened the door, and jumped out the Jeep. When I made it in front of her, she was looking at me with wide eyes. Without a word, I opened the door for her.

"Hurry, and watch your step," I instructed her impatiently. So far, no one had passed by, and I wanted her inside before anyone saw us.

Once she had climbed in, I closed the door and went back to my seat. No words were exchanged as I drove to school; she watched with wide eyes as Royal Infinite Academy came into view.

"Get out." I broke the silence as I came to a stop near some trees far enough away that no one would catch a glimpse of us.

Servant girl didn't flinch; she just nodded, exited the car, and walked away. This time, I wasn't trying to be a dick; I was doing her a favor.

I might be part of the Order, but soon enough, this servant girl would see just how highly my parents thought of me.

At the end of the day, it didn't matter; our names already dictated our path in life.

Once my car was parked, I stayed inside it until the first bell rang. I couldn't help but wonder how her first day of school would go. Everyone here was out for blood.

It had been a year since the last time I walked these halls, and a part of me had hoped I would change, come back a changed man, but that shit did not happen. I was the same short little fucker, but no one outside of the circle dared mock me.

With those inside the Order, that was a different story. They had free range on me. Were they really that bored that they got off on bullying me?

By lunchtime, everyone had heard about the new girl who had transferred into our school. It was expected, especially when you had the body of a model and the face of an angel. It wasn't hard to notice her beauty; I wasn't blind. But there was something else when you looked at her. Not loneliness but not anger either—either way, it fascinated me. Or I was just pathetic because she was someone I could have the upper hand with.

"Hey, Imp!" someone shouted that lousy nickname I hated. People giggled, and I walked over to the table where the rest of the Order spawns sat.

"What do you want?" I asked, sounding bored. At this point, correcting them wasn't even necessary anymore. All of them could think of me however they wanted, but as soon as we set foot in the real world and I took the reins for my father's company one by one, they would all kneel.

Liam King was sitting there like the king he thought he was. All the girls flocked him. He had the looks and the money, while I only had the money.

"Tell me, Imp, does servant girl suck good dick?"

His question irritated me more than I thought it would. I had expected their reaction to her, and I thought it wouldn't bother me, but I fisted my hands under the table. When my father told me she was coming to school—for a brief second, I got excited—thinking I finally had someone on my side. Stupid, right?

Liam got up, and I practically heard the self-centered floozies sigh at the sight of him doing anything.

He walked toward the center of the room and shouted for the whole cafeteria to hear.

"Hey, new girl, come here." He pointed a finger at the servant girl and motioned for her to come toward us.

Everyone in the cafeteria stopped what they were doing to watch the exchange. This nobody, new girl had gotten the attention of King himself and was invited to eat with his disciples.

They didn't know we were just playing a game our ancestors left for us.

Servant girl came up to us, walking timidly. She smiled shyly at me when her eyes found mine, but I gave her no reaction. Would she break under pressure?

"Hi." She beamed up at Liam. I didn't know if it was because she was an idiot and genuinely thought he wanted to be her friend or she wanted to fuck him.

"You're hot," he complimented her in a tone no different than the one he used on all the other girls.

I could see the rest of the girls at our table glaring at servant girl for taking the attention of prince charming. They didn't know that, unlike them, she was fucking doomed. She might know of our world, but she was the scum beneath our shoes.

Servant girl blushed, and I rolled my eyes. I didn't know why part of me thought she would be different. All women liked to use their beauty as power.

"Thank you," she whispered, looking up at him through hooded eyes.

"She's my property," I found myself interrupting their cozy exchange, and every single head at the table turned toward me. Fuck, why did I say that shit? "She belongs to my family," I added.

Liam and his friends threw their heads back and laughed.

"Did leaving make you forget your place, Imp?"

"If your dick is small, just say that, Liam." I got brave and talked back to him. I could have brushed him off, but I wanted to make him angry.

"Bathroom. Now." He glared at me and pointed to Jason so he could drag me along.

I knew what that meant, and I felt numb to it. By now, the whole lunchroom had gone quiet.

"Lead the way," I said as I got up. I didn't fear pain; I welcomed it, and at this point, Liam was doing me a favor.

Liam King smiled at me and dragged servant girl with him. Jason, Connor, and Erin all followed. I could only assume Erin was who Liam was currently fucking, and she felt like it gave her a right to be here.

We all headed toward the boys' bathroom by the locker rooms since it tended to be empty during classes. As soon as I walked in, Liam pushed servant girl to the corner and came for me. With his hands at the collar of my shirt, he pushed me against the wall.

"You want to say that again, Imp?"

"No one made you king, Liam," I spat.

His fist connected with my mouth. Pain radiated from my jaw, spreading to my cheeks.

Fuck, that shit hurt.

Servant girl screamed my name, and everyone laughed. I didn't dare turn to her, but I did look at her in my periphery. She was being held back, and she seemed genuinely concerned for me. Her brows were scrunched, her face a reflection of pain.

My attention returned to Liam, ignoring the feeling I got from knowing that she cared if I was hurt.

"Is that all you got, asshole?" I said, sounding braver than I felt.

The laugh Liam gave me was almost maniacal.

He ignored me for a second and looked at the servant girl.

"Come here, hot girl," he demanded as he motioned for

his friends to bring her over. When she was within reach, he touched her face. I wanted to snap his fingers and hear the bones break as I did so.

That feeling was coming back. The one I couldn't ignore that made me feel too much at once. Like my skin was crawling, and I was about to explode.

My breathing was jagged, and I focused on Liam and what he said to servant girl since I needed him to help me numb the pain.

"I know who you are," he told her. "Here, you are at my disposal."

Servant girl seemed to hang on to his every word to see if he could shed some light on this mess.

"If you want to succeed, you need to know that there's a hierarchy in this place, and Imp is at the bottom."

"She's my pet, Liam, not yours." The words came out before I could filter them.

Liam's head turned my way slowly, and I braced myself.

"Funny you should say that, Imp, because you're my pet."

That was the last thing I remembered before I blacked out. When I came to, everything hurt. Fire burned in my lungs, but for some reason, the floor wasn't cold.

"Oh God, you're awake." The voice was docile, concerned, but full of sweetness.

Gold—this girl was pure gold in a world full of fake diamonds. Her eyes were the kind that you could get lost in for days, and you wouldn't care. My head was on her lap, and I stared up at her trying to comprehend all the different emotions she was making me feel.

"You're...an...idiot," I hissed.

She smiled at me, and damn if it didn't blind me and make me feel warm inside.

"That's not the thanks I was expecting." She scrunched her nose, and somehow, I smiled.

"You should do what Liam wants if you want to survive this place."

A look I couldn't decipher crossed her face, but quickly disappeared.

"I might not have many privileges, but I can choose my friends."

My laugh quickly turned into a wheeze, but, man, how fucked up was this. Servant girl was going to be my first friend.

I didn't question it; and perhaps I should have, but I was blinded by beauty like all men.

THREE

GOING TO SCHOOL WAS NOTHING LIKE I HAD IMAGINED IT
would be. People were vicious—worse than animals. You
gave them some power, and they trampled all over you to
make themselves feel better.

My parents were over the moon due to the fact that I was
getting an education, so now, it seemed like their previous
fighting took a back seat. School was great, but I couldn't
help getting the feeling it was just the beginning of my
problems.

There had to be more kids my age that were in the same
situation as me, right? Why weren't they in school with me?
Or perhaps they were younger? There was so much I didn't
know about the world I lived in, and it scared me. My world
was so small, a tiny little cage, and anything that rattled it
shook me to my core.

My father walked into our room. His hair was messy.
There was red all over the collar of his shirt. I looked at him,
and he looked down at me.

"Go help your mother with the laundry," he demanded.

I put my schoolwork aside and walked out of the small

living quarters I shared with my parents. I understood that he wanted some privacy and something inside of me cracked. Was this any way to live?

My mom was in the laundry room, tears streaming down her face as she hand-washed Mrs. Stiltskin's delicates.

"Are you okay, Mother?"

Her eyes slid my way, and I took a step back. Her tears weren't out of sadness but out of anger.

"One day soon, this will all change," my mother spat.

There wasn't anything I could do or say, so I nodded my head because it would take a miracle for our situation to get any better.

"Go fetch the young Master's things," she told me.

Slowly, I backed away and made my way to Mason's room. My job was helping my mom with all her duties. She was the one who was training me, and lately, the cook had started giving me classes. Time didn't stand still, and they were growing older; someone had to take their place one day, and that someone was most likely going to be me.

What good was an education when at the end of the day, I was a ghost? My records were handled by the Stiltskins, and once I graduated high school, it would be just one sad memory of what could have been.

Mason had a whole wing dedicated to him. As I made my way down the hall that led to his living quarters, the doors opened, and his mother walked out.

I always thought she was beautiful and refined, but that moment when our eyes met, there was something else there. Something dark lurked deep within her brown eyes. She looked down at me, and her lips curled.

"You," she addressed me. "Do not make eye contact with my son. Get his shit and leave."

I bowed my head and ran past her. She hated it when

the servants spoke to her. I slowly opened the door to Mason's room and made a beeline for his hamper.

The moment I was in his room, I felt lighter; my stomach felt funny. His smell was everywhere, and it calmed me. Despite everything, Mase had a close relationship with his mother. She was constantly coming in here. So, I guess his close relationship with his parents is why he didn't care about what went down at school—he had his parents' love.

He was still part of the popular kids even if he was their punching bag, and I wondered why he didn't do anything to change his circumstances.

Just as I was picking up his clothes, the door on the far left opened and Mason walked out, followed by a bunch of steam.

"Ohmygod," I yelped as I took a step back. "I'm so sorry, Master."

He came out of the shower wrapped in a black towel. My cheeks flamed. Up until that moment, I don't think I ever thought about Mason as a guy. Sure, I knew he was a boy, and I around all the other guys at school, but they were all something pretty to look at. Pretty things weren't meant to be touched by my servant hands.

His face wasn't much to look at. It was harsh, full of imperfections and acne, but if you looked past all of that, you could tell he was going to come into his own. His body, on the other hand, looked like the male sculptures they had around the house. All perfectly chiseled.

"Call me Mase," he uttered.

"W-what?" I was flustered; I must have heard him wrong.

"Stop calling me master, and call me Mase."

My response was to nod. I didn't think it was possible for me to call him by his name. Scratch that, his nickname.

Warmth spread through me for a second when I realized he wanted me to use a nickname for him.

"You lose something?" He raised a brow.

I shook my head furiously.

Then my brain went back to why I had yelped in the first place. His skin was bright red, as if he was showering with scalding water.

"Aspen." The word came out harsh and demanding and I wanted the earth to swallow me whole.

"Colorado?" He raised a brow.

I felt so stupid.

"Excuse me," I told him as I took his things and ran out. As soon as I was out the door, I leaned back on it and sighed.

I didn't understand the feeling that was coursing through my veins, but I didn't like it. At the end of the day, I shouldn't feel too deeply or think too hard when I was just someone's property.

When I made it to the laundry room, my mother had already calmed, acting like nothing had happened.

"Can you finish his load? I need a break." She walked away before I could even say yes.

Blood. That's what I noticed the most on Mason's clothes. There was always blood on them, and I felt so guilty about how everyone treated him at school. Not that I kept an eye on him, but when he was around, I always knew where he was. Sometimes I wished I had a class with him. Would he be a real friend?

The thoughts I had were filled with sadness. If my masters knew I felt this way, I'm sure they would keep me locked up.

What made me the saddest was that Liam King treated

me, a servant girl, better than he did Mason, and I wondered why.

Sleep did not come easy that night. My parents had another argument.

"If the master asked the same from you, you would do it without hesitation," he told my mother.

I wasn't privy to what they were allowed to do, and I just wanted to stay in denial for a long time. Ignoring my parents, I went to sleep. The sooner they learned their place, the better all of this would be.

Every day I started out walking only far enough that no one in the estate would be able to see me get in Mason's car. Our rides were usually quiet with a comment here or there. It was easy being around him because, unlike everyone else, he didn't have an ulterior motive.

It was hard to talk to people when you were raised to look up to everyone. Especially when you knew you were at the bottom. I kept shifting in my seat, nervous to glance at Mason since I remembered his body. Most of all, I knew what his heart was like. It was beautiful.

"Something on your mind?" he asked as he drove us to school.

Maybe it wasn't wise of me to speak and say what was on my mind, but something in me told me to push my luck.

"Why do you let Liam treat you that way?"

Mason turned to look at me, and I felt the heat of his stare on my face. I immediately looked down and started to play with the hem of my uniform skirt.

"Look at me," he demanded.

Shyly, I lifted my head. Mason was gripping the steering wheel so hard his knuckles were white.

"You worried about me, Aspen?"

Two things had my stomach sinking. First, his soft tone;

but the second was the use of my name. This feeling was joy, something that I hadn't felt before.

"I mean, you're my master—"

"I'm just Mase, and you're Aspen." He cut me off.

Our gazes locked, and I couldn't help but smile. I was going to cry tears of joy. His answer made me feel human.

He stopped the car once we got close to the school, and I opened the door. Before I jumped out, I turned to look back at him.

"I don't like seeing you hurt," I told him.

This time Mase smiled, and it changed his whole face that I stopped breathing for a moment.

"Don't worry about me; once we leave this place, Liam won't touch me."

I didn't know what he meant by that and didn't want to intrude more than I already had. I started to close the door again, but he spoke once more.

"On the other hand, you're free-rein, so while we are in school, don't talk to me. It's better for you."

The walk to school didn't take that long. And now it made sense why Mase didn't speak much to me during school hours. In the stolen moments we had, it was as if he was someone else.

I was probably the only person excited to be at school every day because it was a privilege to step foot inside an actual educational institution. Even if I didn't get to do anything else, I would excel and not take for granted this wonderful opportunity.

"Hottie." I stiffened when I heard Liam's voice.

He made his way toward me and put his arm around my shoulders.

I hated when he touched me. All the girls glared at me.

"Hi." I smiled at him because he was my superior, and

one must never look at their superiors with anything other than content. In all honesty, Liam made me nervous.

"Did you hear? There's going to be a party at the Stiltskin's estate soon. You'll be there, right?"

My nod was slow because this was news to me. Either way, I had to be there. I was going to be the one who would be serving my classmates.

As soon as the last bell rang, I sprinted out of the school and made my way to where Mase would pick me up. This was my favorite part of the day. His Jeep was already there, and I halted because something was fluttering in my stomach.

"Are you okay?" Mase's concerned voice was right there, and I looked up, at a loss for words, but I felt my cheeks burn.

"Yes, sorry, cramps." My hand came to my mouth as soon as the words were spoken.

"That sucks?" There was confusion on Mase's face, and if I wasn't so startled, I would have laughed.

"Come on, let's get you home." He led me to his Jeep and opened the door for me. It was a little awkward having him attend to me but nice at the same time.

When I made it to the room I shared with my parents, they were both there and jumped up when I opened the door.

"I'm back," I said, startled.

"Good, you can help us finish our chores," my mother told me.

Right. Homework would have to wait. You'd think that they'd be interested in how my life at school was going since they were all over the idea.

"Um, is there going to be an Order party soon?" I asked, and my parents looked at each other.

"They haven't told us anything. Why do you ask?" my mom prodded.

"One of my classmates told me."

My eyes followed my dad's as he put something in his sock drawer.

"Who in the Order talks to you?" he asked, not concerned but with interest.

"Liam King," I told them, knowing how much power that family carried, and when my parents smiled, I knew they thought it was a big deal.

Too bad I didn't agree with them.

FOUR

MASON

My face was flush with the cold toilet as I heaved into the bowl, trying to get all the bile out. The white marble was stained red, and I couldn't bring myself to care. Red angry marks glared back at me as I looked down at my arms.

I thought being away for a year would make everything better, but I was foolish. You could escape your hell, but its scalding flames would always be there, ready to welcome you back with open arms.

As soon as I thought that I had gotten my shit together, all I had to do was look down and stare at the imprint of my dick that was tenting through my boxers and all those faint white scars that adorned my thighs, and I felt sick all over again.

Laughter erupted from my voice box, maybe because my body knew I needed another outlet other than spilled blood, and I refused to cry.

I don't know why I was surprised at what Hilda was up to. Money corrupted your morals, and hers had been tainted since the moment she stepped foot in this house. Not that I remembered when that shit was. My mother died when she gave premature birth to me. The Order didn't need useless things, and since the only thing she did was leave an heir, she wasn't spoken of again. Hilda came to be the perfect fit for my father—a young new bride for him.

After school, I was wandering the halls of the house, hoping that I would come across *my maid,* but what I did find was high-pitched moans that made my skin crawl.

My body was in a trance as it made its way toward the room from where the noises were coming from. The door wasn't properly closed; all I had to do was push it, and it opened. I could feel the pounding in my heart vibrating through my whole body, and my throat constricted from lack of air.

Sure enough, Hilda was there, but that's not all. She was with another man—or rather, the help. Her slutty dress was pulled so he could pump in and out of her. The top was bare as he feasted on one of her tits while he played with the other. Hilda's head was thrown back in pleasure.

I barely made it to my bathroom before everything started to spill out. Looking at her like that was something I never wanted to see. I already had enough—I didn't need to see that shit from another point of view.

Yeah, getting away from her hadn't changed shit; she just found other people to play with her when I wasn't around.

Being lonely made me feel like a pussy. I had all the money in the world; it wasn't fair for me to ask for more. My father was barely home, and my mother, well, she wasn't my mother at all. She was just my father's new wife.

After my tutor left, I made my way to my room and got ready for bed. Soon I would be in high school, and I was looking forward to the privileges that came from getting older. I could have my own car, and my father would give me a card to start managing my money better.

When I came out of my bathroom, I noticed my stepmom was in my room.

"Mom," I said the word that sounded strange even to my own ears. I typically only called her that during social events, because our inner circle knew how much of a farce they were.

She smiled at me and laid down on my bed. I never had a mother, so I didn't find it strange. "Come on, Mase, time for bed."

She patted the spot next to her, and I greedily went to her side. I didn't know what I was looking for—maybe some motherly warmth? I didn't care; I was finally being shown affection by one of my parents. I laid next to her, and when she wrapped her arms around me, I felt warm and longing.

I had never slept so peacefully. My mood had gotten better, school wasn't as bad. I think that's when Liam King took notice of me.

Despite his constant bullying, I didn't give two shits. His words were temporary; the countdown to the rest of our lives rested over our heads. He could no longer torment me like before because I now had something to hold on to.

I'm sure that's why he snapped. He needed me to submit to him. He wanted to prove that his family was still the one in charge. My family was dependent on the Kings' success for many years because our stocks were tied to them. My father changed that, and with the new age, he was sure to surpass them, meaning that Liam King would one day bow down to my name.

That first beating was the worst. I was thrown into a new world I had never wanted to be a part of. People like me were not meant to know pain. I'd never broken a bone, had a cavity, and rarely did I get stomach aches.

The school had to call my father so they could pick me up because I couldn't walk. I was so scared I smelled like my own piss. That's when I learned just how weak and frail my body was.

Liam nicknamed me "Imp" shortly after that.

My father was furious, but not on my behalf. He was mad I let "that little shit" get one up on me. I needed to learn how to man up, and he took me to my room and let me be. I wondered if my father ever had to man up? How could he so easily give me advice on something he had never done.

The maids had been instructed to not treat me any different. I was in pain, and no one cared. I kept gasping for air, and everyone around me kept on living like it was nothing. Bruised ribs were a bitch to have. By nighttime, my pillow was soaked in my tears.

I was pathetic.

I disgusted myself.

I was weak.

Then the door opened, and I hoped that my mother didn't shy away from me either. Relief flooded through my veins when she came toward me. She laid down on the bed next to me and wrapped her arms around me.

I couldn't help it and began to weep. I was such a pussy, but this feeling was new to me, and I wanted to bask in it.

"What happened?" my mom asked, full of concern.

"N-nothing," I hissed because I was afraid if she knew the truth, she would call me a pussy like Dad.

"My poor baby." Her words were soothing, filled with a mother's love, or so I thought.

My eyes were starting to flutter since I was tired, but they sprang open the moment I felt warm lips kissing my temple, so tenderly I thought I must have dreamed it. Mother's lips trailed down my temple to my cheeks down to my jaw, and I began to feel uneasy.

This was new territory for us.

We had only cuddled at night. She would tell me stories about when she was young, gossip about the other families, but she had never given me a goodnight kiss.

"Does everything hurt?" she whispered in a tone I had never heard her use.

Something was stirring in my stomach; it wasn't good because I felt cold, and the blanket and her embrace weren't doing a damn thing to keep me warm.

"I'm fine," I lied.

Now all I wanted was to sleep. I'm sure I was just tired and in too much pain, and there was no reason to panic.

I closed my eyes, trying to relax, when one of my mom's arms wrapped around my waist. Since one of the maids wrapped my ribs, I was in only my boxers. Even though her hands were delicate and smooth, her touch felt like sandpaper on my skin.

"I'll make you feel better," she rasped.

My head turned her way, but she was no longer looking at me. Her gaze went to where her hand made its way down my hip bone.

Just thinking about that memory made me heave. I had nothing in my stomach to even throw up, but my body still tried. As if doing so would remove all that shit.

In one night, she went from Mother to fucking Hilda, and I learned to yearn the pain because it took away from feeling the things she did to me. If I was in pain, it diluted the fucked-up pleasure she brought me.

When I convinced my father to send me away, I felt free, like I could finally be me, except she was always there in the back of my mind. She had taken all my firsts and tarnished them.

Now I was so fucked up I couldn't live without the pain. It had become my favorite clutch. That's why I welcomed the beatings Liam gave me because they made me feel relief, but also hated them because that's when Hilda wanted to come to console me.

FIVE

NEWS ABOUT THE UPCOMING PARTY SPREAD LIKE WILDFIRE IN the Stiltskin household. It had been so long since the Order had gathered at the manor. It was rather pathetic how all the staff, including myself, were looking forward to this event. We were like children denied affection. To see other people, even if it meant to kiss their feet, was something to look forward to.

My stomach churned, and I wondered if I was slowly turning into my parents. Had school started to fill my head with impossible ideas? No matter how much I wanted or tried, I could never be like the rest of them. I wished I would have stayed in my ignorant little bubble because the sadness I had inside of me was morphing into rage day by day, and it scared me.

Now all of us were lined up in the house foyer. Every single servant that was in servitude to the Stiltskins was present. The madam of the house made her way down the line without saying a word.

I made sure to have my head bowed. Something about the way she looked at me didn't sit right with me. Her gaze was too sharp and calculating. My hair was up in a tight pony because she commented about how the dull color disgusted her the last time I had it down.

My parents were next to me, but unlike me, they refused to bow. I wondered what went through their heads that made them act brave.

"As you all know, we will be having a party," Mrs. Stiltskin said in a haughty tone. "I want the house spotless. Every nook and cranny must be impeccable; polish all the silver and gold. I want them all to walk through those doors and die of envy."

Her statement made something inside of me crack. Was she enjoying waving it in our faces, something we could never have, and having the audacity to still want to have more when she already had the world at her feet?

"My husband is in the middle of a new launch, and he doesn't want to be bothered with your nonsense. Any questions about the party must be run through me."

"Yes, ma'am," we all responded in unison.

She stopped and looked at all of us, her gaze lingering on my father, then on me. Slowly she brought one of her hands up and started to remove her diamond ring. She extended her left hand and let it drop.

The noise the diamond made as it hit the floor pinged through the lobby. Everyone was quiet.

"You dropped my ring, pick it up," she demanded in a cold tone as she looked at me.

It took all of my self-control not to say anything back. I felt humiliated in front of everyone. They all looked at me and wondered what I had done to offend the lady of the house. I started to bend so I could pick up the ring, but she put one of her fancy heels on top of it.

"On your knees," she mocked.

My body was burning up—this is what it felt like to be so angry that your vision went blind. I looked at her as I kneeled, and only once my knees were touching the cold marble did she stop stepping on her ring. I remained kneeling as I gave it back to her. Mrs. Stiltskin smirked at me.

"You're dismissed." She waved a hand in the air as if nothing had happened. Roger," she called to my father, "I need your assistance."

I heard my mother's heavy sigh as she turned on her heel and left.

My father made his way to the madam, but he must have felt the weight of my gaze because he turned back to look at me.

"Go clean," he barked.

Something in his eyes told me he wanted me to get out of there. I made my way to the backyard for some fresh air, but I still couldn't help and look back. I saw my father following Mrs. Stiltskin, and he didn't seem to be bothered by it.

There was no privacy in this house—or anywhere. I knew the meaning of being lonely while being in a crowded room. I didn't know about the privilege of having my own room.

I had nothing.

I was nothing.

The backyard was full of people fixing the lights, shearing the bushes, polishing the fountain. There was nowhere to escape from this hellhole.

So I ran back inside, to a place I knew no one would dare touch at this moment because everyone was too busy elsewhere.

I would lose it all if I got found out, but I felt as if I was suffocating; I needed to fucking breathe.

The servants watched me go without a second thought as I smiled at all of them carrying fresh linens. For all they knew, the young master needed new bedsheets. God knew they had to keep changing his bedding regularly. Had the other maids seen what I had seen? Why wasn't anyone speaking about it?

My ears had gone deaf from how loud my heart was beating. Even if someone caught me in the act, I might not hear them. Only as I entered the threshold to Mason's headquarters did my treacherous actions hit me.

My feet shook, and my knees felt weak. This was the first time I had done something that was considered rebellious. Is this what it felt like to think for yourself? It was liberating as it was scary.

I walked deeper into his hallway away from the entrance and found the first room. The air seemed too thick here, but maybe it was just me. My body felt cold, and I couldn't believe what I had done.

For the first time in my life, I felt like I could sympathize with my parents.

Leaning against the wall, I brought my knees up to my chest and took steady breaths until I felt calm enough.

My life was spiraling out of control, and it terrified me.

I needed to get it together.

I hadn't done anything wrong. It's not like I betrayed the Stiltskins. Everyone had these thoughts, right?

The light from the outside illuminated the room. From what I could tell, it was some sort of game room. It had a luxurious wooden billiard table that shined, a poker table, and a bar stocked with liquor.

I straightened up, fixed my dress, and wiped the tears

from my eyes, so I could go back and rejoin the others.

"Is something wrong?"

I turned around when Mase's deep voice startled me.

Shit.

I knew we were sort of friends on school grounds, but not here.

"I'm sorry, Master," I said, flustered as I bowed down to him.

The cold pad of his finger touched my chin. Shivers went through my body, probably a reaction to the adrenaline of being caught.

Slowly he lifted my head so I could look at him. A light ray from the window illuminated his face, making his green eyes shine. They looked like jades—too pretty to belong to a boy.

I blinked furiously, trying to erase those thoughts from my brain.

"Didn't I tell you to call me Mase?" He gave me a half-smirk.

I was looking at him so intently that I noticed his face was starting to clear out. Not completely, but he didn't have as many bumps and rough spots on his skin.

"I'm sorry for intruding." I bowed my head again because I didn't know how to act around him right now, not after his mother reminded me of my place.

"Why were you crying?" He cocked his head as his thumb trailed up my cheek and wiped the remainder of a stray tear.

"Nothing important." I refused to meet his gaze again.

He hummed. "I could always make you tell me."

"I am your property after all." The words slipped past my tongue venomously.

I froze. This wasn't his fault. He had done nothing to me,

so it would be unfair to take it out on him. Slowly I turned my face his way, scared to see what I would find in his stare.

Mason wasn't mad, hell, he was smiling, but there wasn't anything sweet about it. Something was frightening about all those white teeth showing.

My belly dipped, and he took a step closer to me.

"Ahh," he said, amused. "You have realized your part in this play."

I didn't answer.

Back in the old days, my words would have cost me my head. I was nothing but a pawn to these people, and the truth was no matter how nice Mason Stiltskin treated me, I was never going to be his equal.

"I should get going," I told him when I couldn't stand the silence.

Mase blocked my path with a sly smile.

"Stay," he said. "It's an order."

Yeah, I got the feeling his mother wouldn't like that.

"Your mother is checking up on us."

He chuckled as he started to walk in front of me and pushed me until I was backed up against the wall.

"Hilda is going to have her fun first, and then she'll pretend like she's the lady of the house."

His comment irked me. I didn't like the way it rolled off his tongue. All I could think about was her with my father.

"Stop." I raised my hand in front of him almost pleadingly.

"Or what?" His tone was stern, and his body was almost flush with mine. I was starting to panic, so I blurted the first thing that came to my mind.

"Or I'll tell everyone about your bloodied laundry."

He lost the smirk and something dark passed over his eyes, but he quickly masked it. He put both hands on the wall on either side of my shoulders. "Maybe that's just what I like while I fuck…"

He enunciated the last word, and something in me dipped violently. If I felt like I was gasping for air before, I felt like I was suffocating now. I dodged from his hold and ran out to the hallway. I didn't stop until I made it to the laundry room. Without thinking, I went through the dirty hampers that belonged to him.

Everything had drops of blood.

Putting it back to its place, I made my way to the bedroom I shared with my parents. My cheeks were flushed.

My mother was in there, already pacing the room like a lion stuck in a cage. She seemed almost desperate.

"Oh, Aspen, you're back." She came to me and, for a second, I stood there startled, thinking she was coming to embrace me.

"Yes, Mother?"

"I need you to put this in your backpack and leave it in your locker."

My eyebrows scrunched when she pulled out a square device. I didn't know what it was. It was black and thin. It had a metal plate on the top, and the reverse side had a metal circle.

"What is this?"

"Nothing important, but I want you to take it."

"Mo—"

"Do as you're told, Aspen!"

Swallowing the lump in my throat, I took the device and put it in my backpack. My father walked in a while later, and my mom took one look at him and walked out. Family didn't have any meaning when you were a servant of the Order.

I was nothing.

And I never would be.

SIX

MASON

DEATH WAS PATIENT, AND SO WAS I.

My body ached as I roamed the hallways at school. I couldn't wait to get out of this shit hole and move far away from this place. I knew my leash would only go so far because sooner or later, the Order would summon.

Those who had no ties to the Order made their way out of my sight as I passed them, and the rest looked down at me.

Every single one of the Order girls thought that I was beneath them. They loved to call me Imp. Sometimes they liked to fuck Liam as I laid there on the ground. They moaned in ecstasy, and I relished the feel of the pain.

We were all just a little fucked up.

And those bitches loved to remind me that I was never going to touch them. Fine by me; every single one of them reminded me of Hilda, just with a little more entitlement.

I came outside behind the school so I could have my smoke in peace when I heard the distinct high-pitch, annoying-as-fuck squeak of Liam's voice.

"—that shit is ancient, Father. Are you sure we can trust it?"

I put the cigarette to my lips and sighed when the sweet smell of nicotine filtered through my nose.

"Yes, she's eating out of the palm of my hands," he bragged.

Once he was done talking, I lit up my cigarette and made my way outside.

Liam stopped when he noticed me.

"What the fuck are you looking at, Imp?"

I wasn't in the mood for his shit right now, so I ignored him. I had more on my mind than to enjoy the pain he brought.

He didn't like the fact that I ignored him.

"I asked you a fucking question!" he yelled at me, and the vein in his neck pulsed.

He really did have a superiority complex. Too bad for him, it would come crashing down when we entered the real world and took over our families' companies.

"I'm not in the mood for this," I said as I exhaled smoke.

He laughed.

"You do what I want, Imp," he mocked with a cruel smile. "Even if I ask you to suck my dick, you do it with no hesitation."

I turned my face to him and glared—if looks could kill.

Something told me he would do it just to prove a fucking point to me. I felt like I was going to be sick. I no longer saw his face but Hilda's. Her head bobbed in my lap, and I could feel her drool all over my lap.

Maybe I was a pussy, but I threw the cigarette away and ran. By the time I made it to the bathroom, I was panting, and I only allowed Liam King to see the weakness I wanted him to see. He didn't need to know any more of the shit that happened to me.

Let him think I was a weak little shit.

Little by little, my body was getting stronger. I could tell. My endurance was through the roof, and I knew how fucked up that was. Every single time, I had to provoke him more so that I could feel numb.

Or maybe Liam wouldn't care. Perhaps none of those assholes would either; after all, my own father did not give a fuck. In his eyes, I stopped being a little pussy and became a man.

I could still feel my old man's punch when I ran to his office the next day after Hilda helped me rub one out. He looked up from his laptop and told me to stop being a fucking pussy.

I was an embarrassment to him, and Hilda had free range to me.

Why was I so fucked up? Would Liam and the rest behave like me? Or would they take what Hilda gave and ask for more? Was I really a pussy?

Shaking my head of those useless thoughts, I walked back inside.

People were standing all around someone's locker. Aspen was breaking down in front of everyone. Her face was flushed, and she was crying. She looked cute. I was fascinated by her crying face, maybe because she kept her emotions hidden, and whenever this happened, they poured out without control.

When I saw the dean with her, I got worried. I knew Hilda didn't want me talking to her, and things around here had a way of spreading to everyone's ears, but I didn't care. I wanted to be there next to her. I wanted to hold her and comfort her. I wanted her to need me because I realized that

I also needed her. She made me feel better; she numbed me without having to rely on pain.

Before I could reach her, Liam made it first. He was full of mock concern for her. He took her into an embrace, and I was more startled than her because the stupid bitch let him wrap his hands around her when I hadn't done it first.

That should be me comforting her.

"What's going on?" I asked as I got closer.

"None of your business, Imp," Erin Waters told me as she looked down at me.

"Someone broke into servant girl's locker," Nate said as he nodded toward it.

It had "trash" spray-painted in red and her contents were scattered all over the place. I looked around to see if someone was watching with glee and if I could pinpoint the culprit.

Everyone had some sort of sick satisfaction at the sight. They didn't say shit to her because Liam had taken her under his wing, but they were just waiting for the moment he tossed her aside. This place was full of leeches that were ready for the moment you stumbled down. The world was a cruel place, and I had reached my limit.

I WAS COMING OUT OF MY SKIN, WAITING FOR ASPEN TO SHOW at the spot I picked her up. I wanted to make sure she was okay, to comfort her myself.

But Aspen never showed.

I was her friend, wasn't I?

My thoughts kept switching between being concerned for her and her safety, and feeling angry and betrayed because she wasn't with me.

As I pulled up to my street, I saw Liam's black matte G6, and it infuriated me. I floored it the rest of the way, and by the time I pulled up to my driveway, all I saw was a flash of her pretty blonde hair as she turned the corner to the maid's entrance.

Why was I so angry? It was fucking pathetic. I might have started to need her, but that didn't mean she needed me.

I walked into the house with rushed steps trying to make it to my room. I unbuttoned the tie that felt like it was choking me. As soon as I walked in the door, I smelled *her* perfume. It was high class, and it reeked of presumptuous wealth. It annoyed me, made me want to gag.

Sure enough, when I looked up, there was the bitch in my bed.

Hilda was wearing a nightgown. If it could even be called that. The material was so sheer you could see everything. Her legs were spread, a perfectly manicured finger between her legs, and she was moaning in my bed.

"Get out," I gritted, tired of her shit.

I was done with her, and Liam, and with my father.

She leaned up and smiled at me. She loved that she had the power over me. I hated her so much, and I wanted her dead. In fact, it was the only thing I could think about at the moment.

"Oh, honey, don't be like that," she kept on going as if I hadn't spoken. "You love me, that's why you keep coming back to me.

My blood hummed, and my ears were ringing. *I kept coming back to her?* She was the one who wouldn't leave me alone.

"You're the one who won't stop coming in here!"

She laughed.

"Was that a pun?"

I fucking had enough. My whole body was shaking and I felt cold. I was ready to walk out of my room—but why should I have to change my life because of her?

Why did I have to keep submitting? I was almost eighteen; I was no longer fourteen. Why did I let her control me?

I stalked my way to the bed, and once I was there, I dragged Hilda by her legs. She yelped in surprise, her eyes were wide, and I bet she was wondering what was going on with me. That made two of us. I was too irrational to think properly, so I couldn't come up with an answer.

"You want to get fucked, Hilda?" I said through gritted teeth.

She didn't answer me, and even if she did, it wouldn't have mattered. I flipped her. I was no longer the lanky kid she had consoled night after night. Somewhere along the way, I grew, and I just didn't notice. Hilda turned to look at me, and the moment she opened her mouth to speak, I finished loosening my tie and wrapped it around her mouth and tied it behind her head. I pressed her body down to the mattress, knowing that I was slowly suffocating her and making it hard to breathe.

"Is this what you wanted?" I hissed in her ear.

She muttered gibberish I couldn't comprehend.

Slowly I started to push up her nightgown. She was wet from earlier when she was playing with herself. Her body was stiff, she kept screaming at me through the makeshift gag, but I didn't care to make out her words.

I reached for my zipper, and my cock sprang free. I was rock fucking hard, and it had nothing to do with the woman in front of me. For the first time, I was the one in control, and that feeling was like nothing I had felt before.

"You like to fuck me so much. Let's see if I like fucking you."

She tensed up as soon as I spread her ass cheeks. She was dry as hell, and my dick was in pain, but the mere fact that she wasn't enjoying having her ass fucked made me want to do it even more.

I lost control, and somewhere along the way, her pleas became screams. Her body started to shake—she was terrified, and I fucking came.

When I pulled out, I knew I was never going to be the same.

"Get the fuck out," I ordered her before I went to take a shower.

Forget what I said.

Death could be patient, but I didn't have to be.

SEVEN

THE DAY OF THE PARTY CAME FAST. SCHOOL WAS A BLUR AFTER my little locker accident. I knew I wasn't going to fit in, but since no one said anything, I had deluded myself that I could make it work. Between getting the house ready for the party, my locker incident, and my last interaction with Mase, it had all started to chip away at my soul.

I lost the trinket my mother wanted to save, but she acted like she didn't care. Was it all a façade? Was she more like me than I had realized? Did we purposely lie to ourselves to not care about anything because the moment you got attached to something, it got ripped from your grasp?

The summer breeze scraped against my skin. It touched my cheeks like claws trying to cling to me. I closed my eyes and let them. I would be the barrier that stopped the wind from aimless wandering.

I hid in the shadows as I watched how one by one, everyone arrived at the manor. All of them dressed in their nicest suits and dresses, adorned with so many jewels that they could probably feed a third-world country if they sold them.

Meanwhile, I was wearing a maid's uniform. Nothing fancy, just a fitted black dress, with pantyhose and kitten heels. My hair was up in a tight bun that was starting to give me a headache.

It fascinated me how everyone arrived with their respective families. I knew I should get to work, but I was mesmerized. I couldn't stop staring at them. I felt uneasy, something turned in my stomach, and the longer I stayed out here to watch, the clearer it became I was full of envy.

Time to get this show on the road.

My thoughts were bitter, and I was afraid it was too late to turn back now.

I made my way to the kitchen, picked up a tray of champagne and then took a deep breath as I joined the party.

The way these parties were conducted, you'd think you were witnessing one of the world's greatest wonders. Idle chatter could be heard over the live music. Serving people who were older than me was easy. They didn't know me. Perhaps sending me to school had been a new way to humiliate me and put me in my place. Rich people liked to drink their champagne like it was water. I kept going back and forth between the foyer and the kitchen.

As I made my way down once more, I realized not once tonight had I seen my parents.

Was this their new way of rebelling?

"Servant girl." I felt an arm wrap around my shoulders. It was Jason, one of Liam's friends.

"May I get you something?" I didn't meet his eyes; I didn't even look up to him. Unlike my parents, I knew my place.

"You want to get out of here?" he drawled.

He took hold of my arm, his fingers digging into my delicate skin. I looked up at him with my mouth open. None of the older kids had touched me before. Not like this. Except for Liam, but since he was their unofficial leader, I thought it was best not to provoke him.

"I'm working," I hissed.

He looked down at me and smiled. One of his hands came to my face and touched my cheek. "Your job is to take care of whatever your master needs, isn't it?"

My stomach dropped, and my blood ran cold.

"I need to go," I said, trying to sound sure of myself.

He kept on going as if he hadn't heard what I said.

"I wish I would have had a maid as hot as you, then all my needs would have been met."

My eyes widened.

Maybe I was still ignorant because nothing like that had crossed my mind. From what I knew, no one here at the Stiltskins' house had been raped. I guess there were still things much worse out there.

"Come on." He started to drag me away.

I couldn't make much fuss because I still had some champagne on the tray. I was torn between causing a scene or following quietly and then thinking of a way out once we were alone.

"Having fun?"

The question came from the person who blocked Jason's path. I looked up to see who had stopped him and if they would be of any help or not.

Liam King stood there, looking more arrogant than ever.

"Let her go, Jason," he said in a dismissive tone.

I held my breath, hoping to God someone called me for a refill, or another maid intervened. That was unlikely since no one would come between a servant and a master.

"Why should I?" Jason asked with defiance.

Liam leaned into Jason and whispered something in his ear. Jason snickered and then let go of my hand.

"Thank you." I bowed my head toward Liam, wishing I didn't have to. I bit the inside of my cheek to see if that would help me look more sincere. I didn't want to have to bow to any of them anymore.

Liam lifted my chin with his index finger.

He smiled at me, but his eyes were vacant, and the unease I felt moments ago came back with a vengeance.

"You look delicious tonight, ready for me to devour you."

Liam didn't say more, he just walked away, and I was left with a sick feeling in the pit of my stomach. Whatever. I shook my head and walked back to the kitchen. I left the tray on the counter and took the corridor that led to the servant's entrance. I needed some fresh air. The party had just begun, and I was already over it.

The smell of tobacco hit me the moment I opened the door. I already knew who it was before I saw him. Mason leaned against the wall as he took another drag of his cigarette.

"How's the party?" he asked, even though I had a feeling he didn't give two shits about it. Or maybe he was trying not to make it awkward since our last conversation had not ended on a good note.

I'd been so busy I didn't stop to think about the fact that he no longer waited for me. I guess I was expecting that. He didn't owe me any favors, and I shouldn't have been riding with him in the first place.

"Everyone's there already."

He snorted.

Everyone else could pretend like they gave two shits

about Liam and the Order, but with Mase, I actually believed it.

"I should go back," I told him because things were still awkward, and I shouldn't forget where I stood with him. He made it clear this past week just how little my friendship meant to him.

"Wait," he spoke, and before I could open the door, he took hold of my hand and pulled me back toward him.

My back hit his front.

My heart started to strum furiously.

"Aspen." His words were low. "I'm sorry for what I said to you."

I turned my head so I could get a look at him, but it was useless. The lighting on our side of the house was down. Or probably the masters didn't want it on while they had such an important event.

"It's fine," I told him.

"You're lying, but that's okay. That's all everyone knows how to do, right?"

He wasn't wrong. People spoke in riddles. The truth was in between the lines. You just had to look for it.

"What is it you want most in the world?" His question caught me off guard. Why was he asking me this now?

"Nothing," I rushed out.

"You're lying again," he said sadly.

"I need to tell you something and you need to listen to me, even if it's for the last time." There was something almost desperate in his tone. Before I could turn to face him once more, he turned my whole body so we could face each other.

Through the darkness, I could make out some of his features. He was shorter than me by an inch, something I know he despised. It was evident in the way he looked at me.

"Meet me by the fountain at midnight," he said.

Guilt assaulted me because he sounded sincere, but according to my parents, I would be busy.

"Please," he pleaded, his breath fanning my skin. "I need you there, Aspen. And I'm going to ask you the same question again, so trust me..."

For the first time, someone was begging me, and it didn't make me feel better, it just made all my broken pieces shatter.

"Okay," I whispered so he didn't hear the lies that came off my tongue.

"I should go now." I tried to pull back, but he didn't let me.

One of his hands wrapped around my waist while the other cupped my cheek. He smelled like nicotine, gasoline, and his cologne. My skin started to tingle. Before I could process anything, his lips touched mine. They were chapped, and they prickled against my soft ones. The kiss wasn't supposed to mean anything—it couldn't. But a selfish part of me took it because I also needed to leave an imprint of myself on him.

He deepened the kiss, and I let him.

Mase was the first to pull back. I could hear my heavy breathing, and it embarrassed me.

"This is important to me, and I want you to have it," he said as he took my hands and wrapped a chain around it. It was thick with a lot of little squares. "Take care of it, okay? And midnight, don't forget." With those parting words, he left me.

I stayed outside for longer than I should have until I heard my mother's voice calling me. As she opened the door, I put the chain inside my bra and in-between my small breasts.

"Where the hell have you been?" she yelled at me.

There was no use in replying to her; I just followed behind her. In a way, I was glad Mason didn't speak to me for a week. I wouldn't have been able to face him if he had.

The music had stopped, and I could hear Mr. Stiltskin's voice as he welcomed the guests and how they all fake-laughed at his jokes.

My mother opened the door carelessly. It made a noise, and heads turned our way. People turned to look at us, but my mother did not bring her head down. I wish I could have been brave like her, but all I had was a *deer in headlights* look. Mr. Stiltskin glared at my mother. He opened his mouth to speak, but before he could do so, everyone's phones started to ping.

I looked around as everyone pulled out their cellphones. I saw some of my classmates covering their mouths as they laughed. Others gasped with disgust, but all of them looked at Mr. Stiltskin. I moved closer to a couple, and I felt the blood rush down from my head to my feet.

The video was grainy and in color. Two people were on the screen. The man was in a servant's uniform, while the woman was draped in silk and covered in gold. I've been watching my parents walk away from me since I was a little girl. Hence, I knew their backs better than I knew their front profiles. It was pretty evident that the man was my father, and since she wasn't next to Mr. Stiltskin, that had to be the lady of the house. I looked up, noticing the person who was behind Mr. Stiltskin, and then cursed myself for not noticing him before.

Mason stood stoic behind his father. One of his hands was in the pocket of his pants as he stared absently at the people before him. There was no reaction on his face. Then I looked at my mother, and they were the only two people in the entire room who didn't seem surprised.

I wanted to throw up.

Murmurs broke out across the room, everyone discussing it as Mr. Stiltskin left the room with fury etched on his face. Seconds later, the feed cut off just as he made it to where my father was with Hilda Stiltskin.

Shouts erupted when my father walked through the doors, his zipper was still open, his white shirt untucked.

That's when my mother moved. She went to where my father was and walked past him, and went to Mr. King.

"We had a deal," she said in a monotone voice.

My father was at her side.

"Was that part of it too?" he demanded from Mr. King.

"That was not me," Mr. King said as he laughed it off.

"What the hell is going on?" Mr. Stiltskin demanded.

Mr. King was the older image of his son. Tall, thin, and blond. Something so refined that it should look delicate but instead gave you goosebumps.

"You're done, Malcolm." His voice was directed toward Mr. Stiltskin.

"I'm done? You don't have the means to end me!"

Mr. King stopped walking and pulled something out of his pocket. Between his index and pointer finger was the black square my mother wanted me to take.

My mind immediately went back to the day my locker got broken into.

Mase was not waiting for me today, and I wondered if it was because of what had happened to my locker. Did he not want people to associate me with him anymore?

With my shoulders slumped, I started to walk back home. I

don't know why I was sulking since this was the way it was supposed to be since the beginning.

Not even five minutes into my walk, an opaque black car stopped next to me, but I couldn't figure out who it was because the windows were tinted.

As soon as the black glass came down, I recognized the blond mop of hair.

"Need a ride, gorgeous?"

I did, but I said nothing.

He lost the smile and raised a brow and looked me up and down. "If you get in, I'll tell you why I broke into your locker."

I stopped looking at Mr. King and Mr. Stiltskin, and my eyes went to Mase, and he was looking at me with disbelief.

With just that look I knew he had pieced it together and knew I had betrayed him.

PART II

SURVIVAL

WE CUT THE HEADS OFF OUR MASTERS AND BATHE IN THEIR BLOOD.

AND SOMEHOW CONVINCE OURSELVES WE ARE NOT LIKE THE ONES WHO JUST DIED.

IF YOU KILL A MONSTER, WILL A MONSTER YOU BECOME?

EIGHT

NINETEEN YEARS OLD

"Welcome to dead island," I muttered to myself as the island that would be my home for the next two weeks came into view.

The Vermont air was fresh compared to the warm summer that had arrived. The water sparkled under the sun's rays, and I could make out the national forest that surrounded the island.

It was lush and green. It looked almost magical. I guess it had to look like something straight out of a fairytale book to at least appeal to the one percent of the world. Hard to believe that I was now part of the inner circle, and in being so, I learned all the things I didn't know before.

You ever wondered where rich people sent their kids for summer programs? Here it was. They shipped them off to an island to attend a six-week program before joining their respected Ivy League colleges. *Ordine Infinite*, or Order of the Infinite, if you want to get technical. It was the secret society of secret societies. Its roots could be traced back to the reign of at least three kings. Once the United States departed from England's reign, the society went underground, and through modern times, it made some changes. Not all the rich attended this island. You had to be from a bloodline connected to the founding members.

Finishing this course pretty much guaranteed your success. The connections it brought were like no other. It gave you power.

Two years ago, my father secured a top spot for the Millers right next to the Kings. Power always came by stepping on the backs of others, and it was no different in this case.

"It looks gorgeous," Erin said as she pushed her wheelchair closer so she could get a better look.

I grabbed the handles from the back and started to drag it toward the exit so we be ready to get off this boat.

Getting used to having money and, a voice was harder than I thought it would be. Maybe the guilt that followed me didn't allow me to enjoy the things I now had. Two years ago, I betrayed the only person who had mattered to me. Being selfish didn't get you anywhere other than in hell, and that night, I learned that lesson the hard way.

Everyone around me acted like our first meeting didn't happen. They aligned with what the Kings wanted, and I was forced to follow their lead. To them, I was no longer servant girl; that was a thing of the past.

Now my only friend was Erin Waters, and that's because I felt guilty that her current state was because of me. It was the reason why I was able to move past the way she treated me before and form a bond.

"Come on, let's go find our rooms and get settled before the rest of the snakes get here," I told her, completely knowing that I was the nastiest of them all.

"Are you excited, Aspen?" Erin asked, full of wonder. Somehow it felt like we were in the twilight zone. The accident humbled her while it made me a cynic.

"It's all bullshit," I replied.

We came into this blind, not knowing what would go down. Once you completed the two weeks, you were forbidden to talk about what went down on the island. My parents planned their exit from servitude to a fucking T; I could give them that much. I was not from the original family, yet I was allowed to come here.

In the last two years, I heard the whispers about what would happen on the island. So many rumors went flying around, but the one I believed was that if you were smart, you could get enough blackmail material to never have to worry about these so-called friends betraying you.

If my parents taught me anything, it was that life was full of opportunities. You just had to know when to take them.

From the looks of it, we were the first on the island. Mr. Waters pulled some strings so Erin and I could arrive first, and so we were ready and waiting when everyone else got here.

About eighty people lived on this tiny island. It housed a park and a chapel, but the rest was closed off to the public, where the Order had their camping grounds. Because of the forest preserve, the nosey people on Google Maps didn't have a clue of what really went down.

"Aspen," Erin said after we sat down and watched as more boats approached on the horizon.

"Hmmm," I said, looking down at my phone and reading up on the gossip columns.

"Is this the first time you'll be seeing Liam in two years?"

My finger stopped mid-scroll at the mention of Liam King. The last time I had any contact with him was at that party two years ago. Sometimes that night felt like it was only yesterday, while other times, it felt like a lifetime ago.

I couldn't help but look toward Erin. Seeing her in the wheelchair rattled me for the first time in months. Maybe I had been desensitized to the feeling I got whenever I looked at her and how I failed to stop the accident.

I shook my head, not willing to take that trip down memory lane.

"Yeah," I replied.

I betrayed Mason for a chance at a future, for a chance to get my parents out of servitude. At least that's the deal I made with Liam when he gave me a ride home. He told me he could make it so my parents and I could live an ordinary life. He made the dream I didn't dare to dream into a possible reality, and like the naïve girl I had been, I believed him.

Too bad my parents had already been working with Mr. King. How cunning had they been to approach Mr. King on one of his visits to the manor and make a deal knowing it could cost them their lives. I guess snakes recognized other snakes because the Stiltskins' rise to power was a threat to the Kings, and the new crypto technology Mr. Stiltskin had been working on was going to change the game. My mom had access to his office; she could get what Mr. King couldn't. The only problem had been communication.

And thus, they had sent all the servant kids to school. Since I was the only child in the manor and the only one of high school age, I didn't take notice. They offered schooling as a gift, and it was all just part of another game they were playing.

Sometimes I still had trouble trying to figure out what was real and what was fake. My parents wanted more than just a good life, so in exchange for the data, they sold me off to the Kings. After we graduated college, I was set to be Liam's wife.

There was no room for dignity when you wanted the world at your feet. My mother was aware that my dad had been sleeping with Hilda Stiltskin and she was still with him. Either both my parents had power or neither of them did, and they had gotten used to this lifestyle over their dead cold bodies before they left it.

"You are so beautiful, and I like to collect beautiful things."

The words Liam said as he dragged me out of the Stiltskins' house that night still haunted me. I was nothing but a possession to him. He made sure everyone knew about it and then he left to study abroad.

My hand came to my neck and I touched the thin gold chain. It was worth thousands of dollars, and I often wondered why had Mase given that to a low-class servant.

"Who's hosting this anyway?" Erin asked, interrupting my thoughts.

"No idea," I said as I looked at the people who were coming our way.

I would be lying if I said that being close to Liam didn't affect me. My feelings for him hadn't changed in the last two years. I still loathed the idea of being forced to marry him.

I sucked in a breath when I realized that the last time we had all been together had been at that party.

All the damn vipers made their way toward Erin and me. The last one to approach was Liam. After all, the damn king had to make an entrance, right?

He looked like such a fucking douche. Salmon shorts, with a lighter salmon polo, and brown Hermes loafers. Black sunglasses covered his eyes, and his blond hair was slicked down with a side part. There was no denying the disgust on my face.

"Be nice," Erin whispered. She was more concerned over my relationship with Liam than I was. In other words, she was more scared than I was if it all went to shit. He didn't see me as a person; he saw a possession, so I was fucked either way.

Everyone parted as douchebag Liam made his way toward me. Our engagement wasn't something that made headlines. All these damn activists in the country advocating rights left and right, and for what? When the one percent did as they pleased. Man-made laws didn't apply when money ruled all.

"Hey, wifey." Liam's mocking tone grated my ears.

I looked up at him and smiled. "You know what I can't wait for, honey?"

Liam put both his hands inside the pockets of his shorts.

"For us to finally fuck?" he said crassly. I heard the other boys snort.

"To be a widow, my darling," I replied sweetly.

"It makes me fucking hard when you talk about killing me, my love."

Just then, a bunch of hooded people came out of all angles. None of us had time to react as our bodies began to get dragged.

"Erin!" I screamed bloody murder as my vision went black.

They put a fucking velvet cap over my face. I couldn't see shit. I could barely breathe. My pounding heart was so loud that it deafened me.

It didn't matter no matter how much I writhed and moaned. The person who held onto me didn't say a word and continued to drag me.

After what felt like three minutes, I started to hear loud thuds. Fuck. By the time I realized what those noises were, I was already falling.

"I'm going to kill you!"

Laughter echoed behind me.

I was finally allowed to remove my hood and then I took a deep breath as my eyes adjusted to the dark room. Red lights were the only thing that illuminated us. I looked around me and noticed that everyone was in the same position as me. We were all on our hands and knees, trying to get up. I didn't spot Erin, but I had to remind myself that they wouldn't seriously hurt her. Not when her father was basically the king of the seas. He controlled sea commerce.

"Rise, my fellow illuminated, and know this is the last time you will ever have to kneel in your life." The voice was deep, poised, and full of privilege.

In front of us was Theodore King. He was Liam's older cousin. I wondered if a member of the King family was in charge of giving us the welcome speech.

"Sorry, cuz," Theo pointed at Liam. "This was one family secret I couldn't share." He then turned to look at all of us. "I know you're mad. Trust me, I was too when I was here two years ago."

My brows scrunched in confusion.

"There weren't any members of age last year," Theo explained quickly. "This rite of passage goes back centuries. The only people who can humiliate us are ourselves. Everyone else is inferior to us. We are truly kings among men."

Almost everyone hooted and cheered at that statement.

Everyone who had been hooded, was now standing behind Theo. They were all older relatives of the main branches.

"Now you're wondering what exactly is the Ordine Infinite? It's power, my friends. Pure fucking power."

The air in the room changed with that statement. His words were like a drug, and everyone was feeding off them.

Did it make me stupid because I wasn't buying it? How could we have power if we were all hamsters in a wheel doing what our parents wanted? By the time it was our turn to teach our kids, we were conditioned to fear something new.

A rattle next to me startled me, so I turned and was relieved to see Erin.

"Did they hurt you?" I asked, reaching for her cheeks. It was useless to try and find a scratch; I could barely see her.

"No, they just bagged me and brought me."

"Good," I replied and focused on Theo once more.

"In these two weeks, you will learn—"

His voice cut off when the front doors to the building opened, and sunlight streamed in. Two people entered. The first was a hooded person. The next was a tall and slim man. They didn't drag them in like the rest of us. Unlike us, he strolled in casually.

"Who the fuck is this?" Theo asked, annoyed.

When we received our instructions, it said to be at the island at 5 pm sharp. I wondered if they had done this on purpose.

Just as the hooded guy went to try and throw the guy he was escorting, the guy flipped him.

"I told you earlier not to touch my arm," he seethed.

I stared in awe at the newcomer and racked my brain, thinking of who it could be since I didn't see anyone missing.

Everyone was enthralled by this person. He had just said fuck you to the tradition.

"Remove your hood," Liam demanded.

I rolled my eyes, knowing damn well he did it to remind Theo that he was the true heir of the King's fortune even though he was in charge of this little activity.

I watched the newcomer closely. Unlike the rest of us, he didn't look like he was ready for a day at the beach. He wore black from head to toe. A black long sleeve shirt which I found odd since it was hot. Black fitted jeans and combat boots. The weirdest part of all was the black glove on his right arm.

He brought his left arm up and removed the velvet cover from his face.

I gasped.

Those jade eyes I'd recognize anywhere. Memories assaulted me, and I had to hold onto Erin's chair for support, but the moment I touched the metal, it scorched me.

I brought my hand to my chest as if I'd been burned. My palm pressed against it, and I could feel the beating of my heart. It was probably wondering if our time had run out—or maybe it had because I was looking at a ghost.

His black hair wasn't short-trimmed anymore. It was faded at the bottom and longer at the top, running in all directions, but it didn't look untamed. It was stylish like he had run his fingers through it a thousand times.

His face was pale, with dark shadows under his eyelids. His lips resembled a perfect cupid bow, but too manly to be considered feminine. The hollowed cheekbones removed all traces of his baby face, and all the acne had cleared up.

"Imp?" one of Liam's little lackeys exclaimed in disbelief.

We were looking at a ghost.

A cruel smile spread across Mason Stiltskin's lips, and at

that moment, I knew that the Mase I knew was no longer there.

After all, I was the one who had betrayed him.

NINE

ASPEN

EVERYONE IN THE ROOM WAS SPEECHLESS. MASON WAS THE last person we all thought we would be seeing. Because two years ago, after my family's betrayal, the party ended. I'll never forget the footage I saw all over the media the next day. The Stiltskin mansion had caught on fire.

Mason Stiltskin was pronounced dead, along with his parents and Jason.

"Sorry, I'm late," Mase spoke in a deep lazy voice. He didn't care that every single person in this room thought he didn't belong.

He was a stranger. Nothing before me seemed familiar. It's like he lost all his softness and honed his body into a weapon. I had no room to talk; there wasn't anything sweet or naïve in me.

"You don't belong here, Stiltskin," Theo said, stepping forward.

Mason smirked and took a step forward. I watched, fascinated, comparing the boy he had been to the man he was today.

"It's my birthright, Teddy," Mase stated, unbothered.

"There are rules," Theo added.

"I wonder what Daddy will think when he finds out his advisor likes to bend you over his desk," Mason retorted, a sinister smirk plastered on his lush lips.

Everyone gasped. Not that being gay was a crime, but when your family builds its reputation on Christian values, and you had to marry off to better the family name. Well, his parents were never going to allow it.

The world loved to talk about progression and modernization but look to those in power, and you quickly realized how all of it was a farce.

"That doesn't matter. If I say you're out, then you are out." Liam took a step forward, making his way to Mase. At that moment, I realized I was about to be the center of their pissing contest.

I looked down and noticed Erin had gone pale. She looked at Mason with fear in her eyes.

"Somewhere along the line, your family thought just because they bore the last name King, it made you our monarchs," Mase told the room.

Liam's face was red from anger, and as much as I loved to see him rattled, I felt powerless. I couldn't savor the moment because if Mase was out for revenge, I would be his target too.

"I can leave." Mase shrugged his shoulders and took a step back. "But our rules state that if one of the founding members is cast out about something trivial, then a restitution fee must be paid."

Liam smiled. "I'll p—"

"You can stay," Theodore cut Liam off before he could speak. Murder was evident in Liam's eyes as he gazed back at his cousin. "The rest of you, the keys to your cabins are on that exit table. Meet in the common room tomorrow morning."

Everyone looked like they wanted to stay and see what would happen between Mason and the Kings, but I couldn't wait to get out of here.

I took hold of the handlebars on Erin's wheelchair when Mason's undivided attention went from Liam to me.

There was nothing sexual in the way his jade eyes washed over me. A hungry look analyzed my every weak spot and tried to gauge how to exploit it.

He moved in our direction, and I braced myself for the impact, but his attention shifted from me toward Erin when he was standing in front of me.

No!

"You look like a fish out of water," he mocked Erin.

Mason bent at eye level with Erin, and all I could do was hold onto the handles for my dear life. There was no denying I was pathetic and a fucking coward.

"Boo," he said, and Erin flinched.

He then grabbed her cheek and turned it to the side. My heart was pounding. Was he going to whisper in her ear?

His eyes met mine, and at one point, I would have bet my life that Mason was the only person who wouldn't look at me with loathing, but how wrong had I been?

The asshole smiled, and I glared at him.

When he stuck his tongue out, I couldn't help and zero in on the piercings. He didn't have one tongue piercing but three. The first ball was small, the middle one a little bigger, and the third was a standard tongue piercing. He then licked Erin's cheek as he looked directly at me.

Erin's whimper was enough to snap me out of my fog.

"Move," I spat at him. I wish I could have said it with full confidence, but he knew how much of a sham I really was.

"Is that any way to treat an old friend, Aspen?" he said as he rose to his full height—he now towered over me.

A bitter taste coated my tongue at his use of the word friend.

"Come on, Erin, let's go." I began to move her chair.

"Leave my fiancée alone," Liam said as he came to stand next to me and put his hand on my arm. A subtle reminder that I was his.

Mason's eyes zeroed on the spot where Liam was touching me, and his smile got wider.

"Hmmm," Mase hummed. "I hear you like to go pretending like your parents did all the negotiations."

My face burned. His statement was directed at me. Even though everyone here knew I was a pretense and I had slithered my way here, no one ever spoke about it. Again, part of my parents' deal. Somehow it was easier to blame everything on them. Liam was the only one who knew the whole truth.

Mason took a step back, and Erin took a deep breath.

"Shame that someone so beautiful reeks like hell," Mase said, looking right at me.

My throat constricted. I don't know why his words affected me so much. Still, after all these years, he was the only person to ever call me beautiful. Not pretty, nor hot, or someone they liked to fuck. Mason had been the only person to see the real me. He tried to understand me, and I had betrayed that trust.

I looked down, not being able to keep my eyes on his for another second. This time when I started to push Erin away, he let me go.

People lingered outside the main cabin, hoping to see

what was going on inside. I paid no attention to them and instead went to the table where they had the keys. I instantly found mine and Erin's since we were the last ones left. The keys were in gold, and as soon as I picked it up, I knew it was the real deal.

Our names and numbers were inscribed on a piece of leather attached to the key. Erin had number five while I had thirteen.

Shit, we wouldn't be near each other. I fucking hated this. I somehow got it in my head that I was her protector. I took the keys and returned to Erin's side. She was playing with her hair as she stared absently toward the woods.

"Hey, I got our keys," I said, trying to get an idea where her head was at. I hoped to God she didn't want to talk about that night. I didn't have it in me today.

"Aspen, did you really not know what your parents had planned?" Erin asked, and I cursed under my breath.

I wasn't a sweet person. I was a fraud. A fucking fake, and the only reason why I was able to pretend with Erin was that my cynicism and my guilt overrode my other emotions.

I headed toward the stone pathway that led to our rooms, hoping that she would drop it.

"Did you?"

Fuck.

"I never wanted to marry Liam."

Erin scoffed, and my stomach dropped.

"It's not like this is my fault," I huffed out.

She pushed the button on her wheelchair and moved away from me. The action caught me by surprise. I deluded myself into thinking I was helping her and that I was doing something for her, but who was crutching to whom here?

Erin turned her chair around and faced me.

"Nothing ever is your fault, Aspen. You got into school,

but you didn't want to. You're going to marry Liam, but you don't want to. There was a line of families wanting to merge with the Kings, and here you come with nothing to offer.... Oh, but you didn't want to!"

My body felt dizzy, and my head felt like it was going to explode. I took a step toward Erin, but she shook her head.

"You got to leave that house unscathed while I'm over here bound to this fucking chair." Her words rattled me. "Give me my key. I can take it from here." She reached out her hand and snatched the key away from me.

I stayed there until she was out of my view. I looked at the cabin number, and it had the number seven on it. The Order didn't spare expenses. The cabins were all separated to give us all privacy. The door opened, and Nate waved at me.

"Where's Erin?"

"What the fuck does it matter to you."

He smiled, his teeth gleaming against his darker skin. "You don't have to get all defensive. You two are usually attached at the hip."

I glared at him. It was mostly just for show. Nate was one of the few people I didn't mind. Like Erin, he was kinder and not all that vapid and corrupted.

"You should go to your room, it's getting late," he said, but it sounded like a warning.

Shit, he was right.

For a second, I had forgotten Mason was in the mix, and I didn't know how much protection being part of the Order would offer me, but I was ready to take all I could get.

Without another word, I headed toward my room. On the way, I took off the necklace for the first time in two years. My neck felt naked without it, but with Mase being here, it didn't feel right having it wrapped around me. I felt people staring at me as I passed by their cabins, but I pretended not to notice. Mostly everyone had slept with each other. Sex made all those gathering a little more bearable. This was probably why Liam was excited to marry me. I was someone his group of friends had not touched.

I couldn't stand the thought of any of those assholes touching me then bragging about fucking me. It's not like they even turned me on. I looked at them and I felt nothing.

I came to a halt when I made it to my cabin. I looked around, and this was where the pathway ended. It was a small cabin but still luxurious. A cabin made of stone and brick, giving it a fairytale look.

Fear wasn't a foreign concept to me. I didn't scare easily, but I felt it now. The forest seemed endless. I shook my head and took a step forward when I heard footsteps. My heart pounded in my chest, and the hand where I held the key fumbled, causing me to almost drop it.

I managed to hold onto the key and ran to the door, trying to get inside my room when I was pushed against the door.

The wood rubbed against my cheek, and the only reason I wasn't going to have a splinter was that it had been delicately polished.

My legs were forced to part as someone wedged their knee between them. One hand was on my waist, keeping me in place while the other came to my nape.

"Did you know the Imp would be here today?" Liam's voice was dripping with anger.

My lips thinned, stopping me from whimpering in pain. When he saw that I wasn't answering, the pressure he had on my neck intensified.

"I asked you a fucking question, Aspen," he seethed.

"No," I hissed. "Just like everyone else, I thought he was

dead." It wasn't entirely a lie because that's what I deluded myself to think.

Liam started to laugh but then stopped.

"Let me find out that you spread your legs for him, and you're not going to like what happens next."

His words were threatening. He liked to ignore me, because we both knew that I had a leash that was going to end up in his hands sooner or later.

"Go play with one of your whores. I'm sure they're waiting for you," I said through gritted teeth. His reply was to make it harder for me to breathe.

"But you see, darling, I don't want them."

"And I don't want you," I managed to spit out.

The pressure he had on me disappeared. I took a deep breath, calming myself, before I turned to face him.

"You left me alone for the last two years. What changed?" I asked him as I turned to face him.

Liam took a step toward me and put his hands on either side of my head, caging me between his body and the door.

"Your pussy belongs to me, Aspen. Keep your fucking legs closed, and maybe I'll show you mercy."

He leaned in closer to kiss me, but I moved my face, making him kiss my cheek instead.

Liam laughed.

"You're lucky I'm still amused by this game we have going on. It makes me fucking hard."

He pushed away and started to walk backward.

"You don't even realize the corner you landed in. I'm fucking all the whores left and right, while you remain there hating everyone. When we get married, you'll only have me, and I'll have everyone."

His words caused me to panic. Freedom was the only thing I wanted, and it still was so far from my reach. When

Liam realized that it had sunk in, he smirked at me and walked away.

With shaky hands, I opened my door. As soon as it was closed, I leaned against it and closed my eyes. Too bad it took me a second too late to realize I wasn't alone.

TEN

MASON

My BLOOD WAS BOILING, AND THE ONLY LOGICAL EXPLANATION I could come up with was the heat. After all, it was a bitch to wear long sleeves in the summer. Yet the more I heard Liam fucking King speak, the more I wanted to go outside and forget all about the art of war.

Revenge was meant to be savored, and if I walked out while he was handing Aspen her own ass, well, that would show my hand too quickly, and there would be no more fun to have.

I retreated to the shadows as I peeked through the curtains of Aspen's cabin.

Liam had her pressed up against the wall, and the action had my body tense. The only one allowed to make Aspen crawl was me. I didn't want to share that with him. The only thing that kept me in place was the fact that I was getting a lot of valuable information from their little exchange.

So, the golden princess was still a virgin.

The information shouldn't have thrilled me as much as it did, but I couldn't help the grin. It was the icing on the cake. I had been planning my revenge for two years, and I would finally put my plan into action.

Two years ago, upper society crucified my family. They had assisted in turning me into a monster. Them, I couldn't really blame. The only good thing the Order members were good at was looking out for themselves. And Aspen proved to be no fucking different. The little bitch played on my every heartstring and got off on it.

Well, now I was about to show her how I got off. She was going to fucking cry.

When the doorknob started to turn, I took a step back, blending in with the shadows. This was comforting. After everything I had came crashing down, the shadows were the only safe place I had, to fall back on. Darkness didn't judge; it was always ready to welcome you with open arms.

Aspen walked inside, and the only thing I could hear was her heavy breathing. Now that prince charming had left, she was allowing herself to feel the fear that his presence brought her.

It was too dark to look at her properly; that golden hair I loved was tamed in darkness. Those amber eyes didn't shine without any sunlight reflecting on them. A lifetime ago, I would be there trying to soothe her wounds in my own fucked up way.

Aspen felt more than she let on. Back then, the longing for freedom was etched on her face. It was intoxicating to watch because she'd never say it aloud. And a dumbass part of me wanted to give it to her—I had planned to give it to her.

She made a deal for her freedom, and I was about to show her just who her life belonged to—sooner or later, she was going to beg me for mercy.

Both my hands slammed against the wooden door. Aspen's eyes sprang open, and I smiled.

"It's been a while," I said with a lazy drawl. My eyes adjusted to the darkness, and I could see the whites of her eyes.

Her mouth parted, but no words came out. The sick part of me found joy in that.

"What's the matter, Aspen? Cat got your tongue?"

It took her a second, but she spoke in her raspy tone.

"W-what are you doing here?"

Having arrived at the cabin before her, I already knew where the light switch was located, so I reached for it with my gloved hand.

We both blinked furiously as our eyes adjusted to the bright light. My hand came back to the position it had been, and I cocked my head so I could see her better.

Her hair was in long cascading waves that reached her waist. It was brighter, probably because she finally had money to take proper care of it. Her body had filled out nicely. In the past two years, she'd been on fashion blogs.

My eyes lingered a little more on her breasts. Teenage me had imagined what it would be like to fuck Aspen; she was the only person I wanted even after Hilda had fucked with me.

The arch of her neck was delicate, and I could see her thyroid vein pumping. I had to force my hand to remain still before I touched her. My eyes finally went up to her lips—still small and pink. Unlike her mother, she didn't have sharp cheekbones. Her face was round, and she looked innocent.

"I asked you a question, asshole," she spat, her pink tongue peeking through.

My face got even closer to hers. It was a mistake. She

smelled as sweet as ever, taking me back to a time when I was weak.

She still smelled like summer. It was a fresh smell that made you feel warm.

Cute, she was like a kitten meowing to a lion. In betraying me, she found herself.

My mistake was befriending her that day. While my dumbass fell for her, she clutched to someone she could use as a stepping stone on her way to freedom.

Unfortunately for her, I was not the same Mason she knew. My gloved hand moved faster than she anticipated and cupped her cheek just as her dip shit fiancé had, but unlike him, I focused on the hollow of her cheekbone so the pain would burn through her cheek.

"Are you sure about that?" My mocking tone went from amused to lethal, and her eyes widened. "I find it interesting that you and Erin are now stuck like glue."

I already knew that. I already knew everything that these fuckers had done. I wished I could have seen the reaction of all the bitches once I walked in, knowing that at one point or another in the last two years, they let me fuck them.

"That was your fault," she seethed, trying to move away from me.

I saw red. The stupid, vapid bitch was still going with that story. She wanted to make me the villain when she made us both into monsters in one night.

Letting go of her face, I used my other hand to pull her and drag her to the middle of the room. I left her there while I retreated to the sofa. I sat down, and she observed me as she rubbed her jaw, trying to soothe it.

"Okay..." I let the word hang in the air as I took my cigarettes from my pocket. "Let's say it was my fault." I paused to light my cigarette, watching the flame, and forced myself to bring it closer to my face. I took a deep breath before I brought the cigarette to my lips. "I should at least tell Erin my side of the story," I said as soon as I exhaled the smoke.

Aspen's eyes went wide with fear.

I took another drag as my eyes roamed over her body. She noticed what I was doing and glared while folding her arms together, causing her tits to push up. I chuckled.

"Strip," I commanded before taking another hit.

Instantly her hands went to her hips and she was now glaring at me.

"In your dreams, Mase."

I threw my head back, my laughter echoing through the whole cabin. I made myself more comfortable on the sofa and spread my legs.

"Don't call me that, you stupid bitch. We aren't friends."

Her eyes flashed with hurt, and the action caught me by surprise. I shook that feeling away. It had no room in my plans.

"Were you the only one allowed to do the betrayal in this so-called"—I put my cigarette in my mouth so I could do air quotes—"friendship?"

Her lip trembled. I had the power to bring down the perfect little world she had created for herself. She was in with them because she was Liam's, and they had accepted that, but with a few words, I could make her feel alone and have no allies.

"Tell you what, I won't tell your only friend how she ended up in a wheelchair."

"You don't think I'm stupid enough to believe that," she replied right away.

"Smart girl." I smirked.

"Is this because of what happened—"

"I'm one stupid comment away from running to Erin's

room," I barked before she could talk about what she did. "Now, if you don't want that to happen—strip."

I took another drag of my cigarette as I waited to see what she would do next. Either way, I was going to enjoy both outcomes.

"In your fucking dreams, Mason!"

She was wrong. I was too fucked up back then to even think about sex with anyone, especially with her. I always felt dirty; I didn't want to stain her with the shit I carried.

"Midnight," I went on like she wasn't having a fit. Aspen was going to kneel at my feet; I just needed to be patient. I waited two years. What were a few weeks more?

"W-what?" Her voice had lost the strong bravado it previously held.

"That was the time I set the house on fire," I confessed.

My seventeen-year-old self had it all figured out. After the party, my plan had been to set fire to half of the manor. My dad's office, their rooms, and mine. It would give the help enough time to clear out and try to make a run for it before the Order came for them. I wanted to run away with Aspen. Somehow in my fucked up little head, I believed that I would purge all those bad memories that followed me by doing that.

Aspen's hands were now wrapped around her own waist.

"You left that house and didn't tell anyone. How would Erin feel about that? You're just as guilty as me for her accident. Actions have consequences, Aspen, and you have to learn to pay the price."

She didn't say anything more. She took a deep breath and squared her shoulders. Aspen criss crossed her arms, then pulled the blouse she was wearing over head and removed it, leaving her in a lacy red bra. My eyes traveled from her face down to her navel, waiting for her next move.

She had changed, and I wasn't sure I liked that. Back then, she was innocent. Whenever she got shy or uncomfortable, her cheeks would be stained pink—that wasn't the case now, and it made me angry.

She bit her lip as she started to pull down the skirt she wore. I brought my left hand to my mouth in a fist and bit my index finger at the sight of her.

Creamy.

Smooth.

Pale skin.

Just waiting to be marred.

The skirt dropped to the floor, and the sound the fabric made had me leaning forward. She wore a matching set of dainty underwear—my floss was probably thicker than what she called a thong.

"There, I stripped. Now you can leave," Aspen declared as she went to pick up her clothes.

"There's still more to be stripped," I drawled. "Unless you need some help."

I could be nice when it was convenient for me.

"Fuck you. I'm not here to relive your teenage fantasies."

I threw my head back and laughed; the other option was to fucking choke the self-centered bitch to death.

"Newsflash, Aspen, you don't have a pussy made of gold," I told her as I made it a point to cock my head and sweep my gaze from her head to her toes.

"Kneel and show me how sorry you are," I scolded with my tone full of venom.

Her eyes went wide, but she didn't do what she was told. I changed the subject while she was deciding if kneeling was in her best interest.

"The press is forbidden to ask about that night, Erin doesn't like talking about the accident, so no one really knows what happened to her," I went on, and that got her attention. She was holding on to my every word. "But you know, right? Jason was found in my dad's office. He was too drunk to move once the fire started. As for Erin, well, you heard all about that too, right? In her tipsy state, jumping seemed like a good idea."

Slowly Aspen started to kneel. Her eyes were watery, and I wanted her to cry. I wanted to see the proof that she regretted what she had done.

Too bad that Aspen didn't break that easy.

Once she was kneeling, I stood up and walked up to her, glad she opened her stupid little mouth. Hence, it gave my boner a chance to deflate and not make it obvious that even though I hated her, I wouldn't mind fucking her.

"Good girl," I cooed as I pet her head.

Her sharp intake of breath made me smile.

I crouched, so we were at eye level. Aspen gauged me with those amber eyes that got you dizzier than whiskey. With my right hand, I touched her cheek. The leather from my glove stuck to her sweaty skin.

"From now until I say otherwise, you're my new...fucking...*pet*."

The last word lingered between the two of us. All Aspen could do was glare, but she knew that one wrong move and the bed of lies she had created would collapse.

I stood up and looked down at her. With sick satisfaction, I took another drag of my cigarette and then ashed it on her head. I turned around and walked toward the door.

"Lock the door once I leave. I don't want prince charming playing with what's mine."

ELEVEN

WHEN THE SUNRAYS BROKE THROUGH MY DARK CABIN, I cursed myself for not getting a lick of sleep. My pillow was wet with all my angry tears. I wanted to scream at how everything had turned out. Our sins clung to us, waiting for the perfect opportunity to wreak havoc, and mine had just joined the party.

One thing was for sure, these next two weeks were going to be hell. What did I expect? Stepping on the backs of others doesn't achieve happiness.

"Now kneel and show me how sorry you are."

Every time I turned to look at that stupid sofa, I saw Mase there looking like the devil on his throne. In a matter of minutes, he had taken over my thoughts. There was no point in crying over spilled milk, so I needed to think and find a way out of this. The cabin was small yet luxurious. A little fireplace with a fur rug near it, a sofa, a queen-size memory foam bed, and a bathroom. The shower head was on the ceiling, and it felt like I was showering under a waterfall.

I'd be lying if I said I was surprised Mason was still alive.

A part of me knew he wouldn't go down that easy. Then as I was changing, something hit me. Something I had never thought about too deeply because I had to deal with putting my trust in the wrong people. Mason was the one who set the house on fire. He killed his father and his mother —but why?

My palms got sweaty, and I felt dizzy with adrenaline. How had I been so fucking dumb to not put it together before? Was it because his mother was having an affair with my father? No, I didn't think so, but I could have the upper hand on him if I found out.

When I betrayed Mase, I didn't allow myself to think about what would happen to him because the only person I could think about was me. I was raised to live for my masters, and thinking for myself wasn't something we could do, and the first time I decided to be selfish, so many people got hurt. Look at me. It didn't matter how much I loved my parents at one point or another; all I got from them was their backs and their own desires. I was doomed to fail from the beginning.

If you'd told me two years ago that Mase would have had me kneeling for him in my lingerie, I'd say you were lying.

I guess I shouldn't be surprised. Not when heartbreak and betrayals were some of the strongest emotions that were capable of turning your world upside down, and in return, fueled you with rage, giving you a drive you didn't have before.

After checking my weather app, I put on a black dress and sunglasses to hide my sleep-deprived face.

As soon as I opened the door to my cabin, his voice greeted me.

"Morning, *pet*," Mase said from where he had a foot perched on the stone wall.

"Since you're here, there's nothing good about it," I greeted him.

Mason had the audacity to chuckle. I tilted my head to look at him; still not believing this was the same sweet guy from my childhood.

"Are you always this feisty in the morning? Or you're just in need of some dick?" he asked, pulling out a cigarette. He smirked at me as he brought the nicotine stick to his lips as if he could look through the tint of my shades, and for some reason, I blushed.

My virginity status wasn't any of his business, so I wasn't going to make a comment about it. Again, I found it odd he was wearing long sleeves and that leather glove. For all I know, he wanted to look cool.

"Smoking kills," I muttered.

"We're all going to die anyway," he was quick to reply.

I sighed but kept walking, trying to get to the main cabin and away from him as fast as possible, but unfortunately, he wasn't letting me.

Now that Erin had a chance to sleep on her feelings, I would talk to her. Unfortunately, I couldn't do that with an angry, tall, sexy—slash that last comment—I couldn't approach her with Mase hanging around me.

"Why are you following me?"

He exhaled the smoke then spoke, "I'm just taking my dog for a walk."

He did not.

I don't care if this new Mason was over six feet tall, hair that looked like he just got laid, better eyelashes than mine, with piercing green eyes—he did not get to insult me.

My hand moved fast with the intent to slap him, but he caught it mid-stride with that gloved hand.

"What did you call me?"

"Do you prefer bitch?" he mocked me.

"I'd prefer if you weren't here at all," I told him, trying to get out of his hold, but he wasn't letting me. Instead, he pulled me closer to him.

"You're hurting me," I said through gritted teeth as I pulled on my wrist.

"Good."

His reply infuriated me.

"What the hell happened to you?" I demanded from him.

A macabre chuckle left his lips, and it gave me chills. Looking at him was like looking into the eye of a storm. Peaceful one minute and vengeful the next.

"Listen up, pet," he said, bringing his face down toward mine. His hot breath scorched my lips, and I had to remind myself to keep breathing. "You do not get to ask me that fucking question."

Mason was angry, and for the first time in my life, I think I was scared. Scratch that, no, it wasn't fear. It was guilt. He was right; I did not get to ask anything.

"What exactly are you punishing me for? For choosing myself for once?"

"Stop talking..." he said through gritted teeth.

I didn't listen to him.

"It's the fucking truth—"

His gloved hand came at me so fast I didn't have time to react. The leather was soft, a contrast against the hold he had on me.

"Your truth and mine are very different," he seethed so close to me that we were practically kissing.

My intake of breath was loud, and I couldn't help looking at his mouth, especially when all those piercings peeked through when he spoke.

Mason's eyes widened for a second before he smiled. I couldn't breathe anymore. How was it that the action reminded me so much of that night when he gave me the necklace? He was my first kiss. It was something I didn't like to think about often, but it was a fact I couldn't change, and despite everything that happened, I didn't regret it.

"You're starting to drool, pet," he said before he tilted my chin away from him.

It's not like I had asked him for a kiss, but I still felt humiliated by the action. I didn't pay him any more attention. One thing I knew was that powerful men hated being ignored, and despite my lack of qualities, it was one thing I had mastered in the last two years.

Mason let me get ahead of him this time, which I quickly wished he hadn't. When I walked into the main cabin, almost everyone was there. Despite feeling like an outsider with my own peers, I still held my head high and went to take a seat right in the middle of the room.

Half of the bitches here hated me already. It didn't matter where I sat, and going anywhere other than the middle would just fuel them.

As soon as I sat down, I crossed one of my legs and scanned the room for Erin. I was accustomed to using her as my crutch; without her, I felt naked.

I found her sitting next to Nate. I was glad he was with her. The accident had changed Erin; she was everything I once wanted to be. No one would have ever thought we would have switched roles.

"Aspen," someone said my name as they lightly tapped my shoulder.

I turned my head to find Katherine giving me a *what the fuck* look.

"Sorry, I spaced out. What did I miss?"

Lauren rolled her eyes. She was a gorgeous, tan brunette living the modeling life my mother wanted for me. Since she was too old to be anything other than rich, she wanted to live vicariously through me. That motherly vigor quickly turned into envy when she saw just how much attention I garnered. The shoots, blogs, everything I did was to spite her. I lived to see her die a little each day while I was living what she thought was her dream life. It killed me a little more inside doing it, but I was already going to die, so I might as well get a kick out of it in the meantime.

"Did you fuck him too?" she asked me, and I looked at her in confusion.

"Who, Liam?" I asked, disgusted.

Lauren rolled her eyes again. "Everyone's fucked Liam."

My lip curled in disgust. It wasn't a lie what she said. I knew Liam was banging all the society sluts. All of them went to him in hopes he would change his mind, and somewhere along the way, I hoped that he did too.

"Then who?" I asked, even though I didn't care who they all had fucked this summer.

"Stiltskin."

"W-what?"

Suddenly my lack of sleep was hitting me. I felt dizzy and sick.

"I met him at a club, the others said either there or at a bar, but in the last year, he made his rounds."

My eyes quickly scanned the room, and I found him in the corner, sitting on his own. He acted like none of us were here. Our eyes met, and a slow smile spread across his lips, and my stomach fell. Why did it hurt?

"None of you recognized him?" I asked through gritted teeth.

Lauren laughed.

"Why should we? It's not like we talked to him, and besides, he was supposed to be dead."

Wow. They were unbelievable. They bullied him their whole lives and then couldn't even remember his face. Sure, I was shocked when I saw him again, but as soon as I looked into his eyes, I knew who he was.

It was hard to forget the face of the person who hated you. It was much easier to deny that they ever meant anything to you. But him being here now terrified me because past and present were about to collide.

TWELVE

MASON

THE SINS OF OUR FATHERS WERE GOING TO LEAD US STRAIGHT into hell. Maybe we were all in a vicious cycle paying for what they had started.

Right now, I felt like I was in high school again. I was with people I had no interest in associating myself with. This was my birthright, and as much as they wished I was dead, they had to deal with me.

My father had many secrets, stuff the Order wasn't privy to. It's not that he didn't trust the Kings, but he was tired of them always being number one.

My original plan had been to run away with Aspen. Setting half of the house on fire gave the staff enough room to leave, and when Aspen betrayed me, I didn't want to go back on my plan.

My father had been humiliated in front of his peers. Since Hilda's fuck buddy had betrayed her, she would be coming after me while my father disposed of her.

Either way, it was too much at risk that I didn't want to be there with them. Leaving seemed like the only option.

Of course, that wasn't as easy as it seemed.

Dying was the only way I could be free until I was strong enough to withstand them. People did all kinds of things for money, and since I had planned to run away, I already had my exit strategy ready and cash on hand.

I gave the coroner almost everything I had so he could pronounce me dead. I didn't care if I had a dime to my name; all I wanted was revenge. A constant voice in my head kept nagging me that it was the only way I would be free of the demons that were chained to me.

If Aspen had come with me, would things be different?

The chatter stopped, and without looking up, I knew Liam had walked in. I raised my head, but my eyes immediately went to Aspen's. She was looking at me with disgust. However, the rest of the girls at her table were not.

At one point, I did wonder if they would feel disgusted once they realized whom they invited to their bed, but they were shallow as fuck. I should have known better.

I scanned the room, and Liam was glaring at me. I ignored him; what I found interesting was that Nate was also glaring at me, and Erin looked at me with fear.

So they all knew I had set the house on fire. Good, I didn't give a shit about that part. Hopefully, the rest of the secrets died along with that fire. It made sure all the pain I suffered because of it was worth it.

Looking at Erin, I couldn't help and think about how I found her.

Pain.

Despair.

Loneliness.

It's like every other feeling became irrelevant. I couldn't see straight, blinded by my rage. Did I imagine things? I thought Aspen and I were a team since we were fucking lonely, but now she was with him.

There was no way for Mr. King to have gotten my dad's files; that was an inside job. Aspen's dad was fucking Hilda, her mother was one of the maids allowed to clean my father's office, and Aspen went to school with Liam King.

It all made sense now why they suggested we allow our servants to get an education as a way to appease them. Just how long had she been planning this? Did she play me for a fool?

But when I looked into her eyes, she looked guilty, and that fucking killed me. Was there any hope for me?

People always did what was best for themselves; why was I so surprised about this if my own father never put me first. I stood next to my father and Hilda as everyone walked out. My eyes were on Aspen, and as she walked hand in hand with Liam, she didn't turn back once.

As soon as the last of the Order members of the party had left, the shouts started. My father was livid.

"You stupid bitch," he yelled, full of rage. He walked up to Hilda and slapped her so hard she fell to the floor.

By this point, I was numb, but a part of me cracked, wishing that was the reaction he had given her when I told him what she did to me.

Since they were busy, I walked to my room, where I had brought a five-gallon gasoline container. My rooms had already been dosed off earlier before my conversation with Aspen.

All that was left was my parents' side of the house.

When I planned to do this, I thought I'd be nervous, sad, pussy out at the last minute, but I had never felt more sure about anything in my life. There was a calmness in me that was new. My head was clear; there were no doubts and self-loathing thoughts. This feeling was so freeing because, for the first time, the thought of cutting myself wasn't front and center. The negative voice that lived inside my head rent-free was not tearing me up, but instead, it was cheering me on, telling me to do this.

Set the world on fire and watch it burn.

When you controlled the flames, there was nothing to fear. No one was in the foyer when I passed by. My father was probably in his office, and Hilda in the room licking her wounds.

The smell of gasoline hit my senses, telling me to keep going. I needed to be quick before I was stopped. All the servants had cleared out per my orders once my father and Hilda started to argue.

It was time to get this show on the road. Once I was satisfied, I walked to the kitchen and grabbed a bottle of champagne, and a wash cloth. I made my way outside and opened the bottle, taking a heavy gulp. Tonight had gone to shit. The Order, no, the Kings would never allow anyone to surpass them. They were so fucking desperate that they made a deal with a peasant.

I was now standing by my room. I had left the balcony door open. I grabbed a cigarette and lit it, then I stuffed the cloth into the champagne bottle and lit that on fire.

"Molotov cocktail, anyone?" I laughed to myself as I threw it.

Everything became bright the moment the fire made contact with my room. It was fascinating watching the flames being born. In no time, they licked every surface. They were starting to spread fast, and I knew I had to be fast as well. Before I walked out of the house, I made sure to block my father's and Hilda's way out.

They were not leaving this place alive. They didn't deserve to stain the world with their bullshit. Soon everything was burning, and the staff was out. I made sure to hide in the bushes to see what they would do.

Just as I expected, there was no need for them to want to rush out and help. They all made their way to the front of the house where the driveway ended, ensuring they were safe, yet they didn't try to run.

We had a back entrance that led to a lone alley between the houses in the area. I knew leaving a car would draw attention, and I didn't know how to ride a motorcycle, but a scooter was easier, and that would have to do. They were cheap, and cash transactions wouldn't leave a trail. Especially when it was under Hilda's name. You couldn't investigate a dead person.

I had made this plan for two in mind, but going solo was the same shit. I should be used to it by now. The sirens blaring in the background were like music to my ears, but by the time they made it to my father's office and Hilda's room, it would be too late for them.

I needed to leave before someone saw me. I counted on the fact that the Order wouldn't let civilians know what really went down. The police department here was on a leash, and making a deal with me would only line their pockets with money. The fumes were heavy, making my head a little dizzy. I looked at the house once more, and I felt nothing.

Since it was a matter of minutes before the fire department came looking back here, I made my way toward my gateway exit, when the sound of something breaking startled me. The noise came from one of the guest rooms. A nightstand lamp broke the glass that led to the balcony in the guest room. I didn't think I'd have to block that one since no one went out there. It was more for show than anything.

A willowy body came tumbling out. They ran to the side of the balcony and jumped. It was in slow motion as I watched the body land on the floor. For a second, I forgot how to even breathe. Everything was red and covered in smoke. I didn't think twice and ran toward them. Opening the door had allowed the wind to blow into that side of the house causing the flames to rush to this side of the house.

I was coughing as I ran, but after seeing that, I couldn't leave them there. First thing I noticed was the body, and when I saw it *wasn't Hilda, I felt remorse. No one was supposed to be here. As I got next to them, I threw up.*

My face was starting to burn. The flames had reached us. I looked at Erin one last time and started to drag her away from there.

Erin could hate me all she wanted. Our actions had consequences; no one told her to stay at my house after everyone had left. We weren't friends, so I didn't owe her shit. Liam and Theo were the last to walk inside, both of them smirking at me.

I held my head high and looked at them, and when the doors opened again, I wasn't even surprised when his father walked in after them.

THIRTEEN

MASON

As soon as Wilfred King walked in, everyone's eyes came to me. Did they think I was fucking stupid and would show up here without a plan?

They thought they took all of my father's assets, but they had no idea.

"Really, Liam, you had to bring Daddy for this?" I mocked. I was not cowering before them. The era of the Kings was coming to an end. I wasn't even looking to take their place. I just wanted to dethrone them so I could sit on their graves.

"You look well for a dead person," Wilfred King said without fear.

It took me being on my own to realize that it wasn't always the people who had it all that were strong. They had pillars of support; they could fall back without fear. It was all of those that were alone, and day by day, they chose to get the fuck up and keep going. Now that was strong because they did it all without having the guarantee of success.

Strength wasn't power, but it was empowering.

"Did you think only you can pay people off?"

He grinned, but it was forced.

"Let me guess since you two are hiding under his skirt, you think you won?"

These social circles they created in high school still followed them around. As long as no one was a threat to their money and lifestyle, they followed like blind sheep. God forbid any of them ever got more than the Kings because then they would be treated the same as my family was.

"Why don't we go talk somewhere more private," Wilfred said.

"I'm fine right here. After all, there's no secrets among the Order, right?"

His eyes darkened by my answer. He didn't like brazenness one bit.

"It will be in your best interest to come with me. After all, if you're alive, you'll be wanted for murder...."

So that was his trump call.

I smiled.

It's not like I wasn't expecting this.

"Actually, I'm not. After all, you paid the media to say it was a gas leak. But hey, if you want to take it back, I can also give them a long little list of things you have paid to have covered."

My body was sweaty as fuck, but at this moment, I didn't give two shits because Wilfred King was just where I wanted him to be.

The rich, politicians, and anyone who thought themselves as God's will always have skeletons in their closets. And if you wanted revenge, you didn't have to fear getting your hands dirty when trying to get them.

I might have been brought up with a golden

spoon, but I knew how to get my hands dirty, and the difference between me and everyone else here was I didn't let anyone else do my dirty work.

"It was a nice little story you had them spin. Wealthy family dies and leaves everything to their faithful servants, isn't that right, Aspen?"

My cold stare turned toward her, and for the first time, she looked unnerved. Everyone was looking at her now. The deal between her parents and the Kings wasn't something they were privy to. As you grow in the world, you start to make connections, and when my family's assets were transferred to the Millers, it was not hard to guess what had gone down.

"Tell them," I spoke to her, our gazes locked. Neither one of us wanted to be the first to look away. Even if I broke her, I don't know if I would be satisfied.

Well, the least *I* could do was try.

"This is just all hypothetical since I wasn't present when you decided to stab me in the back."

Aspen's lip trembled; her face was stoic, but she was too stiff. I could bet my pack of smokes she had her hands under the table.

"To secure the deal, you needed the information from my father..." I stopped looking at her and turned to Wilfred and Liam. "Congratulations, I heard King Industries had a great launch, and thanks to that, it was the innovation the company needed to stay relevant."

Wilfred couldn't stand anyone outshining him. And by the looks of it, neither did Liam.

It was time I wrapped this up for now.

"So the Millers handed you my father's next big launch, and the fact that the house went kaboom worked in your favor. That's why you had it labeled as a gas leak, wrapped it up nice and pretty, so when you took all of my family's assets, there wouldn't be a delay." My gaze went back to Aspen, and I felt my mouth run dry, even though I still hadn't said the part that hurt the most. "And after you marry Liam, you'll be handing him over everything my family had owned."

It really was a brilliant fucking plan. It worked for everyone. The Kings got to take over everything through a marriage-merger.

Appearance had to be kept after all, and this wasn't a hostile takeover.

I started to clap, and the sound echoed in the cabin. I probably looked a bit unhinged, but it was okay. I had waited so long for this day, and seeing the unraveled look on their faces made it worth it.

"My father didn't like you, and he had money the Order didn't know about," I told him.

That shouldn't be surprising to him. If everyone was wise, they would do the same thing. The Order was supposed to be a union between families, but somewhere along the way, The Kings wanted to rule over them. My father might have been a lot of things, and a part of me hated him, but he was still my father. He lost himself in trying to grow our empires to surpass the Kings.

Aware that everyone was watching me, I casually got up and walked right through where the Kings were standing.

I had been weak my whole life. I let others do whatever the fuck they wanted to me. I cut myself up a thousand times because I couldn't deal with the pain I carried. Humans have a breaking point, and mine set my whole world on fire. No one had to know that the person they knew was gone when I rose from the ashes. They say killing stains your soul, but I was okay with it because it had also set me free.

"Don't test me," I spoke right next to Liam while I looked at his father. "If I killed my own parents, I won't hesitate to kill you."

FOURTEEN

ASPEN

MASON STILTSKIN WENT FROM DOCILE AND WEAK INTO someone who wreaked havoc in their path. I held my head a little higher as he went on and talked about the deal.

It was his money that had given me everything I had.

It was his money that funded the freedom I thought I wanted.

He once had asked me what I wanted most in the world, and I had refused to answer him, but the world gave it to me in the most twisted way.

In his eyes, we were his enemies; at the end of the day, who was I to judge him. You didn't have to physically kill a person for them to be dead.

While I had been wallowing in the fact that my own parents had fucked me over and handed me off like a prized mare, Mason had been plotting his every move to take us all down.

I slowly turned my profile so I could get a better look at Mr. King. The only thing Liam was good at was using his name to get what he wanted. No one took him seriously. You take his last name from him, and he had nothing.

He wasn't a worthy opponent.

On the other hand, Mason had lost everything. They wouldn't say they feared him, they certainly didn't trust him, but for right now, they wouldn't cross him.

Mason whispered something only they could hear. Mr. King's jaw tensed, and he put his hand inside his pocket. It was something I've seen him do to act nonchalant when in all reality, he was losing it.

No one dared say a word as the doors slammed on his way out.

"Everyone is free to go and explore the grounds," Mr. King said with a charming smile.

"Later, I'm going to go see if Stiltskin wants to work out his rage with me," Rachel told us as she left.

My stomach felt queasy.

Once upon a time, I would have been confident he wouldn't go near them, but it seems the only one he hadn't tried going after was me.

Everyone started to clear out fast; the only ones who remained were the King men, and that's when I also stood up, ready to get the fuck out, but before I could make it to the door, Mr. King spoke.

Fuck.

Liam was easy to handle; he had a big mouth and wouldn't move two steps before clearing it with his father, but Wilfred King, he was on a whole new scale. My parents were puppets to him, but they didn't care because their attached strings came with lots of money.

"Aspen." His tone was cold, but it always had been. My only saving grace was my so-called beauty. But then again, beauty was only from perspective, and I never understood how was it that Mr. King went along with my parents' demands.

"Mr. King." My words came out soft and with respect.

One thing I had learned in the past two years was that the rich were so bored with their mere existence their moral compass was broken. Once I stepped foot in his estate, I realized why he agreed to marry me off to his son.

Yes, he was going to be able to control my parents, their new money, but he also wanted me to keep his pretty little blonde lineage going.

"Take a seat," he motioned to the chair that was in front of him.

He stayed standing and pretended to fix his tie. I slowly took a seat, and I hated to look up at him. He always made sure to throw it in my parents' faces just how they had achieved what they wanted. He made us feel inferior every chance he got. I think he got off on it. That wasn't a problem since I grew up looking up at everyone. The problem was that now that I was at the top, I had him at my back, reminding me of what I had done.

His mocking gaze bore witness to the knife I had stabbed.

"Theodore, make sure everyone is at ease," Wilfred instructed Teddy, but in reality, he didn't want him to be part of this conversation.

Family didn't mean anything to anyone here; they would throw them to the wolves in a second if it meant they would survive.

As soon as the door closed behind Teddy, I braced myself for what would come.

"I'm beginning to think you lied to me, Miss Miller," Mr. King said in a calm voice that had chills running down my spine.

"I wouldn't dare," I said without meeting his face.

You didn't hear your loneliness cry out until you were alone in a room, and for the first time in my life, mine was crying out. I had a room to myself. The bed was king-sized, the mattress was soft, and the pillows were fluffy. I had a bathroom to myself, and for the first time, I had the option to take a bath instead of a shower.

None of this mattered; all I could see was Mason's face as I left with Liam.

There was no one around. I was alone, free to lie in the bed I had made for myself, and yet I looked at it like it was made out of spikes. I sat on the floor right by the door and looked at the room, just wondering if it was worth the price. In the end, nothing turned out how I had envisioned. Everyone had cut their own deal, and I was the one who lost. Funny, because a couple of weeks ago, I didn't think I could lose anything since I had nothing, but how wrong had I been.

My thoughts came to a halt when the door to the room I was given a few hours ago flew open. Light filled the room, and I looked up at Liam who stumbled inside.

"Come with me," he spat as he bent to grab my arm, pulled me up, and then dragged me with him.

He was hurting my arm, but I didn't dare say a word. As soon as I had followed him, once my fate had been sealed, he showed me his true face. I was just a conquest to him—an object. He was only putting a façade because deals looked more tempting when they were dipped in gold and covered in lies.

We walked down to the first floor, and then he opened the door to his father's study.

"What was your relationship with Stiltskin?" Mr. King asked as soon as I walked into the room.

It caught me off guard. Yet, there was nothing to say. Whatever sort of friendship Mason and I had was now over. He was not going to forgive me, not after the way he had been glaring at me.

Then that kiss—no, I wasn't going to think of it now.

"He was my master, and I was his servant."

As I said those words, I recalled all the times he told me not to call him master.

"So there was nothing special?"

My heart skipped a beat, but somehow, I managed to keep my face stoic.

"No." The lie was flawless indeed.

"Very well," he said as he leaned back in his chair. "Don't forget you're going to be a King one day, and with that comes certain expectations."

His words were a warning. There was no need to worry; either way, I had burned my bridge.

"I understand," I reassured him.

"Not like it matters." Mr. King waved a hand dismissively. "The Stiltskins are now dead."

Blood drained from my face, my feet went shaky and weak, and my body felt cold.

"Does that surprise you?" Mr. King's tone was mocking. "Take her away."

Liam took me back to my room. I didn't know what he said or how I even ended up in the room they had given me. My brain was trying to process the fact that Mason Stiltskin wasn't in this world anymore, as my heart refused to believe it.

"Imp went and died when I didn't get a chance to kill him myself."

My head snapped toward Liam as he uttered those harsh words, but I bit my lip until blood coated my tongue because I was in no place to say anything.

"How did they die?" I somehow managed to ask.

"They burned."

I think that's when I knew deep in my heart that Mason had not died. Not when every time I thought about our kiss, I could smell the gasoline that stained his fingertips.

"As you said before, I'm set to be a King one day. I know my expectations."

What else could I say? You had to learn to play the game or be played, and with the Kings, I had to adjust quickly.

"You're a smart girl." He smiled at me.

He wasn't praising me or even complimenting me because, on other occasions, he had said my parents were ignorant. I couldn't disagree with him there. It wasn't stated, but it was implied. I was my parents' money cow, and if I stepped out of line, not only would I suffer, but so would they.

"If that's all, may I leave?"

Mr. King gave me a nod and pointed toward the door. I got up immediately and almost forgot that Liam had been in the room with us.

"Excuse me, father, I need a word with my fiancée."

The use of that word was nothing more than a mock. I refrained from glaring at Liam, not in front of his father. I was currently at their mercy, and I wanted to get away from them.

Liam grabbed my arm and led me outside.

As soon as the doors closed, he pushed me against the wall and caged me in. He always filled me with unease. I had a feeling that he didn't try to take from me what I wasn't willing to give because soon I wouldn't have a choice, so that gave him patience.

"You're so fucking hot when you are cornered," he taunted.

I said nothing; he was the type who liked to hear themselves talk.

He looked at me for a few seconds then bent to kiss me. I

turned my head, but he cupped my cheeks with his hands and forced our lips to meet.

"It just makes me harder, Aspen," he whispered.

I glared at him.

"I have a proposition."

I was about to tell him to go to hell when I saw two people walking into the forest. He took it as a cue to keep on talking.

Mason and Rachel.

Jealousy was an ugly emotion. It made you act crazy, irrational; most of all, it made you weak.

FIFTEEN

MASON

NOTHING IN MY LIFE HAS EVER GONE ACCORDING TO PLAN, AND now that all the chips were falling in their place, I didn't know how to relax without feeling like it all was going to fall apart. I had this feeling once, and then it just went to shit, so I didn't want to get comfortable.

I knew I could only push Wilfred King so far before he decided to hell with being cautious and killed me. When you were addicted to power, you'd do anything to keep it. I'd embraced hell for a second, had its flames lick me and caress me, but instead of lying down, I decided that there was still a lot I had to do before I went there.

People started to filter out, and only The Kings and Aspen remained. I wanted to go to my tent and lie down for a second, but curiosity got the better of me. I could feel the stares of those stuck-up bitches clinging to my skin. I clenched my hands.

They served a purpose. I couldn't even remember their faces as we fucked. It was always the same thing—push them down on their knees, fuck them, and leave. I had hoped to humiliate them a little bit, but it seemed that as long as revenge came attached to something pretty to look at, it made it okay.

"Hey, Mason," a whinny, high-pitched voice said next to me.

I looked down to my right to where Rachael was standing next to me. I took a step to the left when I noticed she was trying to press her body against me.

Pussy and tits didn't really entice me. That wasn't what got me hard. Rachel smiled sultry at me, and all it did was turn me off.

"What?" I questioned, even though I already knew what she wanted.

"I thought maybe we could have a repeat, and this time I could do all the work."

I was about to say I wasn't interested when I saw Liam walk out with Aspen. I had the urge to go and pull her away from him. The only person who could torment her was me.

When I felt Aspen's gaze on me, I dropped my profile to give Rachel my undivided attention.

"Tell you what, if you can keep up with me, I'll fuck you again." My smirk was anything but pleasant, and she ate it up.

I made my way to the forest trail entrance, letting everyone see she was on my heels.

"Where's your cabin?" she asked as she noticed I deviated from the trail.

It amazed me how ignorant they could be. Instead of answering her, I walked faster and then hid in the bushes.

I watched her huff in annoyance at the fact that I had ditched her. I was about to leave when she pulled out her phone.

"You better come get me. He fucking ditched me."

I cocked my head, somewhat confused. Her interest had

been real; of that, I was sure. Girls like Rachel were always down for a good time.

A little later, I heard footsteps coming, so I crouched lower to not be seen. I wanted to say I was surprised when Liam walked up to her, but it was just the type of move he would make. He thought everyone was his property.

"Took you long enough," Rachel huffed.

"I was busy." He shrugged it off.

"With your fiancée?" Rachel scuffed.

Every time I heard that word, it grated on my nerves—it was a constant stab in the back.

"Don't start," he told her as he got closer, his voice now gentle. "You know I have to marry her."

Rachel rolled her eyes but still wrapped her arms around him. I know I should leave, but it always fascinated me to see other people fuck. How they gave in so quickly and trusted the person they were with so carelessly.

"You better not do to me what you did to Erin," Rachel said as she removed her shirt.

That caught me off guard. Erin was a victim, no matter how much of a bitch she had been. It seemed the accident had changed her. But back then, she was stuck with Liam like she owned him.

"As soon as she became an inconvenience, you let your friend have her."

Well, this certainly was interesting.

There was a lot of kissing and groping that I got bored of and quietly left them. My campsite was a little bit deeper. I just wanted to take this damn glove off for now. Blonde hair caught my eye—not just any blonde, the type that shined like gold in the sunlight.

Without hesitation, I went after it. Liam was too engrossed in fucking that he wouldn't notice if someone else was around unless they were right in his path. Self-centered people never noticed anyone else.

I managed to grab Aspen before she went toward Liam and Rachael. My hand wrapped around her waist with ease. She was small but no longer frail. She had gained some weight, and it didn't look bad.

"Going somewhere?" I whispered in her ear.

"Le—"

I put a gloved hand over her mouth before she could yell. Excitement spread through my veins as I realized I had her all to myself. The first thing I wanted was to give her a dose of humility. With one hand wrapped around her and the other to her mouth, I moved us, so we were close enough to see Liam and Rachel, but hidden from their view.

The moment she heard moaning, she became still in my arms.

"What's wrong?" I whispered in her ear. "Don't tell me you're a prude."

Usually, I wouldn't be talking, but right now, I couldn't help myself. Like I said earlier, I didn't get excited easily. That wasn't the case now, though. My dick was rock hard. Number one, I was in a position of power against Aspen. Having her in my arms, being the one in control, and having my hand covering her mouth thrilled me. Second was the fact that I was about to shove some humility down her throat.

We hid behind a tree. I pressed Aspen up against it; she was wedged between the trunk and my body. Then I tilted her head so she could see the scene that was unraveling in front of us. Rachel had her skirt hiked up to her waist. She was bent over, holding onto a boulder while Liam fucked her from behind.

"That's who you're going to marry?" I mocked in her ear.

Aspen's breathing was still, and her body stiffened. Was she angry that her fiancé was fucking someone else? Based on their earlier conversation, I didn't think so, but I also knew Liam, and he enjoyed taunting her. He hadn't forced her because he knew sooner or later, he would have her. This was just a cat-and-mouse game that he was sure he would win. That made me angry, and my blood boiled.

"Look how much they're enjoying it," I groaned in her ear. Without thinking, I rested my head on the crook of her neck. My tongue peeked out, and I licked the soft skin of her neck, adding pressure so she could feel the little metal balls rubbing against her.

Aspen's back arched, and I wondered what she would sound like if I flicked her clit with my tongue. I pulled back before I could have more idiotic thoughts. This wasn't for her; it was for me to get off on her pain.

I didn't remove my hand from her mouth but instead slipped two fingers inside. "Don't make a sound, or else he will see you…" I itched to make her gag around my fingers. I wanted to see her eyes water and hear her muffled cries.

"Harder."

Rachel's scream startled Aspen. Her body jolted, and I had to press up against her more. I was careful so she wouldn't feel the imprint of my dick on her ass.

Liam pulled Rachel's hair, causing her head to fall back.

"You like that?" he groaned.

Slowly my fingers started to move in and out of Aspen's mouth, and I don't think she noticed the moment she began to suck them. All it did was make me want to replace them with my cock. How would it feel? Having her pink lips stretched as I fucked her mouth?

"Do you want to be fucked like a whore, Aspen?"

SIXTEEN

Have you ever done things without thinking? It's like your body is on auto instead of manual, and it knows your innermost desires, hence following them blindly? That's how I felt right now. I followed behind Mason and Rachel without thinking.

I could say I needed space from Liam, but I could have just gone back to the cabin or gone off to the lake with the others, but I didn't. I wanted to see with my own eyes that Mason was so changed that he was fucking the same girls who belittled him. I wanted to feel disgusted by him, but in reality, we wouldn't be so different. I now dined with them, so what difference did it make if he fucked them?

Now I was trapped here, with him holding me while Liam fucked Rachel. The forest was quiet. I could hear the wet noises perfectly, and it made my body hot. I itched to get closer to Mason if that was even possible. The leather entered my mouth with ease, and it made me feel full of him. I wanted more. I wanted to feel his lips pressed against me again, for him to kiss me with desperation and ask me again what I wanted most in the world—what I wanted the most was to turn back time.

My mouth started to move on its own, a slow fire spreading within me. Seeing what was happening in front of me and being engulfed in Mason's smell drove me crazy.

"Do you want to be fucked like a whore, Aspen?" Mason's husky voice was the only indication that he was just affected as I was, but like hell would I let him have the upper hand.

I bit his fingers, but the leather prevented me from doing any damage.

He chuckled softly. The sound made my stomach drop. Without realizing it, I turned my head hoping I could see it, but by the time our eyes met, his lips were once again in a flat line. His green eyes were unguarded, and it made his face look a little less hostile. Why did I take this look for granted back then? Since the moment I met him, he never looked at me with arrogance or like I was beneath him. Maybe indifference, but that had changed as the years went by.

I pulled my head away from his fingers since he eased up.

"You're not touching me," I ground out.

His eyes became cold once more.

"Are you saving it for Liam?" He sounded disgusted.

Before I could say more, he brought his gloved hand down between my legs. I could feel the wet leather trailing up my thighs.

"What are you doing?" I hissed.

Mason didn't reply right away. Instead, he angled us so I could see Liam fuck Rachel harder and faster.

"Proving that you're no different," he whispered maybe more to himself than to me.

The moment his finger rubbed my clit, I lifted onto my tiptoes from the sensation and let out a soft moan.

Mason held onto me tighter while his finger rubbed me in slow circles. The way the leather felt against my clit was divine. Subconsciously I started to grind my hips against his hand. I wanted more. I now understood why everyone was so obsessed with having sex if it felt like this.

Mason removed his finger only to press the tip against my entrance. I moaned, not in pleasure, but not in pain either. It was different. Mason removed his hand that was wrapped around my waist and brought it up to my neck. He wrapped his hand around it like a choker.

"I suggest you stay quiet...unless you want your fiancée to see how you're rubbing your pussy against my hand like a bitch in heat."

His words were harsh and crude, and instead of being offended or turned off, I was thrilled. Or maybe because I was lost in the depths of his green eyes that I couldn't control my reactions.

I heard Rachel moan again, then Liam praised her, and just for a second, I wanted to lose control like that too. I never had anyone. I had to rely on myself. My mistakes were my only companions.

"*Mase,*" I hissed his name.

His eyes flared, and he brought his hand to my mouth, covering it tightly as he inserted his finger in—this time, deeper and with more force. I screamed against his mouth.

"Don't call me that. I'm not your friend," he seethed.

I couldn't answer when his hand was wrapped so tight around my mouth. Mason's fingers slid in and out, the stinging and burning slowly fading with each thrust.

"You're so fucking tight," he groaned.

His voice made me melt into him.

"Let's see if you can handle two fingers," he taunted.

My body stilled for a second, preparing for more.

"You're so fucking wet."

He was affected as much as I was; I could hear it in his voice. This time when he entered me, he did it slowly. I knew I was soaked because the leather slid in with ease. There was still discomfort, but it was starting to feel good.

The way he was looking at me now, I wanted to remember this look over the hate. I wanted him to kiss me. I was so desperate that I started to lick his hand. His eyes widened in surprise.

He removed the pressure enough so I could talk.

"Please," I begged.

I don't know if it was for a kiss, for him to let me finish, or for him to forgive me. It really didn't matter at the moment.

Mason removed the two fingers, making me feel empty, then brought them to my clit and started to rub against it. The friction felt so good that I wanted to seek more and be submerged in it. I felt hot where he touched, gradually losing control over my emotions. My body knew what it wanted and sought it. I rubbed my pussy against him and bit my lip, but still I could hear the soft mewls that escaped.

I could feel Mason's heavy breathing. A part of me wanted to have some dignity that I tried to move my face so he wouldn't be able to see me.

Mason didn't allow that. He gripped my chin and angled my face so we wouldn't break eye contact.

"Look at me," he demanded in a low voice.

I wrapped one of my hands around his neck and pushed him down toward my face without thinking.

Mason went still for a second. We just breathed each other in. Rachel's cries got louder, and Liam cursed, but I didn't care to focus on them anymore. I waited years to feel Mason's mouth against me again.

Last time I couldn't savor it because all I could taste was betrayal on his lips. This time I was ready to swallow his rage and match it with my own.

His lips were no longer chapped; they were soft and moved with precision. My mouth parted the moment he began to move his hand again.

"Rub your pussy against my hand. I want my glove soaked with your release," he whispered against my lips right before he kissed me.

My hips began to move furiously against him. We were in perfect sync. I could feel my release coming, and I was desperately chasing it. The moment I felt my release start to wash over me, I pulled on his hair, and Mason shoved his tongue inside of me, swallowing my moans. Those three little balls in my mouth made me jolt. I didn't have the chance to focus on that because he shoved one lone finger deep inside of me. My pussy gripped onto it as my release started to subside.

The desperation in our kiss was fading because when Mason tore his mouth away, I realized I could no longer hear anything around us.

"You're just as easy as the rest of them, *pet.*"

Rage and humiliation washed over me. I tried to move away from him, but he held onto my waist. He lifted me up a bit and then shoved me down on the finger he had inside me.

I started to thrash against him, but it was no use. He wasn't letting me go anywhere. I sighed in relief when he pulled his fingers out. It was short-lived when he dragged me out of our hiding place and walked toward the place

Liam had just been. There was no sign of him and Rachel anymore.

Mason shoved me against the boulder Rachel had been bent over a moment ago.

"Did it make you jealous to hear I fucked every single one of those bitches?" His voice was cruel.

I didn't have a chance to catch my breath when he pulled down my underwear and shoved a finger inside of me. This time it felt different since he did it with his other hand—more personal, if anything.

"Answer me," he seethed when I refused to make a sound.

He then added two more fingers. Blood coated my tongue from where I was biting my lip so hard.

"It's okay, don't answer." He chuckled. "But your pussy is begging for more."

Maybe I should have been scared, but a part of me wanted it. Perhaps it was something he could take and then call ourselves even. Or even if he never forgave me, I'd have something to remember him by.

He pulled his fingers out, and I braced myself to feel him at my entrance, but that didn't happen. Instead, he turned me around and switched spots with me.

I was left standing with my underwear halfway down my legs while he sat on the rock with his legs spread. I could see his dick tenting through his pants.

"On your knees, pet," he ground out.

We had been here before—him showing his dominance over me.

"N-no," I told him.

Maybe because I didn't want to give in too quickly, or I wasn't ready to admit defeat.

"Unless you want me to tell prince charming how tight your pussy is, you'll do as I say."

Liam would go apeshit over this.

"I can also let everyone know you knew I was going to burn the house down. It might have saved a life...or three."

My hands went to my underwear so I could bring them up, but he spoke.

"Leave them like that," Mason commanded.

I let go of my panties, and with shaky legs, I began to get on my knees.

"Good girl." Mason smirked.

My belly dipped for all the wrong reasons.

Last time, he had me naked in front of him, but it wasn't as humiliating as I felt at this moment. If someone were to walk out here, there would be no coming back from this. Still, I couldn't bring myself to move.

My knees were starting to burn from the dirty ground, but without saying a word, I reached for his zipper.

"What are you doing?" Mason asked as he held onto my wrist.

I didn't answer him.

"Open your mouth," he said instead.

We looked at each other for a second. Maybe I was waiting for the old him to come out, but that wasn't happening.

My mouth parted, and he smiled at me. I'll admit it made me bring my guard down.

He brought his left hand to my cheek and caressed it, his thumb lightly tracing my lip.

"They're swollen," he whispered.

He pushed his thumb inside.

"Pretend it's my dick."

I wrapped my lips around it and swirled my tongue

against it, and then I pulled back. Mason cupped my cheek, then moved his hand to my head and ran his fingers through my hair. The action was tender and that surprised me. He did it again, and when he rubbed against my nape, I couldn't help but lower my guard and close my eyes.

Affection—that's what I was feeling.

I felt my face being lowered, and I let him. Mason slowly removed his hand from my nape then tenderly brought it to cup my cheek again. I opened my eyes when he tipped my chin up.

"Like I'd let your mouth near my dick," he spat.

I froze, and my body went cold. Before I could move, he gripped my jaw and added pressure against my cheeks, forcing my lips to open.

"Lick my glove clean," he groaned as he showed the two fingers that had been inside of me into my mouth.

My eyes watered as I gagged against them. If I wanted him to let go of me, I had no choice but to do as he said.

When he had his fill, he removed his hand slowly. I could see my saliva dripping from them. I didn't care about the sight; I was trying to catch my breath.

"Fuck—"

"I'll pass," Mason said as he left me before I could curse him out.

Once he was gone, tears streamed down my face at how stupid I had been. Every single action had consequences, and this was the repercussion of mine.

SEVENTEEN

MASON

I COULD FEEL EVERY SINGLE CELL IN MY BODY VIBRATE WITH need. I don't know how I kept my composure and managed to get out before shoving my dick down Aspen's throat. The moment she had reached for my zipper, I almost let her. How would it feel? Before, the feeling was terrifying; I didn't know what to do with my body. Torn between disgust, fear, and wanting Hilda to take me deeper. Ultimately it made me feel so used that even if I came, the post-orgasmic feeling was drowned out by shame.

As soon as I crawled inside my tent, I removed my leather glove and threw it. The fresh air felt amazing against my sweaty hand. I proceeded to remove my shirt and then just threw myself against the sleeping bag. It was a bitch to keep hiding my burns in the summer. I learned not to mind them. The scarred skin was just another reminder of what I had been through.

"Fuck," I whispered to myself.

Without a second thought, I pulled down my zipper and stroked my dick. I wrapped my left hand around it and began to jack myself. I was so fucking hard I knew it wouldn't take long. Especially not after recalling the way Aspen had looked. The moment she started to grind herself against my fingers, I lost it. I thought that by using my gloved hand, I could put some sort of barrier against us.

I've thought of Aspen many times before to try and remove Hilda from my mind, but I could never get it right. The image in my head never did it justice. It always felt too fake, and in the end, memories of Hilda won. But now, Aspen was fresh in my mind, her cries, the way she looked at me. I couldn't control myself. I was supposed to be teaching her a lesson, and my need for her took over.

The moment her wet pussy touched my skin, I almost came in my pants. No woman had ever made me feel that way. Still, the look of disappointment and regret at the end was what had me coming right now.

My release coated my hand, and I quickly reached for an old shirt to wipe it off. My heavy breathing echoed inside the tent, and I waited for that feeling that always followed me around, but it didn't come. For the first time, I didn't feel shame.

I needed a shower and better sleep. The first was an easy solve; I could go down to the lake early in the morning. As for sleeping, I knew that wasn't going to come easy, it never really did. It just felt worse under the open sky.

My family had never been one for camping. My parents kept me close, and in return, it made me sheltered. My dad didn't want me to depend too much on the Order. Maybe in a way that contributed to the fact that I got ostracized by them.

This trip was supposed to be secret and elusive, letting us all know the big sins of our forefathers in due time. By the time you arrived at this point, you were used to it all; you wouldn't want to give it up.

My father had told me that each of us would receive a book containing information on all the things the Order has taken a part in. It was the initiation. You knew the secrets of what made it tick, but in return, it made you an accomplice.

The Order was supposed to be an all-for-one and one-for-all kind of thing, but everyone looked out for themselves. That's why in the book, you'd never find all the side deals each family had made. I, however, had received such a booklet, along with information on my father's other business, when I came back from studying abroad.

Maybe my father thought that because I had fucked Hilda, I was a man. I snorted and put my arm over my head.

The world was a fucked-up place, and you either lived or drowned in it.

By the time the sun had come up, I was already showered and making my way to Aspen's cabin. Technically speaking, my family's cabin since that was just another thing she had stolen from me.

Usually, no one was around this early, so when I bumped into Erin and Nate, I wasn't expecting them. He pushed her even though her wheelchair was adapted to move her. He looked content, and she was smiling at him. Both of their carefree smiles vanished the moment they saw me.

"I guess saying good morning is out of the question." I shrugged.

Nate glared at me, and Erin just stared at me stoically.

Since neither of them said anything, I just kept walking.

"You should have died." Erin's voice was loud enough that I could hear her.

I chuckled.

Had I died in that fire, so would she.

I turned around, and Nate was giving me a warning look. Probably so I wouldn't offend her. Tragedies happen to people all the time. She was in a wheelchair, so what? She still had so much more than everyone else. She needed to get over herself.

It was time to test the new information I had overheard.

"Senior year, you were Liam 's favorite, weren't you?" I asked in a condescending tone. Her mouth parted open, but neither of them said more.

"Maybe you should have left him before he tossed you aside."

Erin flinched.

"No one told you to stay around and hang at my house. We weren't fucking friends."

With those words, I walked away. My hand was fisted so tight I had fought the urge to show her the scars I got for saving her.

I was too weak to carry Erin, so my only option was to drag her away, except that was also going to be a bitch because of my lack of oxygen. Still, I needed to try. At this moment, I had never cussed myself more. I was an imp, and I couldn't get anything right. Had I been stronger, I would have been able to carry her away.

I was coughing and wheezing, scared that I would get caught any second and all of this would be for nothing. Even if I got caught, would it even matter? Nothing turned out like I had hoped. The smoke fog wasn't as heavy—my only indication that I was moving in the right direction.

Step after step, and each was heavier than the next. I just needed to finish dragging her, and I could leave. I was so close I could feel it.

They say adrenaline makes you do stupid shit, and it was true. I was almost done getting Erin to safety when part of the roof collapsed. The debris went flying around us, and I protected Erin with my body. Luckily we had been far enough, so we weren't submerged in it, but it still managed to reach us.

My arm was hurting like a bitch. I howled when I couldn't stand it anymore, scared that someone was going to hear me. Still, I hadn't stopped because I didn't want Erin to die for what I had done.

It took months for my hand to finish healing. Without going to a proper doctor, the scarring never healed right. The nerves in my hands still caused me pain from time to time, but that shit was to be expected.

Pain has always centered me, so I didn't mind it.

I needed to get off this island soon. I had a meet I could not miss. After my father died, it took some time to prove that I could take over the reins of what he had left behind.

If my father was correct and we got our book, then the rest of the time would be like a vacation. Concluding the welcome into the Order.

Things were sure to get interesting soon.

EIGHTEEN

I was crying, and I didn't know why. A part of me refused to believe that Mason was dead. He couldn't be. I clutched the chain he gave me close to my chest. Is this what he had tried to tell me before I spat on his face?

It was delusional of me to think that he would come back and save me. We were so many things, but at the same time, nothing at all. He was my master, but not really. I was his friend, but not truly. There had been feelings, but we never released them. We were just a bunch of little incomplete, broken pieces.

And here we are again—all those broken, jagged pieces cutting each other over and over again. I clutched onto his chain because it still brought some comfort, and I felt naked without it.

Yesterday I had lost my fucking mind. Mason was not here to save me or set me free; he was here for his revenge, and I needed to fucking remember that.

Whether I was rich or a servant slave, my life was no different. I still had to bow down to the same kings.

It was another day of pretending.

As I showered, I began to get angry. This feeling, I

remembered it all too well. It was laced with injustice and repression. I was part of the in-crowd, but I would always be the outsider that stabbed someone else in the back to get in. I sat on top of a small fortune that was stolen. I was going to marry America's number one bachelor, and the idea terrified me. Was there anything I could do?

The hot water burned gliding down my skin, and all it did was add fuel to the rage that had always been inside of me. I was always the victim, and when I tried not to be, I was the villain. Time passed by, and the leash it had around my neck kept closing in.

On the one hand, I had Liam, who I was sure was going to make me miserable. I never believed in love or anything like that. What even was true love? Having parents who sold you off? Backstabbing a boy only to have some freedom? Sleeping with a married woman so you could get your wife and child out of being slaves? It was all just a bunch of bullshit.

I got out of the shower and wrapped a towel around my middle. I cleaned up the fog and looked at my reflection.

What stared back at me was a coward. The more I looked, the more disgusted I was with myself. The clothes, the house, the money—I felt guilty about it, yet I hadn't tried running. I knew the Order could find me, but I still could have found a way around it.

If I had cut back on the bullshit, I would have realized deep down in my heart Mason was alive. He had set fire to that fucking house and wanted me to go with him. My knees went weak, and I held onto the sink for support.

Knowing he wanted to bring me with him—that was what hurt the most. Had I trusted him and told him the thing I wanted the most, maybe, just maybe we could both be somewhere else living a normal life.

Regret was one hell of a bitch, wasn't it?

"What do you want from me?" I whispered as I looked at myself.

He could have told Erin what went down that night between us the moment he got here. I mean, at this point, would it even matter? Erin wasn't even talking to me. She was the only person I clung to because she was the only one who had somewhat accepted me.

I opened the door and walked out of the bathroom, ready to get another day over with. As the steam poured outward, I realized the water had been burning. It brought a memory front and center of the time I had walked into Mason's room. His skin had been bright red. Then I remembered all the blood, and I felt stupid to have forgotten such an important detail.

"Washing away your sins?"

My head snapped toward where the voice was coming from.

Mason sat on the same chair he had been the other day. One brow was raised while the rest of his face was stoic.

"Get the hell out of my room," I spat at him.

On the one hand, I was angry for what he had done to me, while another part of me was embarrassed.

He threw his head back and laughed. I was fascinated watching the way his Adam's apple wobbled by the action. When he looked back at me, there was a chilling look on his face.

"It really took you no effort to claim everything that had been mine," he stated. "The cabins are assigned by family. You only get one because they gave you mine."

My throat constricted.

"The Kings tried to sweep my last name under the rug and give you everything that once was mine."

I didn't know what to say. Any apology would make him mad. It was too late for that.

"Why did you burn the house down?" I surprised myself by asking that dreadful question.

The way his eyes glimmered with sick satisfaction was not fair.

"What fire?" he drawled. He tilted his head, and I could feel his gaze trailing down my skin.

It made me hot, and I prayed to God that I wouldn't blush.

My arm came to the top of the towel, making sure it stayed in place.

"None of the servants got hurt," I murmured. That fact still got to me. Mason wasn't stupid or did half-ass shit like Liam. He had a purpose for everything. "The only casualties were your father..." I observed his reactions, trying to gauge anything from him. "Your mother." Nothing, he straightened his head and looked me dead in the eyes.

"And Jason," he finished for me. "Oh, and according to official reports, yours truly."

He was so blasé about it all that it pissed me off.

"I don't think you meant for Jason to get hurt," I said, something that everyone already speculated.

"You're saying this as if you're sure I started that fire."

I wanted to rattle him. Make him feel the way I had been feeling these past few years. Stuck with nowhere to go.

"You smelled like gasoline," I told him. I closed my eyes and sighed. I could recall that night perfectly, but I never liked going back there. It was just a big what-if in my memories. "You wanted to take me with you..."

For the first time, I said the words aloud. I wasn't confronting him about it, just stating a fact. His face morphed. There was no evil smirk or cruel smile; his whole face straight up looked lethal. "Shut the fuck up and don't speak about things you know nothing about."

I glared at him. I don't know why I was desperate to prove to myself that he had cared. That our past was still playing in his mind. Our insignificant moments were just enough to shape our broken souls into who we were today. Because there was no denying Mason Stiltskin was broken.

"You wanted me to go with you, didn't you?" I took one step closer to him. He gritted his teeth. Those jade eyes blazing with so much repressed rage.

"You could have burned the whole house down and left on your own, but you only had two targets in mind..." Another step, and he was holding onto the sides of the sofa like he was trying to make sure he was clawed to it. If I was smart, I would have backed out and stopped pushing, but I needed to hear it from him that he had wanted me with him.

Until this moment, I didn't realize I harbored a sick desperation to feel wanted just for being me.

"Stop talking," he growled.

I didn't listen.

"No one ever came by the house. No one ever visited you guys. For the most part, it was only the staff there. You wanted your parents dead, but the real question is why?"

I was now in front of him. His reaction told me everything I had already suspected. He wanted to burn down something else with that house.

"What were you trying to hide?" I taunted as I leaned down.

Mason sat up and took hold of my wet hair. He pulled it down, making me twist my body at a weird angle. He kept pulling until my head was at eye level with him. My scalp burned, and I whimpered in pain.

"Guess you'll never know," he breathed against my ear.

He got up, still holding onto me. I could feel my head throb, and I knew I was bound to have a migraine for the rest of the day.

"What are you up to, *pet*?" he asked before he let go of me. He used that nickname to show his power over me.

I could still feel his hold on me as I watched him walk out the door. It was silly of me to think I could make a crack on the armor he wore.

Truth be told, I was getting desperate. Sometimes it felt like everyone's future was at my back. Very ambiguous of me to think that way, but it was true.

No matter how hard I tried, I couldn't seem to fuck over my parents as they did me.

I quickly changed then made my way over to the main cabin. I could sit with the rest of the girls, but for what? They would make small talk with me because it was beneficial for their future, but would laugh at me when I was not with them.

The doors opened, and the same people that had put a bag over our heads were here. They all carried a journal— old and leather-bound—with them.

They handed them out one by one. The room was silent, and this was the moment all of them had been waiting for. Everyone got one except for two people.

Mason and myself.

NINETEEN

THE FIRST PERSON I LOOKED AT WAS LIAM. BY LOOKING AT HIS face, I would know if this had been a mistake. He smiled at me, and that told me everything I needed to know.

I stayed quiet as people started to open their journals and murmur to themselves. My eyes found Mason, but unlike me, he didn't seem bothered.

"You forgot me," he raised his gloved hand and asked.

There was no way this had been a mistake; it had been planned, and I wondered if it had been all along. Since the moment we stepped foot on this damned island, nothing went according to plan.

Liam stood up, and everyone turned to watch him.

"Now we are all probably wondering why two people didn't get their journals," he shared with the room. He turned to look at me first. He cocked his head, and there was a wild look in his eyes. It reminded me of his father, and that terrified me. I held on to my arms, glad that the table offered coverage.

"I'm afraid I've been too lenient on you," the asshole chastised me. "In indulging your wishes, you seem to have forgotten that you don't belong. You weren't born into this role. You didn't earn it. All you're good at is backstabbing."

I fought the urge to flinch.

"As my future wife, there's no need for you to have any of this. You're lucky to be standing behind me."

Everyone started to snicker. Their true colors showed now that the little protection I had from Liam had faded.

"As for me?" Mason asked in a bored tone. He had his elbow resting on the table while he supported his head on the palm of his hand. The action was almost childish that it warmed me.

I would have thought he would have been the first to cast stones my way. He wanted to see me on the ground, and I wasn't so far from it now.

Liam smiled as he turned toward Mason.

"A dead man has no use of this."

Mason straightened and then smirked at Liam.

"Is that a threat?" he asked as he stood up. He took the journal from the person who was closest to him. No one dared say anything as he flipped over the pages like he was bored.

"Following the old ways will really be the death of you," Mason said as he threw the journal back. "You think I care about the amount of shit our family members have done? The rise and fall of the economy, fucking with the stock market for their personal gain. Getting involved in politics to make laws for their benefit. Treating healthcare like it was a game to be played and profit from those in need? I don't really give a shit about men pretending to be God."

He made his way toward Liam, and for the first time, the roles had been reversed. Mason was now taller, broader, and most of all, he was no longer afraid.

"You can't bully me. And your daddy can't solve this

problem with a snap of his fingers. You wanted to ruin my family, but I'm still here, and I don't play by the same rules. The past few years, I wasn't just fucking my way around the world. I was getting every single piece of information I could to dethrone you."

What had I been doing? I had given up on myself. I got comfortable with what I had and let myself be led, all the while complaining that I had no other choice. I really was a snake, and I already knew that.

"Should we relive old memories, Imp?"

"You really think you can lay a hand on me?" Mason put his hands on the table and leaned into Liam.

Liam smiled. I braced myself for them to start going at it and punching each other, but that didn't happen. Liam started to whisper something in Mason's ear. He went stiff, and I wondered what was going on.

"And what makes you think I care?" Mason questioned him.

Liam shrugged and sat back down.

Without looking at anyone, Mason walked out. I stayed in my seat as everyone began to talk among each other. They looked at their journals, and since Liam didn't seem worried, neither did they.

I felt their stares, and I wondered what I was doing here. I regret ever wishing for freedom because nothing good had come from it.

"Aspen," Liam called out to me.

I looked at him, and I waited to see what he would do. He moved to the side a bit, and Rachel sat on his lap. Maybe if I had feelings for him, I would have felt humiliated, and perhaps that's what killed him too—that I didn't care because he couldn't get off on my humiliation.

"This meeting is only for Orden Infinite members. Leave."

Subconsciously I had been waiting for this moment since the day my parents and I walked out of the Stiltskin's house. With my head held high, I made my way out of that room. These people had never accepted me, and they never would. My parents could delude themselves all they wanted, but sooner or later, their stolen castle would also burn to the ground.

I didn't go to my cabin. It didn't matter where I went; I was always alone. You'd think I'd be used to it by now. I ignored the last conversation I had with Liam as I made my way into the forest. Some demons you just had to face head-on, and it was past time I met mine.

I walked, and climbed up the uneven terrain, knowing that sooner or later, I would find him. I had taken everything from him, even his cabin, yet he could have kicked me out the moment he stepped foot in this place.

My body felt hot just thinking about being alone with him. Is that what I wanted? To be touched by him? He brought me pleasure, but he also was the only one who could bring me pain.

The deeper I went into the forest, the harder my heart pounded. I was scared and excited. Maybe this was what I needed to be freed from—the shackles that bound me.

I came to a halt when I found a clearing. There was a small tent set up on the ground, footsteps surrounding it. So this was where he was staying? I didn't like the idea of him alone here at night.

Hesitantly I took a step forward. My hands began to sweat as I reached for the flap of the tent. Just as I was going to get it open, something gripped my hand, and I screamed. My body recognized Mason's arms because when he put his hand over my mouth to stop me from screeching, I began to calm down. Pathetic, right?

"What the hell are you doing here?" I didn't say anything; I was waiting for him to remove his hand. Surprisingly, he didn't grab me with his gloved hand this time. The leather could get a little suffocating. When he saw I wasn't even trying to answer, he pulled his hand away. He was still at my back. Not a guardian angel, but my own personal demon from hell; one I had created myself.

"Why are you staying here?"

I was the queen of asking stupid questions; I knew it. I wanted the truth to drip from his lips, and maybe it would be enough to set me free.

"It's not like I can just lay on the ground," he replied, without giving me the words I longed to hear.

When did I get so prideful? Ever since I could remember, I had been bowing down to those of the Order. Now the moment that it mattered most, I didn't even think about doing it.

"You're Mase, and I'm Aspen," I said, completely changing the subject.

Mason's reaction was expected. His hands went to my arms, gripping me.

"Don't," he warned.

"Do you remember what you had asked me?" I asked as his fingers dug into my skin. "The thing I wanted most in the wo—"

Mason turned me around so I could face him. He was glaring down at me. Those green eyes had always been expressive, and even if they were full of loathing, they still shined.

"Too late," he warned.

"All I wanted was to be f—"

I didn't finish speaking because Mason's lips were on mine. They were brutal, trying to silence my confession. Ironically as our lips touched, I felt like I soared. This was a taste of the freedom I had been chasing. Nothing mattered right now. I felt so light the world could end, and it didn't matter because I had touched heaven, even if just for a few seconds.

He pulled back, and we were both gasping.

"I don't want to hear your lies anymore," he hissed. It lacked the usual venom he usually spat at me.

I reached for his hand, the one with the glove, and I could feel his gaze piercing me as I touched it.

"This is from the fire, right?"

He started to pull it back, but I held onto him tighter. He stopped moving, and I looked up at him, my eyes not leaving his as I pulled off the glove.

His heavy breathing was my only indication that he was uncomfortable. I didn't break eye contact with him as I touched his hand. I felt every ridge and bump that the flames had produced. I wanted to ask him so many questions, but I didn't have a right to know. I could only push myself so far before I broke completely.

I closed my eyes right in front of his face and then slowly brought his hand to my lips. My lips were much more sensitive to the texture of his hand. There were no hard calluses to prevent me from really feeling just how much he had been through.

Mason's intake of breath was loud enough that I could hear it.

I put his hand back down and opened my eyes again, scared of what I might find. He had every right to tell me to fuck off, and that terrified me for more than one reason.

He didn't trust me, and I knew that maybe he never would. Trust was earned, and I had done the opposite.

"Why didn't you ask for your cabin back?"

"Because I don't need anything that has been tainted by you."

I flinched.

A part of me hoped to hear something different. I smiled sadly at him. "For what it's worth, I've gone back to that night a thousand times. In my search for freedom, I lost it all."

TWENTY

MASON

MY HEAD WAS IN A FUCKED-UP PLACE. I WAS TORN BETWEEN following the plan I had set out or risk it all again. Liam's words taunted me, but not as much as Aspen's body did. There had always been something about her. The silent way she was just there giving me comfort in my darkest moments.

I could still feel her lips as they kissed my bare hand. The softness against my marred skin. Coming here had been to prove a point. Aspen wasn't even my main target; the Kings were, but she was an added bonus.

She was right; I could have asked for my cabin back. It was mine since birth, but in doing so, I risked her being out in the cold, or even worse, she would be stuck with Liam. Just thinking about him touching her the way I had drove me insane.

As much as I hated to admit it, I have thought of her as mine since I met her.

I rubbed my temple because I knew Liam had something up his sleeve. Knowing that worked in my favor for now. At least I knew he wouldn't be stupid enough to try and kill me. I crawled into my tent, and I slept for the first time in the past three days.

"ASPEN!"

My voice was raw from screaming in pain, and as always, it was her name. It flowed flawlessly from my lips. Growing up in that house, I had always been alone. I wasn't very social, so I wasn't close with my peers. My father was always working, and Hilda—I stopped myself from thinking about her. In my current state, it would just make it worse.

Then I remembered seeing her—the little blonde girl that lived in my house.

When I was little, I wondered why she didn't go to my school. Why she lived in our house. When I asked my father, he told me that one day I would understand. I used to wander around the house, trying to get a peek at her. She was always with her mother, hiding behind her, and I was fascinated. She was beautiful. A ray of sunshine in our gloomy house.

Then after Hilda started coming into my room, I forgot all about her. There wasn't anything in my mind. All I wanted was numbed bliss, but she stumbled outside, and the girl with hair like sunshine was drowning in that fucking house just like me.

My hand burned like a bitch, and there was nothing left to do but scream. Maybe I wouldn't be in pain if I had more money, but I just had to pull through before getting the rest of my father's assets.

I paid off the fire department and cops.

I couldn't help and think of what would have happened if Aspen had chosen me?

The loud rumbling of thunder echoed all around the forest, jolting me awake. I gasped for air. Shit, just my luck that the storm was coming. I didn't need to look outside the tent to know it was nighttime.

Rain started to splash against the tent, and it gave me the excuse I needed to get out. As soon as I was out, the night was illuminated with lighting. I made my way down the forest, heading to the path I had memorized the moment I arrived here.

"For what it's worth, I've gone back to that night a thousand times. In my search for freedom, I lost it all."

Her words were fucking with me.

No one was around where I walked. I could see lights from the other cabins, but I just kept making my way toward Aspen. When I found myself outside, I raised my hand and knocked.

"Go away, Liam," she screamed.

Her words enraged me.

"Open the fucking door, pet," I shouted over the rain.

I was prepared for her to tell me to fuck off as well but found myself smiling when I heard the door begin to open.

"You could have broken in like last time."

"Is that what you want?" I asked, pushing my way inside. "For me to barge in?"

She bit her lip and didn't answer my question. Instead, she took a step toward me. "You're soaking wet."

"That will be you in a few minutes," I countered.

Now that I was here, my dick was throbbing. I wanted to sink myself so deep inside of her and forget about everything in between.

"Let me turn on the fire," she said without meeting my eyes. She took a step toward the fireplace, and I stopped her.

"Don't," I whispered.

Even if it was contained, I didn't think I could handle the flames.

"But you need to warm up."

"Not like that."

My voice was strained, and I didn't want to come out and say it. I hated that the incident had made me weak.

Aspen seemed to understand because she dropped the subject.

"Come on, you need to shower." She took hold of my hand and led me to the bathroom. It wasn't until I felt her touching me that I remembered I never put my glove back on. She let go of me, and I instantly wanted to reach back for her. Aspen turned on the water for me, and as she adjusted the temperature, she turned to me.

"Can you handle hot water or just warm?"

"Warm's fine," I said without looking at her.

Back then, I used to take burning showers to numb myself and feel like I was washing away the pain. Now, if I did that, I would be reminded of the flames.

"I'll get you a towel."

She left without another word, and I briefly wondered what the fuck was I doing. It was too late to back out now. Maybe life was finally giving me back some of what it had taken from me.

Once I was done, I noticed a towel right by the door. I was so lost in my thoughts that I didn't see her open the door to leave a towel. Wrapping the towel around my waist, I made sure it was secured before I walked out.

The lights were off, and the only light came from outside. It wasn't much but just enough to make out her features. Aspen was sitting on the sofa, and her undivided attention was on me.

"You can take the bed," she said in that soft spoken voice that I had yearned to hear.

"Stop being ridiculous and get on the fucking bed." My dick jumped at my suggestion.

She didn't say a word but slowly got up, made her way to the bed, and crawled under the sheets. I followed behind her. When I got next to the bed, she pulled the covers to let me in.

"Why didn't you come with me?"

My question hung heavy in the air as I slid beneath the covers. I laid down and looked up at the ceiling.

"I've never had anything, so when the opportunity for my freedom presented itself, it blinded me from everything. I didn't know the exact details of what I was exchanging for that so-called freedom until it was too late."

A humorless chuckle left my lips.

"I was ready to give you everything. You were the only person I wanted with me after that place burned to the ground. I couldn't compromise my plan or be talked out of it, but I also didn't want you to hate me, so I didn't intend for the help to get hurt."

I could feel Aspen's body going still next to me.

I knew she would be asking questions, and I think I was finally ready to answer them. I wanted her to not think of me as a monster.

"What's the thing you want most in the world?"

The question slid off my lips easily. Maybe the world didn't give you second chances. You had to take them, and I wanted so desperately to reach for mine.

"We could have run away, but why did you burn it all down?"

She answered my question with one of her own.

As I reached for her, it felt as if my heart was about to beat out of my chest.

I never had friends except for the weird relationship we

had. I had never confided in anyone. So when I reached for her hand, I knew shit was about to get real. I looked at the ceiling, trying not to overthink about how she would react.

"What the hell—"

She started to cuss me out as I put her hand on my naked thigh. She stopped what she was saying as her palms felt all of the scars that remained. The one constant reminder that all that shit I felt was real, and at one point, it had consumed me to the point that I wanted to tear my skin.

I let go of her hand and laid still as she started to move it on her own. She gasped at all the marred skin that she came in contact with.

"The blood," she whispered.

"Yeah..."

What more could I say.

People didn't usually understand why another person would harm themselves. It was an addiction, and like all addictions, it gave you an outlet to put all your effort into, so you wouldn't see the fucked up reality that was in front of you.

"W-why?"

I could hear frustration and sadness in her tone.

"Because I wanted to feel some pain."

It was the honest truth.

"That's why you never did a thing about Liam..."

I didn't answer what was already evident.

"Can I see them?" she asked, and my body froze.

My chest kept rising and falling rapidly. I had never given anyone access to my body, not more than I wanted to give. I didn't care to see faces because, in my head, it was always the same.

"No." My tone was harsh.

I sat up and hovered over her. My hands went to each

side of her hair. It was dark, but those golden strands still shined.

"I want to forget they are there." I cupped her cheek gently. "I wanted to burn all those memories, but because of you, I couldn't do it." I gripped her chin and lowered my face closer to the point where I could taste her minty breath. "You didn't come with me, and all those demons kept on trailing after me."

Gently I took her lower lip into my mouth. Tasting it, teasing it, and lastly, biting down on it. She howled in pain.

That's why it hurt so much when she left. I had deluded myself that with her by my side, everything would have been fine.

"You wouldn't understand," she said without looking at me.

A humorless chuckle left my lips.

"You're a spoiled little kid," she spat at me.

Anger spread through my body, but slowly faded. I grabbed both her hands and put them over her head.

"Why are you so beautiful?" the question slipped out, and I hated myself for the attraction I felt toward her. It was one thing I wished time had taken away.

TWENTY-ONE

HUMANS WERE MEANT TO BE SELFISH CREATURES. THAT'S WHY cheating, lying, and stealing all came so easily—but always at a price. I was so dizzy I could barely breathe, but I didn't care.

Mason's heat surrounded me. It made me realize just how cold I had been. He had always been such a mystery, and I never wanted to unravel him more than I did in this moment. I didn't expect him to show up so soon, but the rain had been on my side.

My palms still felt every lash, every scar; it was imprinted on my hands. More than anything, I had the urge to see them and soothe the pain he carried within him. Unfortunately, he didn't let me. Maybe it was for the best. He already blamed me for his demons that I couldn't help and lashed back at him.

Mason had it all, and to learn that he liked the pain Liam gave him, took him down from the pedestal I had put him on. He could change the situation he was in, but I never could.

"Why are you so beautiful?" he asked.

He had both my hands pinned above my head. I cocked my head, waiting to see what his next move would be.

It broke my heart the way he had walked in here; there was a wild look in his eyes that I wanted to soothe. When he refused to go near the fireplace, I cracked. I reminded myself that these were my actions, and I was going to give him my all.

I leaned my head up and kissed him. The kiss tasted like heartbreak, and I hoped to God he didn't notice. I deepened the kiss, trying to get anything he would give me. His tongue snaked into my mouth, and I moaned against it as soon as those silver balls touched my tongue. By the time I pulled back, we were both panting. Without another word, Mason flipped me. I stayed still as he removed my pants along with the panties I wore.

"I'm going to fuck you with my mouth," he groaned, and I felt spasms going through my legs. Shit. I was already wet. Since the moment he walked in here, all I could think of was the way he had fingered me.

He rose above me, and I felt the imprint of his dick poking me since he didn't bother to put on the towel. My belly dipped with anticipation. His hand wrapped around my waist and slowly lifted my hips until my ass was in the air.

The position was embarrassing, and I was about to protest when I felt his mouth on the curve of my ass. He was giving me small little kisses that tugged at my every nerve. He switched to the other side and did the same thing.

He had me squirming, and he hadn't even touched my pussy. All of this was new to me, and I couldn't wait. I had resigned myself to the fact that Liam would have my first; glad that at least he didn't get my first kiss.

Like I said, selfish.

This was probably the only opportunity I would have to decide for myself.

"I don't need to taste you to know just how wet you are," he said against my skin. "I can fucking smell it."

My cheeks burned. I pushed my hands up, ready to move, but he was faster than me. He collared my throat and held me down.

"Don't," he warned.

Next, I felt his tongue above my waist, tracing the path my spine made.

My knees were shaking from the sensation he was evoking in me. He covered my back with kisses, soft bites, and licks. Those metal balls kept making me shiver every time they rubbed against my skin. They were coated with his saliva, leaving traces of him all over me. With his free hand, he rubbed up and down my ass, and my legs spread on their own, trying to get him where I needed him most.

The pressure that was on my neck disappeared.

I froze when I felt the top of Mason's dick rubbing against my ass.

He didn't say a word as he removed my bra and shirt. His cock kept rubbing against me, and I took a deep breath steadying myself for what he would do next. Once he was done with that, he bent low so he could whisper in my ear.

"Keep that ass in the air," he groaned against the shell of my ear. "If you move, I'll shove my dick in your pussy so hard you'll feel like you're choking on it."

Goosebumps spread across my skin, but it wasn't from fear. I didn't answer him, and I didn't think he was expecting one.

I buried my head on my pillow the moment he spread my ass cheeks. Knowing him, he was going to humiliate me as much as he could. His hair brushed against my skin, and I waited with anticipation, wanting him to touch me.

"Fuck," I moaned into the pillow the moment his tongue sneaked in. Those metal balls glided their way through my folds, and I instantly lost my mind.

He did it again and again with no set rhythm. He was exploring, and my body kept getting hotter and hotter. I could feel my clit throb and my wetness starting to spread down my thighs.

"Mase!" I screeched when he started to lick my clit. He moved his tongue back and forth, and there was no time to recover as each ball added pressure as they glided. I could tell he liked my response because his pace increased and he added more pressure. My knees trembled, and I didn't think I could keep my position.

"Shit," I hissed when he neared my entrance.

"What did I say?" he asked in a husky voice.

I was trying to catch my breath. Mason wrapped an arm around my waist and lifted my hips again. I prepared myself for his tongue once more, but the loud echo of his hand against my ass registered first and then the stinging on my skin.

"I wanna—"

I didn't get to finish my sentence because he spanked me again.

"Did I say you could talk?" he growled.

I bit my lip and stayed quiet. I was on edge already.

"Good girl," he praised against the skin he had hit. He gave me a small peck, then I felt his finger pushing inside of me.

"You're so wet; one won't do," he told me before he pulled it out and added two.

My body jolted at the fullness. He scissored his fingers, and it stung. I gritted my teeth, and he chuckled.

"You're loving this, aren't you?"

His fingers began to move in and out again, this time slower and with more precision. I didn't think he wanted my answer, so I didn't give it to him. The slow burn that had been on edge since he started this was now spreading, and I was ready for the pleasure to consume me.

I started to chase the feeling on my own, my hips moving against his hand. He cursed, then sat me up while he fingered my clit. He was right behind me, his tongue licking my earlobe. I couldn't help but moan as I laid my head on the crook of his neck.

I was so close. He stopped moving his fingers. Instead, he cupped my pussy. His heavy breathing fanned my ear as I humped his hand that rested on top of my mound. I should be embarrassed, but I was so close already I couldn't stop.

"What did I say would happen if you moved?" His harsh voice was low.

I stopped moving, and Mason pulled his hand back so his fingers could play with my clit. I whimpered because I knew I was so close to coming.

"My hand is fucking soaked...."

Without thinking, I reached between our bodies. Mason went still. He wasn't expecting me to touch him. I bit my lip as I took hold of his dick. He was hard, and the tip dripped with pre-cum.

My heart was pounding so hard as I moved my hand up and down. Mason hissed.

"Let me see your face and do it slow..." My words were low, but I knew he heard them because his hand that was across my waist became tighter, and his fingers gripped my hips like he was trying to claw his way in.

"No," he spat.

My chest rose and fell. I tried to move to force him to look at me, but he wouldn't let me. Mason wedged one of his thighs between my legs. He wrapped his scarred arm around my waist, and the other came to play with my breast. He kissed my neck as he maneuvered my body. My pussy spasmed against his skin at the friction he was providing. I moaned, and he moved me fast, his leg moving higher up, so every time I moved, my clit rubbed against him.

When I couldn't take it anymore, I started to grind against him on my own. He let go of my lips as I came. He let go of my waist and played with my breast as I kept humping his leg.

I was panting in anger and embarrassment.

Mason threw me down on the bed, gripped my ass cheeks and shoved his dick between my folds.

"Fuck," he cursed his release.

I felt his cum drip from my ass crack to my pussy.

Tears sprang into my eyes. I gripped the bedding, and all the other feelings that had taken a back seat to my lust started to come back. He made me feel so much when I was used to the numbness of my life. He brought out my feelings and instead of wanting to deal with them, I just wanted to get lost in pleasure. Because like all things, pleasure was only temporary—then I could go back to my numbing bliss.

"Get. Out," I told him, hating that I heard the hurt in my voice.

I half expected Mason to get dressed and leave. I didn't care that it was raining, that he had nowhere to go, that this would be a setback. I wanted to cry, and I didn't want to do it in front of him.

Instead, he turned me around, this time gently, as if I was going to break.

I turned my head so he wouldn't see my face. Out of all the things I acquired when my family gained some power, pride had been the one I had been the most comfortable keeping.

Baring my body to him was better than giving him my soul.

Two fingertips touched my cheek, and he used them to turn my head so we could face each other. His chest was rising and falling rapidly. He scanned my face then used the pad of his thumb to trace the outline of my eyes—waiting for tears to spill.

"I didn't want to give her a chance to ruin this moment for me." I scrunched my brows in confusion at what he was saying. "Hilda has already ruined all my firsts; I didn't want her to taint the ones I'm making with you."

My mouth parted open in shock. All of a sudden, all those puzzle pieces I had collected made sense. My body went cold, and I shivered in fear. Mason turned his face, and I reached up to cup his cheeks so I could force him to look at me.

"Stupid, right?" He laughed bitterly, and my heart broke for him.

A tear sprang down my cheek. A part of me wished he had never shared this part of himself with me. Because once someone bared their soul to you, it was all that much harder to let them go.

I shook my head.

"I'm sorry," I cried. Not in pity for him, but it was an apology for everything that happened since we met.

He looked at me as I sat up. Slowly letting my intentions show, I wrapped my hands around him. He smelled fresh, like cotton linen and spring. Tentatively, his arms came around me.

Even though we were naked, there was nothing sexual about our embrace.

"Come with me?" he asked, and my heart stopped. "I'll give you the thing you want the most."

I hid my sadness with a smile, and I kissed him. This kiss was different. It wasn't full of pain, deception, or lies, but it shared our souls, and that exchange hurt all the same.

We didn't let go, not even to go to sleep. In his arms, I memorized the feel of his skin, the way his heart beat and how he wrapped his arms tighter around me when he spoke about a future with me in it.

TWENTY-TWO

MASON

THEY SAID FORGIVING SOMEONE COULD SET YOU FREE, BUT I didn't think that was true. How could you let someone walk all over you and tell them it was okay? I didn't understand that concept until last night. Forgiving someone wasn't about them; it was about yourself. Forgiveness is about accepting that they brought you pain and deciding to leave it behind and not carry it around with you.

I was surprised I could sleep so easily with Aspen next to me. I usually had nightmares, but I guess I was just too exhausted. The room was cold, and I felt somewhat pathetic at the fact that I couldn't bring myself to start a fire.

She didn't mock me about it when she asked.

"Does it scare you?" She ran her fingers through my hair. I closed my eyes and focused on her voice. I didn't think Hilda would come between us at this moment, but I didn't want to risk it. Sensing that it was a question I didn't want to answer, she moved on to the next thing.

"How about smoking? Are you okay with small flames?"

"I don't particularly enjoy having to light up," I answered her.

I was fucked. I knew it could happen, but now that I had

a taste of her, I didn't want to let her go. Aspen Miller was mine, and I was ready to go against everyone to keep her. I might not have known the weight that my words implied when I was in school, but I was prepared to prove them.

First, I needed to get us off this island. And for that, I needed to deal with Liam. The more he realized I wanted her, the more he would try to keep her.

I looked down at where Aspen's head rested against my chest, and I felt at peace. I reached for the tendrils of her hair and played with them.

Leaning down, I kissed the top of her head. Then slowly, I moved away from her. I needed to go back to my tent and get a change of clothes. Before I left the cabin, I looked at Aspen once more, and a slight grin formed.

Was this happiness?

"Why don't we make a bet," Liam whispered in my ear, and I knew his gaze went past me and toward Aspen. I knew she was seated alone behind me. I always felt her whenever I walked into a room.

"Sure," I said, indulging him.

"If you can make Aspen walk off this island with you, you can keep her."

When he said that, I knew it wouldn't be easy. I didn't even know if I wanted to keep her, but when I saw him with her, I knew I'd rather she was with me than with him.

This wasn't the do-over I had envisioned, but the rest would come easy with Aspen by my side. I changed my clothes, put my glove on, grabbed a lighter and my cigarettes, then made my way back to Aspen's room, ready to get prepared for what the day would bring.

One time was a coincidence but twice was on purpose. That's what I thought as soon as I saw Nate, this time without Erin.

"Can I help you with something?"

"You got burned helping Erin, didn't you?"

His eyes went to where my gloved hand was at.

I didn't answer, so he kept going.

"It's hot as shit, but you don't bother with short sleeves. You always look at your lighter before you flick it on and bring it to your lips almost forcefully."

I didn't like that he had figured me out easily. I didn't say more and began to walk away.

"Stiltskin," Nate called out.

I stopped mid-step but didn't turn around.

"Be careful."

It was a clear warning but not a threat, at least not from him. He wasn't telling me something that I wasn't aware of on my own.

By the time I made it to the cabin, Aspen was gone. I was a little disappointed, but it's not like I wouldn't see her later. I was slowly becoming obsessed again, but this time I was ready to dive right in.

SINCE THE ORDER HAD GIVEN OUT THEIR BOOK OF SECRETS, the rest of the time spent on the island was like a vacation. My father once told me that at the end, all the members would gather here and pass on actions and stocks to the business. There was nothing to get passed on to me, and based on how Aspen got threatened, it was the same for her.

Wilfred King may have given the Millers my family's money, but he didn't let them control it. He knew damn well that they would be just as happy living comfortably. Too bad for all of them. I'd rather see all of my empires burn to the ground than allowing them to have it.

I got the feeling Aspen had been ignoring me today, and I didn't understand why. I've barely seen her. And when I did, she just smiled and kissed my cheek, but something was missing, like she was trying to hold back from me. After last night, I would have thought we'd be on the same page.

Now it was dark again, and I was making my way to her cabin because we needed to talk about what would happen when we left this place.

Her lights were on, and the door was ajar. I didn't think, I just pushed it open.

Fuck.

I couldn't breathe.

This wasn't real.

Looking at the image in front of me, I felt all the tattered pieces of kindness still harbored inside me disappear.

Liam was smirking at me. He reached for Aspen's head and ran his fingers through her golden hair. He pulled her head back, and the popping noise her mouth made as she released his dick echoed through the room.

I ran toward him, ready to punch him, but I was pulled back. Two people held onto me, one at each side. They could barely contain me.

"You son of a bitch!" My voice was desperate. "You're going to pay for this."

Aspen—she wouldn't even look at me; she just stayed kneeling at his feet.

"Sooner or later, everyone kneels for their king," Liam said triumphantly.

I moved my body, trying to break free, but the more I tried to move, the more pressure the assholes at either side of me added.

"Let. Her. Go."

Liam laughed.

"What are you going to do? You're nothing but a ghost."

I was like a bull trying to strike. Liam zipped up his pants, but I needed Aspen to get away from him. Or him to be so disgusted by her and push her off.

"Ask her who had her panting and moaning last night," I spat, sure that it would make him lose control.

To my surprise, he stayed calm.

He grabbed her face and forced her to look at me.

I was hoping to see tears, anything that would make me feel better about this whole situation, but there weren't any.

"Is that true?" He cocked his head as he asked her.

Aspen looked at my face for five seconds, and then she nodded her head and looked down.

"You did exactly as I asked and didn't disappoint me," Liam told her.

Every single part of me was breaking a thousand times over. Why did we continue to give the same people our broken pieces if they didn't bother to fix them?

"Why?" I seethed, looking straight at her. I wanted it to come from her lips because this time, she couldn't hide behind her parents. This time, the betrayal had been all hers.

"Isn't it obvious," Liam answered for her. "She wants a real taste of power, and she'll never get that with you."

I brought my hands together in rage and then pulled them fast until the people holding onto me let me go. I punched the first and then the second. Pain radiated from my fist, but I didn't care.

Liam didn't move, and neither did Aspen. I pushed him away. The asshole let me move him and didn't even try to fight back. Ignoring him, I kneeled in front of her. He didn't say anything as I gripped her chin.

"Tell me, why?"

Those golden eyes that I could get drunk off just by staring at them burned bright.

"Because I want to be free," she said between gritted teeth.

Her answer was like a blow to the stomach. I would have granted her that wish and done it for free, but she didn't want to trust me.

"You want power, is that it? Fine. I'll make this easy for you, Aspen," I told her. "Everything that was mine is now yours. You can fucking keep it without feeling guilty that it's stolen. I don't need it." I stopped to control my breathing. I leaned down and whispered in her ear, "In return, you'll give me the thing you love the most."

She didn't say a word and wouldn't even meet my eyes.

I left her there, and I was almost out the door when Liam spoke again, "Did you think I was letting you leave this place alive?"

I didn't get a chance to answer him when I felt someone hit the back of my head. As I went down and started to lose my conscience, I could have sworn I heard Aspen scream.

Maybe it was just wishful thinking on my part.

ASPEN

Blood coated my tongue as I watched the island become smaller and smaller. Mostly everyone had left—except for Mason Stiltskin. I didn't think he was dead because Liam's number one objective had been to humiliate him.

I felt someone sitting next to me, and I didn't have to turn around to know it was Liam.

"Six years," I spoke, my words harsh and full of venom.

"A deal is a deal," he said cockily. He reached for my face

and turned it so we could face each other. "I'll keep my word, and I won't touch you, but as soon as those six years are up, you're mine."

I pulled my face from his grasp and remembered what he had said to me that day.

My focus was on Mason and Rachel, and it was an emotion I wasn't used to, but it was jealousy. Liam had me pinned against the wall, and I pretended like the words he was saying weren't real. Maybe if I acted like it didn't matter, the weight of his words wouldn't be a burden.

"Are you listening to me, fiancée?"

"Mmhmm."

"Find out why Stiltskin burned the house down, or else..."

I looked up at him.

"Or else what?"

His smile was cruel.

"I finally get to have some fun with you, and while I'm at it, I'll share that fun with my friends."

That was the first time that it sunk in just how helpless I was. You could throw money at me and dress me in fine silk, but I would always be a toy for him to play with.

Liam had not been pleased that I didn't manage to get the real reason why Mason had burned the house down. So instead, he decided to taunt him another way. My options were simple. I got on my knees for him, or he made his threat into a reality. I didn't regret not telling him the real reason why that house burned down.

Mason Stiltskin now hated me because once was a mistake, but twice, he wouldn't be satisfied until I was dead. I surrendered myself to the fact that I would be taking his secrets to my grave.

Part III

DESPAIR

*AND IN THE END, THE ONLY PEOPLE WE
COULD BLAME WERE OURSELVES.
LOVE WASN'T EASY; LOVE WASN'T FAIR
BUT IT WASN'T MEANT TO BE CRUEL
AND FULL OF DESPAIR.*

TWENTY-THREE

Twenty-One years old

Time was really a funny concept. It was probably one of the most important things. Something we shouldn't take for granted, yet we all did. We sat around waiting, whining, reminiscing, all while the clock kept ticking.

All while the consequences of our actions were right there, waiting for the perfect moment to return.

And here was my moment.

No one woke up one day and decided to be a heinous bitch; life made you that way. You chose to wear thick skin because you could either keep getting cut up over some bullshit, or you could own it and hurt others before they hurt you.

Life wasn't easy. It was fucking hard. Sometimes it felt like the more you tried, the more it weighed you down. The choices that were best for you fucked up everyone else. Mine certainly had, and I was done apologizing for them.

The engagement ring on my finger didn't even weigh me down anymore. It was just a steel band that was a reminder of everything I had done.

One lesson I learned the hard way was that you shouldn't apologize for breaking someone's heart if it meant setting yours free. Not that it was really free, but the choice I made saved me, and I needed to stop feeling guilty for it.

I gave Liam what he wanted. Neither Mason nor my parents could have protected me from him having me. My parents didn't even bother to try.

I took a deep breath and made my way to the edge of my balcony. Everything looked golden now that the sun started to go down and casted its shadow on King's tower.

My perfectly manicured hands held onto the brick wall as I peeped down below at the kingdom I had conquered by backstabbing the others. The people walking downtown looked like ants. From up here, they looked vulnerable, squishable like bugs. In all reality, I envied them. They wandered around town with freedom. Sure, they were chained to the world, but their choices were their own. That was more than I could say for myself.

"Mrs. King, your mother is calling."

I rolled my eyes. I wasn't married to Liam—not yet. I had asked him for time, and for breaking Mason's heart, he had rewarded me. He gave me six years before I was set to marry him. Six years where he wasn't allowed to touch me. Three down and three to go.

It didn't matter to me if I lived with him or at the so called place that was my home. For the most part, he left me alone, so I preferred being here rather than my parents' home.

You'd think they'd get the hint that I wanted nothing to do with them, but my mother continued to call.

"You may leave." I waved a hand to dismiss the servant.

I walked back inside the penthouse, my heels echoing as I went. The servants all ran when they saw me, probably because they already figured I wasn't going to be in a good mood.

"What do you want?" I barked as soon as I picked up the phone.

"Aspen, that's no way to speak to your mother."

I laughed.

"Don't test me. With one word, you'll be out on the streets."

She started going on and on about her sacrifices.

"I'm sure your husband had such a hard time fucking himself away to a better life." I hung up the phone before she could give me a headache.

She was mad because I had cut her off. She thought she could live forever with the fortune she had stolen, but she didn't count on the fact that I would want to see her suffer.

Maybe it was stupid on my part to sell myself off for their well-being, but back then, I was still weak and scared. I was done fucking myself over for people who didn't deserve me.

I couldn't be like them. They offered their parents easily without remorse. If I could do the same, maybe I wouldn't be here, but it was too late to think on that now.

My smartwatch started to beep, alerting me that I had a meeting to get to. The only reason I would show was to see a few people squirm. I walked to my closet and changed into a dress, a black pair of Louboutins, and the newest Birkin's bag Liam had gifted me.

Everything about me shined. If the media had adored me when I came into the spotlight, they fucking loved me now. I was the Upper East Side's "It girl."

Maybe that's why my mother was dying a slow death. I was pictured everywhere having brunch with members of the Order but never her.

I smiled as I applied my lip-gloss.

"Watch me become everything you ever wanted, and more, Mother," I whispered to my reflection.

Once I was satisfied, I made my way out of my room. The penthouse Liam and I shared was on the other side of his parents. I suspected this was because they wanted to keep an eye on me.

I was making my way down the stairs when the elevator door opened, and Liam walked in. I grabbed the sunglasses that were in my purse and slid them on.

He stopped walking when he saw me and just watched me. I felt his gaze slide through my body.

I got off on it—on the fact that he would not touch me. It made me feel in control. It gave me power.

"You look sexy." He smirked. "The purse suits you."

I walked past him and pressed the button for the elevator to open. Then I turned my head so I could look at him.

"Expect a call from your mistress soon." I smiled at him.

The elevator door opened, and before I could set a foot inside, he pulled me back by my arm. His face came down so close to mine, I stopped breathing. I loved pushing him, but the moment he came at me, my heart stopped. After all these years, it still felt wrong.

"I love that you're such a fucking snake," he taunted so close to my lips that we were almost kissing.

I pulled away from him, then closed the elevator door.

The smile on my face was as fake as my mother's new tits, but the media didn't know that. I had worked hard to become America's sweetheart. I always felt eyes on me. I was okay with it. I knew it was the only thing protecting me. If the media loved me, no real harm could come to me.

The restaurant where lunch was being held was new

and trendy. There was a line to get in. My driver stopped right in front of the door. I waited as he got out and opened the door for me. The hostess took me to where the group of women I came to meet had already gathered.

Bingo.

I smiled as I took off my shades. The only spot empty was between Rachel and Erin. I guess they wanted to fuck with me too. I no longer spoke to Erin; our friendship died on that island. As for Rachel, she was someone I tolerated.

"Sorry I'm late; Liam wouldn't let me leave the apartment."

Some of their stares came to me; others looked at Rachel since it was no secret they were fucking. But none of them would dare to ask me what I meant.

I now basked in the protection the Kings offered me. The shiny ring on my finger was like armor. I went to my chair and put the bag right in front of Rachel while I took a seat.

"A present from the fiancée." I smirked at them as I noticed their stares.

It was barely there, but the moment she scrunched her face in anger, I wanted to throw my head back and laugh.

"I don't know how you do it, having a fiancée that doesn't keep it in his pants," Teddy's girlfriend muttered.

I pursed my lips. "I guess it's different with you since Teddy is the one who's getting it in the ass."

Her face turned red. She was nothing more than a beard. The real difference between them and me was that I didn't delude myself. The rest of the lunch went like that. A bunch of sly insults and backhanded compliments.

It's amazing how easily you get used to feeding off others' pain. It was my source of entertainment, and I relished every second that I got to make them miserable.

TWENTY-FOUR

MASON

TWENTY-THREE YEARS OLD

Patience was a virtue that I no longer had. Sometimes it felt like I spent my whole life waiting, and for what? People were going to do whatever the fuck they wanted, and it was better to have the upper hand.

I was in one of my warehouses, sitting down as I heard another excuse from one of the men who worked for me. I pretended to listen because lately, I lived to shred that little bit of hope that fed the human soul.

Given a chance, humans would cheat, steal, and lie if it meant they could escape death.

"That's a great story and all," I said, referring to the lie he had just fed me. "But I don't see what that has to do with my stolen merchandise."

His face turned even paler.

Strong emotions could sway a heart; too bad for him, I no longer had one.

The warehouse was empty. It was primarily used for meetings or new proposals, never for exchanges.

"Pp-p-lease, p-p-p-lease," the man started to sob.

It was pathetic. He was twice my age, and he was begging me. He probably thought I was a stupid kid, and that's why he felt the need to steal from me.

Some people learn better the hard way. I know I did. Your body doesn't get the memo until it remembers the pain and doesn't want to feel it again.

"I'm a generous man," I told him as a lethal smile spread across my lips.

The two men who were on either side of me went tense. They would probably advise against what I would do next, but lessons had to be taught.

"T-t-thank you, s-s-ir."

You should never thank the devil until you know the fine print of the deal you made with him. With my gloved hand, I motioned for one of my men to come forward. In his hand was a briefcase.

I got up from the metal chair I was sitting in. I fixed the lapel of my suit. It would have been hard to do it with my right hand, but I've worked hard to make my left hand the dominant one for years.

You'd never see me in anything other than in all black, from my shoes, to my tie, to my suit, and the shiny gleam of my hair. I was the demon of the underworld, and those who took me seriously knew not to test me.

I took the briefcase, then crouched to be at eye level with the weasel who thought he could steal from me. The man watched as I opened it up, and he knew he was fucked when he saw the three firearms.

My father had many secrets, and this had been one of them. He knew his new technology would take him to the next level, but he had been obsessed with surpassing the Kings, so he made his way into the underworld. Nothing sold faster on the streets than firepower.

I had been disgusted with this when he told me about it. It was right after I came back from studying abroad. I quickly stopped my train of thought because the memory of what happened after came attached with golden strands of hair.

"Tell you what," I said. "If you win, you get to walk out of here, not only with your life but with the briefcase."

Like the rat he was, his eyes gleamed at the possibility of walking out of here victorious. My lip curled in disgust, but he was too busy looking at the briefcase to notice.

"So, are you in?"

"What do I have to do?" he asked, sounding a little less scared. Probably already counting his riches in his head.

I reached behind my back and pulled out a revolver. His eyes went wide. "Whoever fate wants to win, lives. Deal?"

Now that he knew what he had to do, he was second-guessing his decision.

"Think of it this way—you would have died before, but now, at least you have a chance to live."

He gulped.

"And if I win, I really get to walk out alive?"

"I'm a man of my word," I told him confidently. It was something I had earned. "To show my good faith, you can go first."

I handed him the revolver, and he looked at it and then at me but didn't take it.

"Y-you go first," he managed to say.

"Sure," I said as I brought the gun to my temple and pulled the trigger.

His face fell when it clicked in his brain that I didn't blow my brains out.

"Your turn."

I took hold of his hand and put the revolver in his palm.

He looked at the gun and at my face again.

"I'll advise against trying to shoot me with it. If you play dirty, so will I. This is between you and me; there's no reason to involve your kids, don't you agree?"

His lower lip trembled. A few seconds passed, and then he brought the gun to his head with a shaky hand. He whimpered as he pulled the trigger. The barrel was at his temple, and his eyes were still closed.

My men snickered when the stench of piss reached them.

"My turn," I told him as I removed the revolver from his grip.

Again, nothing happened.

This time he put the barrel to his temple a bit more confidently. I stood still as his finger started to press against the trigger. The sound of the shot deafened me. I felt splatters of blood hit my face, and his lifeless body dropped with a loud thud on the floor.

I reached for the briefcase, stood, and began to walk away.

I removed my tie with my other hand, then used it to wipe the blood from my face. One of my men was right behind me.

"What would you have done if he wanted to go first?"

"No one is ever eager to die," I said.

Death was an illusion. Of that, I was convinced. What was living when you had nothing to live for? Wasn't that just another form of death?

The ride back to my house was quiet, or maybe I was still somewhat tone-deaf from the ricochet. When we pulled up to my driveway, I sighed when I saw the car that was parked in my preferred spot.

"Master Stiltskin." The servants who saw me on the way to my study bowed.

I just glared at them.

I was tired of telling them not to call me that anymore. I guess old habits die hard. I wanted nothing to do with my old life, but it wasn't as easy to move on, not for someone who was supposed to be dead. Stealing my old staff from the Millers was a fuck you to them for what they did and a reminder to the Order that I was still around.

"Why are you inside my house?" I barked as I opened the door.

Nate was sitting down and drinking my scotch.

"Because we're friends," he answered like it was obvious.

Thanks to him, I didn't have to swim off the island. He took me back to shore and has been trailing around me ever since.

"I assume you came here for something and not here to listen about the man I just killed," I said dryly.

"Jesus," he muttered. "Maybe you should keep some things to yourself. Lawyer and client privilege only gets us so far."

I shrugged. "If we are being technical, he killed himself."

Nate rubbed his temples. It didn't matter how hard I pushed; he didn't budge. I knew he was with me because he wanted to take away the power the Kings had. If you weren't in their good graces, you were against them, and his family was fed up with them.

I knew his reason probably involved Erin, but I didn't care to ask. Instead, I reached for the tie with my gloved hand and set it on the desk. Someone needed to burn that.

"They set a date," Nate said.

I could feel his stare piercing me.

"You don't say." My reply was calculated and

monotonous. Most days, I could forget all about Aspen Miller. It was hard to do when that bitch was everywhere on the news.

I reached for the scotch and then poured us a drink. Nate kept looking at me, wondering if I was going to snap.

I was past that.

Aspen had everything she wanted, so I was going to let her keep rolling in the pile of shit she had created for herself.

"To the happy couple."

TWENTY-FIVE

TWENTY-FIVE YEARS OLD

Thump.

Thump.

Thump.

The day I have always dreaded has finally come. In all honesty, I thought I would have felt nothing. For the past few years, I've blended myself in my new role. For the past few years, I've thought of anything but *him*.

Maybe because it was my wedding day, I was feeling nostalgic.

Every time I felt my heart beat inside my chest, I knew I was one step closer to hell. There was still an invisible link that held me to him. A link that chained our souls— no amount of time or blood spilled had managed to sever that. I'd be lying if I said I wasn't nervous; I was terrified. I told myself I learned to live with my actions all those years ago, but the severity of them was about to slap me in the face.

Sometimes we make decisions knowing how much they will break the other person, but in the process, we turn them into iron-clad steel. For the person doing the damage, well, they learn to live with the brokenness.

Do you know what it's like to live without half of your heart? You feel nothing. You become nothing. You see death, and you invite it over.

Have you ever wished for death?

Morbid, right? The girl who had it all wanted to die. It was what was supposed to be the happiest day of my life. All I could see was white everywhere. My heels, the fucking princess dress I wore, and the veil.

My hands glided down the bodice. Every bump and ridge was a testament to whom I was marrying. It should be a crime to waste this much money on a wedding dress. I still remember how we came from nothing, living at the mercy of others, but here we were.

My Walmart flats became Prada heels.

The fresh smell of flowers overpowered the room. Nothing but the best for me. This was the wedding of the century. Old money's prince charming marrying new money socialite princess. If only the media knew I had always been part of the Order Infinite, but we were just their slaves.

Enter my parents, whose cunning ways surpassed their masters. Now we, the lowlife Millers, got to stand beside them. My parents could have given us freedom; instead, they tied us to the families we have been enslaved to for the last century.

Men like my father were easily seduced by pussy and power. It was him who I had to thank for the step I was about to take today.

Aspen Miller was finally going to get married. Thus, proving that you couldn't escape your fate, just prolong it. My mother was already at the church, making sure the servants didn't fuck up. Acting as if she wasn't beneath all of our guests' shoes in the past. There was no love lost between us. My mother was a bitch. She encouraged my father to go with his betrayal and sacrificed me for some pearls.

Let them dress me in all white and offer me up to their new gods. What was the point of living life when you were already dead on the inside? My life didn't have any meaning, so I might as well just hold on for the ride.

I had to come back to my parents' house since media coverage was going to be everywhere.

My father had been locked in his office all day. All his hard work had paid off, and I was about to seal the deal for him. It was nice to know one of us slept soundly at night after stabbing a knife.

As flawed as our old life had been, I couldn't say it was terrible. Our old masters never laid a hand on us.

When I heard the tapping on my door, I didn't bother to look up.

"Miss Aspen," one of our maids said. "Your father said it's time."

A sense of hopelessness washed through me. It spread through my body, and when it reached my heart, I became numb.

Why are you so beautiful?

His voice startled me. It haunted me, and a selfish part of me welcomed it. It had been so long since I heard the rasp of his tone or the deep husk of his voice. Something that scared you but kept you on your toes—it made you feel alive.

It was ironic that I heard it today of all days. Or maybe it was a punishment. Dressed in all white today, but I was still covered in his blood.

I wondered if this was how birds felt when they got their

wings clipped. Did they wish for death, knowing that they would never again be able to soar the open skies?

That's why I wanted to die. What was living if it was all a farce? Why be alive if it was just a lie?

"Coming," I replied in a vacant tone.

My head slowly lifted, and I felt nothing when I saw my reflection. The sweetheart neckline was lovely and complimented my breasts. A diamond choker rested on my neck. My hair was in loose curls cascading down to my back.

Hair like gold.

My gold strands had been the talk of the media since Liam and I first announced our engagement. My amber eyes stared back at me, and they looked lifeless.

William "Liam" King was about to win, and there was nothing I could do about it.

Sooner or later, you will kneel for your king.

His words mocked me. I had made a fool out of him, but he was patient, and he was about to call checkmate in front of the whole world. This is why peasants and kings didn't mix—there was no way in hell we could win.

"Aspen!" This time, my father's voice rang through the other side of the door.

Looking at myself in the mirror one last time, I stood up and made my way toward him. I stopped before I opened the door and looked around my room. This was probably the last time I would see it like this. Not that I cared much. This house was new, but it didn't feel like home.

Home had been in the servant quarters of *his* house. Home had been late-night walks to the kitchen to prepare him a meal knowing he would glare at me for doing so. Home had been when he was near.

I knew that as soon my mother was done with my wedding festivities, she was going to remodel this room, and everything would be gone. I wasn't the sentimental type. I was trading one cage for another, so it didn't matter.

Worldly things faded. At the end of the day, it didn't matter how much money or gold you had when you died. You didn't get to take it with you.

I would trade my life in an instant if it meant I was in charge of my own destiny. Unfortunately, it wasn't so easy to disappear. I went to the best schools, yet all I got was a fancy degree that stood for nothing. Education didn't mean shit when your family and their friends ruled the world.

There was no place to run. No place to hide.

My hand touched the gold knob, but I walked back to my bed before opening the door. Inside the pillowcase was a thin gold chain. Without thinking, I took it and put it between my breasts.

"Aspen!" my father shouted as I opened the door.

My father was a tall man, so I've always looked up to him, but not because I admired him. Since he came into power, he has been meticulously put together, not a strand of light brown hair out of place—alluring but not warm. Growing up, I've always wondered if he loved me or if I was just an opportunity.

"Let's go," he said as he checked his phone. "The media is already outside waiting to get a shot of you."

No words were said besides that. My father wasn't going to bother with praise unless others were around to witness it. I followed behind him, looking at the house he paid for with the blood of others, waiting for a pang of nostalgia to hit me, but it never came.

"Make sure you smile at all times. This is the happiest day of your life," my dad said as we stepped foot in the elevator.

As the elevator descended, so did the bit of freedom I

had. As we got to the first floor, I put on my veil so no one would see the horror on my face. My fiancé could get the honor.

The people in the lobby of our building stared, but I paid no attention. As soon as we were outside, I saw flashing lights. My father put on a protective hand on my back because the paps were watching. Still, it felt nice to feel protected and cherished, so I focused on that feeling as I climbed inside the Royce.

When the door to the Rolls Royce closed, my father dropped the act. I scooted closer to the window and focused on the buildings, counting each, waiting for the dreaded moment I made it to the chapel.

"What's taking so long?" my father asked as he pushed the button so the chauffeur could hear him.

"Apologies, sir, there seems to be an accident."

At that moment, my numb heart chose to perk a beat. A signal that we were alive.

I looked at my father, and he was not happy about the news. His jaw was set, and I briefly wondered if I spoke up, would it matter?

I opened my mouth to say, "I can't do this," but the words didn't come.

"You'll give me the thing you love the most."

His voice came again, and I sat up straighter.

I really was a fucking hypocrite and a coward. I hated Liam King, but my marriage to him was the only thing that kept me safe from *his* revenge.

Before I could get caught up in the past, the car came to an unexpected halt. One of my hands reached to the window for support. I heard a commotion, and my father brought the partition down just as a car slammed into the driver's side.

My throat was clogged, and a mixture of adrenaline, fear, and relief coursed through me. I was a monster, wasn't I? My first thought should have been the driver, and here I was, glad for a few more seconds of freedom.

I was so caught up in my own head that I didn't hear my father yelling and the door to my side opening. A flash of light hit me before I was engulfed in darkness.

The feeling was familiar, and maybe that's why I didn't fight it. After all, this was not the first time a hood had been thrown over my face, except last time, it had been velvet.

My heart accelerated even more as I felt strong hands wrap around my waist; sadly, they didn't seem familiar. My half-a-million-dollar dress was getting ruined, and even in this fucked up situation, it gave me satisfaction.

The noise of the city crashed into me once more, as did my father's hysterical shouts and demands.

"Do you not know who we are?" he screeched, his voice sounding farther with every step I took. *You think we are more important than we really are, Dad. Your king will throw us under the bus as soon as he gets the first chance.*

The man who took me didn't speak, and since he saw I wasn't resisting, he stopped holding me so tight. We came to a stop, and I heard a door opening.

It suddenly became real. The way our bodies fight when we are drowning, that survival instinct kicks in. I wanted to die, but I didn't want to be murdered. How foolish was I? The Order had enemies everywhere.

Fuck.

I thrashed, and the man who was escorting me instantly reacted. It was too late for me to do anything, and the cowardly part of myself wondered if I only did it so I could face myself later on and say at least I tried.

With ease, the man picked me up and threw me inside

the car. The first thing that happened; my sweaty hands made contact with the leather on the back seat. Second, the smell of cedarwood engulfed my senses. And third, a chill went down my spine all the way to my toes when a gloved finger made its way into my hood and caressed my cheek.

"No," I gasped, speaking for the first time since being taken away.

The hood placed over my head was removed, and the only thing I could see was jade eyes glaring at me.

How was this possible?

"Surprised to see me, pet?" he spoke in that lazy tone that used to do funny things to me.

I blinked a couple of times, and I knew that walking down the aisle would have been a safer choice.

Mason Stiltskin was out for his revenge, and I had no one to blame but myself.

He tipped my chin up with one finger, and I couldn't help but be mesmerized. So much hate and loathing swirled in those jade eyes, and all of it was for me.

Looking into his green eyes, I couldn't help but think of the past—our rocky beginning down to the hellish ending.

TWENTY-SIX

MASON

GOOD THINGS COME TO THOSE WHO WAIT, OR SO THEY SAY. I couldn't say it was easy to hold myself back when the first thing I wanted to do after leaving the island was go in search of Aspen, and fucking wring her neck.

But looking at her through someone else's lens wasn't the same.

Now, after six years, she was finally within reaching distance from me. The limo reeked with her scent, and it was driving me insane. I chose this car because it was spacious, and I knew exactly what I needed to do before taking everything away from her.

The moment my right hand made contact, she froze, and that thrilled me. Good, she knew the devil had finally come for her. I removed the hood, and all that golden hair came into view. She looked like a princess, ready for the ball. She resembled purity when we both knew she reeked of hell. Our gazes met, and every cell in my body jolted.

"Surprised to see me, pet?" My voice was low and controlled, but inside I was already burning up.

"I'm America's sweetheart. You can't kill me," she spat at me.

I cocked my head and smiled. So that was her plan. My cock twitched with her scheming. Her mouth parted at my smile. She looked at me and tried to reach for the handle of the car, but I grabbed onto her waist and then put her on the side seat.

You had to love big productions because they planned everything down to a T, making it easier to manipulate them. The car was moving, already blending its way into the traffic. If my time on the island taught me anything, it was that revenge could only get you so far. You needed money, time, and people behind you that stood for the same cause.

The only thing fucking with my plan now was Aspen's wedding dress.

"You're not going to get away with this," she hissed.

I stared at her tits. Especially the way they stood out from the neckline of her dress.

"Oh, don't worry, I'll take you to meet prince charming soon."

The way she froze at my words was satisfying. She had no idea what awaited her, and I was barely able to contain myself anymore.

"What do you mean?"

"Has your life gone according to plan?" I asked her, changing the subject. She sat quietly and just stared, but I could feel her intense gaze all over me. "Come on, pet, we are wasting time."

"What do you want from me? Are you here to kidnap me, is that it?"

A dark chuckle left my lips.

"We'll be there in less than fifteen minutes, sir."

My driver's voice could be heard through the intercom.

With my right hand, I loosened my tie then removed it. I leaned forward and took off my jacket.

When I looked up again, I noticed Aspen was breathing heavily. She really looked fucking beautiful. And I reminded myself that she was on her way to marry someone else.

"I have no intention of bringing you with me," I told her in a husky tone.

The moment I rose from my seat, she tried to lean back as if that would save her from me. I grabbed my tie and then went for her like a lion threw itself to a gazelle.

"What the fuc—"

She didn't finish her sentence because I cut her off with a kiss. The more she cursed at me, the more brutally I kissed her lips. After a few seconds, she finally kissed me back. I pulled back because this was my show, and I couldn't let her win.

Our loud panting was like our very own symphony guiding us to the next phase in our relationship. Before she could compose herself, I grabbed both her wrists and tied them.

Her lips trembled but in anger, because her face was flushed, and her eyes were void of tears.

"You used me at the island; how about this time I get to use you?" My tone was cold. I waited for a moment for guilt to assault me, but it didn't come. The way I saw it, I was just getting even.

"Touch me and you die," she hissed.

"And who's going to kill me? Prince charming?" I ridiculed her. I leaned forward and brushed my nose against the curve of her neck, trailing from her shoulder up to her ear. She smelled so fucking sweet, and I wanted to take that smell and bask in it.

"Don't worry, Aspen, you can still walk down the aisle

with him," I whispered against the shell of her ear, and she shivered. I angled my face in the crook of her neck, and then I licked her. A small whimper left her mouth, and she arched her neck to give me better access.

I wondered if she remembered just what those balls could do against her pussy.

My self-control was being fucking tested, and I could only blame myself. I didn't want to kiss her lips anymore because her lips would be swollen. If I kissed more of her neck, I would leave hickeys. Anything to try and leave a trace of myself.

I put my hand on top of her breast, and she watched as I slowly pushed it down and pinched her nipple. The dress was so tight, that I couldn't do much else. My time was running out, so I removed my hand from her breast.

"Stop," she pleaded between gritted teeth.

I ignored her and instead buried my head on top of her breast and licked her there too, at the same time as my hands made their way under her dress. I hoped her material didn't get too ruined, or else it would ruin all her pictures.

"But I don't want to stop." I looked up at her as my hands glided leisurely up her thighs. "You didn't stop when you broke my heart."

Her mouth fell open, and she looked at me with surprise but also with wonder. My fingers traced the path her garters made, and I wished I could see her without the dress. What would she look like laid out in white on my bed?

"Have you been fucking Liam?" My voice was harsh.

"That's none of your business." Her voice was full of rage, and I bit my lip when I could see moisture gathering in her eyes.

My left hand made contact with her silk panties. My

finger went to the slit, and I looked back at her triumphantly at how wet it felt.

"My hand in your pussy makes it my business." Two fingers went inside the silk material, and she gasped just from having her pussy stroked. "The way you get wet for me makes it my business..."

"S-s-top," she managed to say as I teased her entrance.

"I'm not stopping—" The two fingers scissored her pussy, and she winced. Her mouth parted with a silent moan as I started to thrust them in and out.

Her hips moved clumsily, but her pussy was eager for my touch. My mouth watered as I remembered her taste and how it felt to lick her pussy and suck her clit.

"You've been a good girl for me, haven't you?"

She looked at me with half-mast eyes filled with lust, but didn't answer me.

"No one has been inside this pussy."

I pulled my gloved hand out and just left the one that was fingering inside the dress. I took some maneuvering, but I managed to grab her chin. "Were you saving this for him?"

My sanity was slowly slipping the more I touched her.

Aspen bit her lip, and I knew she was getting close. I pulled my fingers out and used the pad of my thumb to tease her clit.

She couldn't help but moan.

"Five minutes away, sir."

That seemed to take Aspen out of the trance she had found herself in. I removed my hand, and she watched me intently, waiting for my next move. I rose as much as I could in the car and pulled down my zipper, and my dick sprang free.

"W-w-what are you doing?" she asked breathlessly.

I didn't answer her question. Instead, I sat her up and then took her spot. Aspen tried to lunge to the other seat, but I didn't let her.

"What are you doing?" she hissed.

I moved some of the tulle and sat her on top of me. She was facing forward, and I could see her every expression, thanks to the mirrors in front of us.

"We're finally going to fuck."

Panic spread through her features. My right hand wrapped around her waist and pulled her back toward me. With my left hand, I moved the dress to the side.

"Don't do this, Mas—"

A bitter laugh escaped me as she tried to call me by my name.

"Why should I listen to you? All you've done is fuck me over, so this time you can at least do it properly."

I lifted her up and then guided my dick at her entrance. She kept on moving, trying to get away from me. Slowly I pushed the tip inside of her. She was fucking soaked. I wasn't even in, and it already felt amazing.

"Ask me why I did it?" she pleaded.

Our eyes met through the mirror, and I could see she was breaking. The only problem was that I no longer cared if she did.

"I don't care," I told her as my dick slowly made its way inside. Both my hands came to her waist, holding on to her as my hips drove into her.

"Please, Mase, not like this," she hissed as I started to stretch her out.

Her voice was so low and fucking needy that I couldn't hold back anymore. I thrusted my hips at the same time I pushed her down against me.

Aspen screamed as her pussy gripped onto me so tight

that it felt like my dick would break off. My thrusts were slower now that I was deep inside of her. She was so wet and warm I felt like I was melting.

"I hate you..." I whispered. "I hate you so much I can hardly breathe."

Her breathing became erratic by my words. Tears started to fall down from her eyes.

"Will this make us even then?" she spat as she rose on her heels then slammed back down on me. I groaned, and she whimpered in pain but did it again and again until she found pleasure in the pain.

"Never," I told her as I kissed the back of her neck. "You were supposed to be mine, Aspen."

Her breath hitched, and she turned her head as much as she could so we could look at each other. Our breathing became in sync, our lungs desperately trying to keep us alive as we tried to tear into each other.

"If you're going to walk down the aisle with him"—my words were full of venom as I pushed my hips deep inside her, causing her eyes to roll back—"you're going to do it with my cum dripping out of you."

We started to fuck each other harder and faster. Aspen's hands were gripping the edge of the seat as she supported herself while I fucked her relentlessly. Her cries filled the cabin of the car, and I knew they would haunt me when she was no longer with me. Her pussy started to convulse around me, and I pushed in so fucking deep wanting to bury all of me inside of her. Now my cum coated every inch of her.

I could feel the limo turning, and I knew we had arrived.

Aspen tried to move, but I stopped her. Instead, I slowly pulled my dick out and rubbed it against her thighs.

My hand went to her cheek, rubbing it gently. "I hope

blood stains all that white," I whispered against her ear, and she shivered. "So when you take off this dress, you'd always remember who this pussy belongs to. *Long live the Kings*."

Before she could say another word, my driver spoke again.

"*Sir, we've arrived.*"

Seconds later, Nate opened the door and helped Aspen out of the Limo. For six years, I held myself back, knowing that I had to bide my time before I could ever lay another hand on her.

I didn't let myself get a second look at her, or else I would not be able to let her go.

TWENTY-SEVEN

My legs were not strong enough to support me anymore. I don't even remember making my way out of that car.

I was cold. My body kept shivering. A warm hand touched mine and pulled me gently away.

"Long live the Kings."

Those four words spread like ice to my heart.

Whatever warmth I had managed to bask in was now gone. For a second, there I was, ready to screw everyone, let the world set on fire, and beg Mase to take me with him.

Someone was guiding me, and I didn't understand why. There was a throbbing pain between my legs. I could feel moisture and something sticky trickling down.

"We don't have much time," a female voice said.

The man guiding me came to a stop, and a female's hand came to my dress and started to fix it. I looked down first, and I didn't think I'd have it in me to be surprised anymore.

Erin was before me. She looked elegant and refined in her peach dress. She stretched out the tulle on my dress, so it wasn't wrinkled.

"Did he hurt you?" the man behind me said.

I should have known it was Nate. He and Erin usually stuck around together.

"What's going on?" I asked, still dazed.

I looked around, and sure enough, we were already at the church where my ceremony would occur.

There was a barricade of cars over here blocking me from view. We had rehearsed this. Once I walked toward the front, my father and I would come into view so the press could get pictures of me.

Liam was going to kill me, and for the first time, I didn't care. I had served my purpose in this world. I lived. My parents lived off me. I betrayed, and now I have paid for my sins.

"She's good to go," Erin said.

I watched as she pulled her chair back. Our eyes met, and I didn't know what to say to her. It was easier to pretend that she wasn't there than try to apologize for something that happened so long ago. Truth be told, she might not understand my reasoning. But I'm glad Mason burned down that house. This future was much better than one where he would have been trapped.

Nate added pressure on my back so I could keep moving. My reflection caught on the window of a car, and I couldn't stop staring at myself.

My dress looked fine. Nothing major had changed. My skin was a bit flushed but could be chalked up to wedding day jitters. My lips were a little swollen but nothing major. The makeup had been light and natural. The only thing I couldn't do anything about was my puffy red eyes. If anything, they looked more appealing. Tears of joy, one could say. I looked like the perfect bride with nothing out of place except inside of me. My underwear was a wet mess.

My thighs were sticky, and I felt Mason's cum leak with every step.

"Liam is going to find out about this," I told them both. It wasn't even a warning. They knew what would happen to them too. His father had too much power.

"Don't worry about that," Nate reassured me.

I wanted to laugh. My father and I had been assaulted in plain daylight. There was no talking our way out of this.

I took another step forward, and my legs shook. I didn't want to go through with this anymore. Maybe it hurt so much more because Mason didn't even ask me to come with him. I mean, why would he? He had asked me on two occasions, and both times, I spat on his face.

The reality that he didn't want me slid off me. He took my virginity and called it a day.

I was hyperventilating.

How could I be so reckless?

My only protection had been the fact that I was untouched. Liam let me do as I pleased because he knew sooner or later, I would be his.

I needed to get away from here.

"Please take me away," I turned around and begged Nate.

His soft features were gone. "No." His words were final. "You have to walk down that aisle. "

The cage I had made for myself was finally closing in on me. Nate started to drag me with more force. A few seconds later, I heard more footsteps, and my father was being dragged along with another man I didn't know.

"You're going to pay for this," he spat at them.

Nate, who always seemed kinder than the rest, looked my father up and down, and his lip curled in disgust.

"And what power do you have against me?"

My father's face turned red. In a matter of seconds, his

life flashed before his eyes. The little money cow he had created was ripped away from him.

"Now go, and not a word to anyone. Unless you want Wilfred to think you're conspiring against him."

My father looked back at him and then at me. He looked me up and down and seemed to come to the conclusion that I was fine. The apple didn't fall far from the tree, did it?

"Smile, Father. This is what you wanted," I told him as I looped my hand through his.

As soon as we cleared the area that was blocked, cameras began to go off. I smiled at them. If they wanted a show, I would give them one. This is what Mason wanted? For the world to see me about to marry a man while my body already belonged to someone else?

We walked up the steps hand in hand, both of us together. The doors to the cathedral opened, and I turned to my father.

"As soon as I get rid of your last name, you are dead to me."

He didn't get a chance to respond because we made our way down the aisle. Everyone stood up and pretended to be happy for me. Others whispered among themselves. All the while I died a little more with each step.

Once at the altar, my father took my hand and gave it to Liam. Their arrangement had finally come full circle.

I looked at Liam, and the smile he had on his face was nothing more than triumph. The people behind us didn't care; this was just a show.

I briefly wondered what would happen if I were to scream that this was a farce. That I didn't want to go through with this. That I was nothing more than a mere pawn. Live cattle had more rights than me.

The minister came, and the ceremony started. I had

expected for the doors to bust open and for Mason to walk through them. To let Liam know what had happened between us.

That didn't happen.

"You may now kiss the bride."

I stopped breathing when I heard those words. My body forgot how to move, but Liam's didn't. He had been waiting for this day.

Everyone cheered as Liam's lips touched mine. It felt wrong. It shouldn't have been *him*. Right now, I wished I got burned in that house too. What was the point of living a life you didn't love?

I turned away from him as soon as he pulled away. My mother was crying, and the thing that enraged me was that they were tears of joy.

I was going to be sick.

Maybe if I told Liam what had happened, he would kill me. I wanted to die. I managed to fool myself for the last six years that it was going to be fine. I managed to believe the lie I had created for myself. They were my choices, and I told myself that they were the best choices I could make.

I had been nothing but a stupid little girl who didn't know anything about the real world. The life I had lived was a pretense. I was constantly bending down to the wills of others. I got blinded by things that were never meant to be mine.

My heart beat faster with every passing minute. We walked out those doors—husband and wife. Why did he let me go through this? Was this my punishment?

What would have happened if I let Liam know why Mason burned the house down? Could I have managed to set myself free? In all reality, that could have never happened. I was a puppet to these people—to my parents. The only person I seemed to defy was the one I loved.

Which was stupid to call it love; it was an all-consuming rage that took over me when I was near Mason Stiltskin. It was full of self-loathing and havoc. Something so toxic that got you addicted to the taste. Like all toxic things, they didn't start out that way. It was always sweet at first. Giving you a taste of what could be, but with each taste, it hooked you in.

Liam was all smiles as he took my hand and opened the door of the car that would take us to the reception.

I looked out the window as the city passed us by. There were no words passed between us. Nothing we both wanted to share. This was an exchange of power and nothing else.

Liam led me by the hand as we made our way inside the reception hall. The guests would be in another room, and it was time for me to change into my second dress of the night.

I saw the bridal suite and dreaded having to go in. Liam walked in first, holding the door open for me. As soon as I walked in, the door was shut with a loud thud, and I closed my eyes.

"Mrs. King," Liam whispered in my ear.

There were no shivers. My body didn't race with excitement at his voice. He wasn't my sweet addiction. He was something I rejected from the start.

"We're going to finally fuck," he hissed. "And this pussy will finally be mine."

I raised my head higher as I felt his fingers touch my back and slowly start to work the zipper. Liam peppered kisses on my neck and my back as he pulled the gown down. The dress pooled at my feet. My breasts were covered in white pasties, panties I was too scared to look at, a white garter went across my hips and the stockings that snapped to it.

"You 're not leaving this room until you scream my name," he moaned excitedly.

I had finally lost it because I smiled. He kissed down my body, and I was waiting for the moment where he realized that my pussy didn't belong to him. Someone else had already claimed it.

TWENTY-EIGHT

THE THUMPING OF MY HEARTBEAT WAS SO LOUD I FELT LIKE each beat echoed in my ear. Liam kissed the space between the dimples in my back as I patiently waited for all of this to blow over.

When he suddenly got up, a part of me was relieved, but the other was disappointed. We were just prolonging the inevitable.

He slowly prowled around me until he was standing in front of me. He took hold of one of my hands and guided me forward to step out of my dress.

"I hope blood stains all that white."

I hoped so too. Mason's voice and words have haunted me through the years, and his latest statement had engraved its way into my heart. It probably wasn't enough to pay back all the pain I had caused him, but I gave to him the only thing that I had—the right to my body. It wasn't even mine to give away, but I wanted him to have it all the same. Knowing his secret, I'd like to think that one day he would learn to cherish the fact that I gave him my first time.

Holding onto Liam's hand, I stepped one foot forward,

eager to meet my destiny. I was beginning to think the real cage was living, and dying set you free.

As soon as I was out of the dress, Liam licked his lips. He removed the black bowtie first, then the jacket. After that, the vest, and then one by one, he undid the buttons of his white shirt.

I couldn't believe people had overlooked Mason just to look at him. If you were to compare them side by side, there was no contest on who was the most handsome. He didn't only surpass his looks but also height; he even looked broader than he had back on the island.

His chaos was coming into its own back then, but now it had peaked, and it was full of dark embraces that you never wanted to leave.

Liam licked his lips, and then he threw me on the sofa that was in the room. I fell on my back, and he was on top of me in an instant. His eyes finally glowed with the evil that lurked inside of him. The vileness he disguised with charming smiles. The facade that he showed the world was gone.

The only devil I feared was the one I had created. I looked into his eyes as he began to open my legs for him.

"I'm going to fuck you so hard you're going to cry," he hissed with excitement.

I bit my mouth so I wouldn't spoil the surprise for him. I felt his gaze like a touch slowly moving its way down my body. With each second that he got closer, my skin burned with anticipation.

The moment his eyes landed between my legs, I felt the room go cold. The air turned so violent you could taste it.

"I'd say you're a little late for that," I taunted him.

He looked like a bull ready to strike. I finally dared to look down, and my insides clenched at the sight. Dried cum was all over my thighs, but the real kicker was the red blood-stain on my panties. There had been no denying what I had done.

His hand came to my neck in an instant like a cobra striking at its prey. He pressed down on the sides, and I gasped for the air that was not there.

"Who the fuck touched you?"

Deep down, I had known that giving my body to Mason would have been the biggest fuck you I could have given Liam.

He let go of my neck and ripped my panties from my body. He held them up so I could see them clearly.

"You fucking bitch," he said through gritted teeth.

"All I could think about was his dick inside of me as I said I—"

I didn't get to finish my sentence as he struck my cheek with such a force, my teeth clanked.

"I'm going to murder him," he seethed. "You should have been grateful and kissing my feet." Another smack this time on the other side.

"You poor girls are all the same," he said more calmly and that scared me even more than his rage. I wanted him to keep hitting me to get lost in the pain so it could block out everything else.

At this moment, I think I finally understood Mason a little more. It was easier to numb yourself than to face your demons.

The coppery taste of blood filled my tastebuds.

"H-he c-came so de-deep i-inside of me," I managed to spit out despite the pain on my face.

"Yeah?" Liam smirked. "I'm going to treat you like the rat you are. Forget the reception. You're not leaving this room until you're brimming with my cum."

My jaw hurt as I smiled.

"It's okay. Mason already filled me up," I hissed.

He grabbed a fistful of my hair, and I felt every bobby pin that had been stuck in there trying to poke its way inside of my skull. He threw me down onto the floor. I landed on my stomach, and I closed my eyes.

I just wanted to pass out. One more hit, and it wouldn't be long now. I could feel my body giving out.

Liam pulled my head back by my hair. It hurt the way my neck stretched. I whimpered in pain, and he laughed at it. "Since you're no longer a virgin, I won't bother with being gentle."

Even if I wasn't, I doubt he would have.

He let go of my hair, and my head hit the floor. I didn't even have the energy to talk anymore. I didn't have the energy to fight, but somehow, I could still cry.

My choices had caught up to me, and I was ready to face the consequences of them.

I heard the sound of Liam pulling down his pants, and I waited. It felt like the room had gone silent. After that, I couldn't even hear our breathing. The tip of his dick poked my ass, and I waited...for the pain or for oblivion; I wasn't sure which. Told myself that it was okay. Before he could push inside of me, the door burst open.

"We've been fucking calling you!"

The voice seemed familiar, but I couldn't place it. Were my ears bleeding already?

"Get the fuck out!" Liam screamed.

Suddenly my back felt lighter. His presence was no longer there. I felt weightless as soon as he was gone.

"Your father just got arrested, and my guess is you're next."

I tried to lift my head to see who was talking, but it was

too painful. More talking went on, and I couldn't make out what they said.

"You need to leave and lay low while this blows over."

"She's coming with me!" Liam yelled.

He tried to drag me up with him, but my actions were sluggish. That's when I saw who was in the room with us. My eyes met Nate's, and he looked down at me, his face stoic, but his eyes told another story.

"She can't fucking move. You get caught with her, and it will be worse for you," Nate said calmly.

"What happened?" Liam barked, looking unhinged.

Nate pulled out his phone and showed it to Liam. His face seemed to go pale. He looked down at me and then punched the wall.

"I'll be back for you." It wasn't a threat but a promise.

The moment he left the room, relief had more tears streaming down my face. Nate removed his jacket and gently wrapped it around me.

"Let's get you out of here," he told me.

I couldn't even say yes or thank you. Just as he was lifting me up, something shiny caught my eye. It was on top of my dress, shining like a beacon. The diamond necklace that Mason had given me all those years ago was begging me to take it with me once more. This necklace had been my companion for years. It had seen my ups and my downs. Through my hardest moments, it had shined with hope. I mustered the last of my energy and tried to reach for it. I wasn't successful, but luckily Nate saw it and handed it to me.

After holding on for so long, I closed my eyes, and I let go.

MY HEAD THROBBED WHEN I WOKE UP AGAIN. I OPENED MY eyes, and I didn't recognize the room I was in. I sat up, and luckily nothing hurt. It was just my face that carried the pain.

I looked down at myself, and I was no longer naked. I wore a t-shirt and some pants. In my hands, I clutched onto those diamonds so tightly that the imprint of the tiny squares was on my palm when I let go. I slowly sat up and made my way out. It was a house that I wasn't familiar with. I had been to most of the Order's members' homes, but I couldn't recall this one.

I was almost down the hallway when I heard a creak behind me. I turned around, my hand to my chest as if that would protect me.

I blinked when I saw Erin, hoping she wasn't a figment of my imagination.

"You should be in bed," she told me.

"Where am I?"

"Nate's penthouse."

My heart raced when I realized that he lived in the city not far from Liam's place. For the first time, I wanted to run. There was nothing holding me back. Liam was currently indisposed, and if he got his hands on me, he would kill me. Mason got his revenge, and my parents no longer matter.

I dropped to my knees, letting go of that pride I had picked up along the way and begged her for help.

TWENTY-NINE

A FEW WEEKS LATER

My life had been a rollercoaster these past few weeks. Everything happened so fast after I was taken away from Liam. The media was relentless that I had not been out in weeks. The Kings were under investigation. Turns out the tech they stole from Mr. Stiltskin was tied to some terrorist groups.

There was no way to clear their name without admitting what they had done. The blame lay at their feet. They were too busy ceasing their fires, they had no time to think about me. But I knew Liam would come, and he would want to continue where we left off.

As for Mason, I hadn't heard from him, and I was too scared to ask Erin about him.

That day when I begged for her help, she looked at me and my bruised face and nodded. We left that house, and she's been accompanying me ever since.

"Where are you going?" Nate was behind as we tried to go down the elevator.

Erin lifted her chin up and looked at him with defiance, a look I hadn't seen her use on anyone since before her accident.

"She needs space," she bit out at him.

And it felt good to have her throw her neck out for me. It almost felt like old times. The island felt like a lifetime ago. Despite the shame and guilt, I did care for her. It was easier to pretend like I didn't because, in the end, all the things I wanted I could never have.

"He's not going to be happy about this." Nate raised a brow at her.

"He owes me one," had been her response.

At first, we didn't talk much. She gave me a room, and clothes, and fed me. There had been no catch. My life kept turning, so much that it made me dizzy thinking back on it. I came from nothing, living off the masters we were born into. I gained the backing of the most prestigious last name in this world, and now that name was tainted.

I was alone in Erin's apartment, the media was wondering where I could be, and instead of feeling lonely, I felt at peace. My name was being dragged to the ground, my wedding day was ridiculed, and I couldn't care less about any of that.

There was a knock at my door, and the older lady that took care of Erin's apartment walked in with a smile. I returned her smile with one of my own, which was odd because I had forgotten how to smile freely. But most of all, somewhere in the last six years, I stopped seeing the servants as people. I was stuck in my own head. I forgot that I used to be just like them.

"Thank you," I told her as I took hold of the breakfast tray she gave me. As she opened the curtains in the room, I took a sip of the orange juice and gagged.

The maid turned back to look at me.

"I think it's past its due date," I said with embarrassment.

"I'll bring you some water," she told me and rushed out of the room.

True to her word, she came back with a cold glass of water for me. She removed the juice right away, but I felt her gaze on me as she went about her chores. Maybe she thought the same thing as me. I needed a game plan because I was overstaying my welcome.

I wandered around the house drinking coffee on her balcony, just looking up at the sky as I enjoyed my drink. It was sad that I could care less how my parents were handling their fall from grace. Their only protection were the Kings, and now they had no one. For the first time, I was glad all their assets were tied up with theirs.

By the time evening arrived, I had decided to take a shower just in case Erin stopped by. I took my things to my bathroom and came to a halt when I found a small box on top of the sink.

I set my stuff down and then went to it.

Time had stood still for me quite a few times that I knew the feeling all too well. This time, it was no different. It was trying to grip on to the past as the present clawed its way out.

"If you're going to walk down the aisle with him, you're going to do it with my cum dripping out of you."

"Shit," I whispered.

I tried to think back on when I had my last period, but I couldn't remember. Since I wasn't sexually active, birth control was something I never bothered with since the Kings controlled my every move.

My hands gripped the edge of the counter as I calmed myself down. There was no way I was pregnant. I couldn't be. I'd only had sex once. I couldn't be that unlucky.

Still, I took the test, and as I waited, I took a shower. As if washing my body would wash this away too. The hot water scorched me, and I let it, as if it would wash me clean from all my sins. Afterward I did all other things but peek at those results. Once I was changed, I reached for the stick with shaky hands.

I staggered until my back hit the wall. I slid onto the floor, holding on to my stomach. I wanted to cry, and I wanted to scream. It's like my body was a fountain of a thousand emotions that I didn't know how to process.

All my life, I've done the wrong thing. Mistake after mistake, but in that moment, I knew that I wanted to do something right. Love wasn't something I ever thought of. It was a luxury that I didn't have, but I knew that I was already in love with the idea of having something that was mine. Something that I could live and die for. They said a woman became a mother the moment she knew she was pregnant, and as for the father, the moment he held his kid in his arms.

My train of thoughts stopped suddenly, and all that joy I had felt earlier was replaced by fear.

"In return, you'll give me the thing you love the most."

For most of my life, Mason's voice had followed me around. Even though it taunted me, it comforted me to hear him, but now all I felt was dread.

One thing was for sure. I would do for this child what my parents never did for me. So I wiped my tears, grabbed that necklace, and walked out of that bathroom like nothing was wrong.

Sitting across the table from Erin, I knew I had been a coward all these years. And it was time to stop running from all my mistakes. I had already paid for most of them anyway. Dinner was quiet, but that wasn't anything new. It was usually like this. I got the feeling neither one of us knew what to say to the other.

"Why are you helping me?"

She stopped mid-bite and put the fork down. "When you showed up at school, I didn't like you. I hated you despite not knowing you."

I looked down at my plate.

"Before you came along, I was the one Liam favored. My family and his were close. We could offer them more than any of the other families. I felt like the world was at my fingertips."

She took a deep breath and then took a sip of her wine.

"The day of the party, he threw me aside. He no longer needed me. And later, I found out why."

The guilt I had toward her was now stronger.

I held onto my stomach under the table and then turned to her.

"I didn't know what Mason had planned, but I wasn't surprised," I admitted. "I met him before my family walked away with the Kings. He asked me to run away with him, and I could smell gasoline on him. If I would have said something—"

Erin smirked at me.

"So that's why you stuck to me like glue? You felt as if you'd said something, I wouldn't be in this wheelchair?"

Erin took another sip of her wine.

"Liam gave me to Jason. He handed me off like I was property he could throw away whenever he no longer wanted it."

I didn't know what to say to her other than sorry.

"I'm glad you didn't tell me any of this before. I would have blamed you, and I'm glad you were with me those first few years. Everyone distanced themselves, and for the first time, I knew what loneliness felt like."

"But if I had said something—"

"I'm glad Jason is dead," she rushed out. "I couldn't say anything about what happened that night because Mr. King wanted it all to be buried. And if I opened my mouth, it would have created an unnecessary scandal."

I had no idea about this. I remembered how I felt under the weight of Liam's power. That feeling was something I didn't wish upon anyone.

"I guess I'm helping you because I feel sorry for you. And I can kill two birds with one stone that way."

That was fair enough. I felt lighter after our talk. We finished our food, and I didn't say more. I waited in my room until all was quiet and Erin had left for the night. With the necklace in my pocket, I silently left the apartment.

"You'll give me the thing you love the most."

For the first time, I had something that was mine. Something to fight for and no one holding me back—it was time to run.

THIRTY

MASON

REVENGE WAS FUCKING SWEET, EXCEPT I COULDN'T ENJOY IT without my final chess piece. It had been almost a month and there had been no word on Aspen. How the fuck did a girl who knew nothing about the real world disappear?

I was pacing my office, annoyed that everything moved slowly. I wanted to see the Kings go down. Preferably dead, but knowing I was the one who had caused their collapse gave me satisfaction. Ever since I found out about my father's other business venture, I knew something else had to be buried deep. I had to invest a shit ton of money in gathering sources and intel. I didn't want to make a move until I was sure that I would be successful.

When I found out that the stolen technology was used overseas by terrorist groups, I felt like I had hit the jackpot. All I had to do was leak that information out, and the Kings would choke by their own hand. It was revenge at its sweetest.

I had bid my time, and it had paid off.

So, I had been dealing with a lot of shit that I stupidly listened to Nate and let Erin keep Aspen. For one, I was going to be busy setting fires left and right. All the people who had been behind my family's demise would pay. And second, I knew Liam wanted Aspen, dead or alive, and I couldn't risk having her with me while I was so busy.

I had seen her face while she was sleeping. I memorized every bruise that had appeared on her face, and it drove me to the point of insanity. Liam King was going to pay for everything.

I didn't count on the fact that the space I gave her would turn against me. One day, Aspen was there; and the next, she was not. My hand went to the cabinet under my desk, and I pulled out the pregnancy test that I hid there since I found it in the trash bin of her bathroom.

She was pregnant with my child.

A thousand scenarios rushed through my head. Kids were not something I'd taken the time to think about. But the moment I had seen that test—fuck. I wanted that child more than anything.

Now I just needed to get Aspen here with me. I was so sick and tired of her bullshit. My dick had led me over the last decade of whatever relationship we had, and it was time for a change.

It was a dick move, but I was the one in power, and it was time to show her who her real king was. I was going to make her kneel at my feet.

Her being pregnant with my child changed things. I was fine with her getting married. I wanted her trapped. I wanted Liam to think he was getting everything he wanted. I sat in my office looking at pictures of their first husband-and-wife kiss, and I had smiled because my cum had been all over her pussy.

Then I had leaked out the information. Like hell if I was going to let that prick get his dick anywhere near her.

Her getting hurt was on me, and I knew I would make him pay.

But the moment Erin told me she was gone and I went to that apartment, and the only thing I found was the pregnancy test, I knew humiliating Liam wouldn't do. I no longer cared because the whole world already knew what he and his family had done. That was the beauty of technology—a double-edged sword that could make or break you.

Now that Aspen carried my child, I wouldn't be satisfied until I made her a widow. His death would lay at my hands, and I would relish in the fact that the chapter that had torn us apart since day one would finally be coming to an end.

Now I just needed to find her because the longer she stayed on the streets, the more risk she ran of Liam getting to her first.

My study door opened, and Erin came in, followed by Nate.

"Since when is it okay to stop by my house without asking me first?" I asked, annoyed.

"Since we found a lead," Erin bit back.

I sat up straighter. "A lead that we wouldn't have needed had you not let her get away."

I tried to leave the venom from my voice. Nate didn't like it when I was mean to her, and right now, I didn't need him mad at me. Not when he was the one trying to get the Order members against the Kings. Most of them didn't like me, but they loved him.

"We're even now." Erin shrugged.

I fisted my hand but otherwise maintained silence. I guess this was her fuck you since I was the cause of the fire.

"What's the lead?" My gaze went from her to Nate's.

"Remember that necklace that you had me tag years ago?"

I cocked my head. I had kept my ear to the ground, trying to see if it showed up, but I hadn't found it. When on the island, I never saw Aspen wear it, so I was sure she had sold it off or not cared for it. It had been my birth mother's —it was the only thing I had of hers.

The night of the fire, I had given it to Aspen as insurance. In case things went wrong and I burned alongside my parents, I wanted her to run away. To use that for cash and start a new life.

"It's this one, right?" Nate pulled out his phone and showed me a picture of it. I hadn't seen it in years, but I remembered it.

"Yeah," I croaked.

Nate took the phone back and zoomed in on it.

"She had this on her wedding day."

My head snapped up at him.

"What?"

He set the phone down and then brought his hand behind his head.

"She was about to pass out, and she tried to reach for it. It was inside her dress."

Something about that statement made me weak. She had it on that day. She took a piece of me with her. And I wondered how many other times she had carried it.

"Give me the information," I demanded.

"I already checked, and it was sold."

"Doesn't matter, I'll get it back." I was confident in my abilities.

A FEW DAYS LATER, I FOUND MYSELF OUTSIDE THE HOUSE OF Aspen's parents. I knew it was a long shot that she would be here or that she would even ask them for help, but I wasn't about to leave any stone unturned.

I rang the doorbell out of courtesy, so they'd know someone was coming. Their staff was no longer there. So now they had to do everything themselves. It's not like anyone was giving them anything anymore.

Aspen's mother opened the door and looked at me with wide eyes.

"Y-y-you," she spat and tried to slap my face.

Surprise bitch, I'm not dead.

I caught her wrist mid-air and laughed. "You're bold for someone who doesn't have anything anymore."

Aspen's mother was not beautiful like her daughter. She had let all that money go to her head, and instead of trying to be smart about it, she spent her money trying to get a new face. It was not hard to see who she wanted to emulate. My lips curled in disgust as I noticed that even her taste was the same as Hilda's.

I pushed inside, and she trailed behind me.

"The staff is happily serving their rightful owner again," I rubbed salt on her wound.

A while later, her dipshit husband came out. Well, if this didn't bring back memories.

"Is Aspen here?" I cut to the chase.

"My daughter is none of your concern," he told me.

I barked back a laugh. He said it with a straight face, believing the lie himself. I guess when you tell a lie long enough, and you believe it.

"The same daughter you sold off for money?" I raised a brow at him.

"I gave my daughter an opportunity to succeed."

I rolled my eyes.

"I should have had my men kill you on her wedding

day," I said so casually. Death wasn't something new to me. It trailed behind me like an old friend ready to jump in if anyone dared cross me.

His eyes widened, and his face went pale.

"I guess no one told you I was alive?" I mocked them.

Their house felt cold. It was nice, but there was nothing to it; just two miserable people convincing themselves that this was what they wanted. But hey, who was I to judge? Being rich and miserable were better than being poor and still miserable.

"Is she here or not?" I asked once more, losing my patience.

"That's none of your business," her mother told me.

I walked over to a chair and took a seat. I then pulled out a pack of cigarettes from my pocket and lit that fucker up. The flames still bothered me, but I learned to crave that fear that came with having fire close to my face. It's what kept me sane and kept me going.

I no longer needed a knife to my skin. Not when I had another outlet. The nicotine calmed me, and then once I exhaled the smoke, I looked at them again.

Their gazes were on my gloved hand.

Everyone who knew about the fire knew why I was covered. It didn't take a genius to guess I had been burned, but none of them knew I was terrified of it. Well, almost everyone. Only Nate and Aspen had guessed.

"Since no one had bothered to fill you in...because no one likes you," I said smugly to them, "let me tell you what's going on. The technology you stole from my father, yeah, that shit was linked to all kinds of terrorist groups. So as you can see, the Kings are done for." I paused to sigh dramatically. "But what about our money? You're probably asking yourselves that, right? I hate to be the bearer of bad news, I really do, but all of the Kings' assets are frozen. Everyone is pulling out of doing business with them, and since the deal you made was only with Wilfred, well, no one respects it." I took another drag of my cigarette. "What I'm trying to say is that no one likes you."

Ah, it felt good to see the fear on their faces.

"I'd say in about a week, the feds will freeze all your assets."

They didn't say anything as I got up and searched room by room. There was no trace of her here. She never treated this house as hers. After all, she was living with Liam for a while. Aspen had nothing that she ever held on to except for the necklace I gave her and somehow that made me smile.

I started to walk out of the house when a hand touched mine. Aspen's mother was clinging to me.

"Help us," she begged.

I raised a brow at her audacity.

"Sorry, I don't trust people who stab knives at my back."

Shrugging her off, I started to walk again.

"We know what she did to you," Mr. Miller said.

This time I turned back slowly.

"Guess as her other fuck buddy, you would know." My voice was calm, but they disgusted me.

"We won't tell anyone," Mrs. Miller assured me.

I looked at both of them, and as much as I wanted to kill them, a fate worse than death for them would be to be beggars. So they could see how poor people really lived. Once they'd be staying on the streets, they would wish that they had never trusted Wilfred King.

"What is there to tell? I'm dead, and the way things are going, you two are heading that way."

THIRTY-ONE

ASPEN

IT FELT LIKE A LIFETIME AGO THAT I HAD DONNED A MAID uniform. Life had gone full circle for me, and I was okay with it. Some may mock my job, think little of me, and I couldn't care less.

Was I scared leaving the confines of Erin's apartment? I had been terrified, but the idea of having a child and having it ripped away from me frightened me even more. I knew the Order was busy trying to cease the fires around them, so one rogue girl wouldn't be an issue.

I didn't care to expose them. I didn't care for that world because I had learned the hard way that everything that glittered wasn't gold.

For the first time, I felt free. And it wasn't what I thought it would be. Freedom wasn't going to a top-notch school nor having all the money in the world. Freedom was making ends meet by working relentlessly with my own two hands.

It was hard selling the necklace I had carried with me for so long. It had felt like a part of me, but it was the only thing I had that I could get some cash for. Being alone in the streets was a stark reality I had not prepared myself to deal with. I knew the amount of money they gave me was crap, but I needed a head start.

My apartment was shitty but the best I could find. I left the city and found myself near the place I was born. I wanted to see the remains of that house, but I didn't dare go near the gated community.

Instead, I found myself on the other side of town.

Looking at myself in the mirror, I didn't resemble the girl on the news. I was nothing like the glamorous Aspen King. My clothes were baggy and simple. My cheeks had hollowed out. I had traded designer bags for the ones under my eyes. My hair was dimmed and brassy.

What helped the most was that being a maid wasn't new to me at all. No one would think that the rich Aspen King was scrubbing floors on her knees. It was fitting and where I belonged.

Had life continued going the same without betrayals, I would still be at the Stiltskins' house. I would be Mason's friend in secret. He would have come into his own, and I would have watched from afar as he was finally accepted into the fold.

"Fuck," I sobbed.

These damn fucking hormones. Just thinking about watching him get married to someone else had me depressed.

Then my stomach felt empty because I was the one who was married. I was the one who had backstabbed him more than once. Will my child understand that one day?

I touched my stomach lovingly and knew that I needed to see a doctor sooner rather than later. I trusted no one and kept to my own at work. My place was furnished with just my bed and enough clothes to get me through the week.

I had no identity other than being Mrs. King, and I didn't

want it. So working for cash was my only option, but going to the doctor would mean questions would be asked. I still haven't thought that far ahead. My only consolation was that some women didn't know they were pregnant until they were four months so I would be fine for a little while longer.

I reminded myself that I wasn't selfish. I was just trying to keep my child and me together. It was motherly instinct.

Once I looked at the alarm, I sighed. It was time to get ready for work. I changed into the black uniform the company had us wear, and then I put my hair up in a bun. Most pictures showed my hair long and flowy. Like this, at least I looked different. If I wasn't pregnant, I would have dyed my hair black.

Not once in my life had I considered myself lucky, but things had worked surprisingly well after running away. I've never had anything of my own, and pawning that necklace gave me cash. Then I stopped in a diner, and the waitress took a liking to me. She gave me a number, and it all worked out from there.

It was obvious I was running from something, and maybe that made them feel pity for me. Either way, I was grateful. I had a prepaid phone that I only used for work. I had no one I could talk to, nor did I want to talk to anybody else.

Today it took more out of me to get out of bed. I was tired and I guess those sleepless nights were catching up to me.

The cleaning van was already at my complex. I went in and smiled at the other two ladies. We arrived at the restaurant we were going to clean at, and I got to work. It was like riding a bike. You never forgot where you came from; most of the time, we chose not to think about it.

"I hate you, Macy. You never sweat."

It took me a second to remember that she was talking to me. I couldn't afford to use my name. It wasn't all that common. I don't know why I gave that one out, but it seemed easier to remember.

"Guess I'm used to it," I told her.

I tried to keep my interaction with them to a bare minimum. I was ready to become a memory at a moment's notice. I yawned. I felt more tired today than usual. More time passed, and they turned on the television.

As usual, I tried to tune it out, but I was always scared they would show my picture. The news went on, and I kept on cleaning. I felt a little dizzy, so I decided to take a small break when the breaking news image flashed on TV.

"Wilfred King of King enterprises has been arrested as new information has come to light regarding the illegal acquisition of Stiltskin Tech. No word on whether his son, William King, has been arrested yet. Now as many as you know this all happened on his wedding day and no one has yet seen his wife."

I started to feel dizzy. I held onto the wall as I tried to make my way outside to get some fresh air.

"This case has been shocking from the start. It's like watching modern monarchy fall."

My ears started to buzz, and I couldn't hear, but the last thing I remembered was seeing my face on television.

A BEEPING SOUND WOKE ME UP. THE ROOM FELT COLD, AND there was a stillness in the air that made me uneasy. My eyes opened drowsily, and I didn't recognize where I was. That beeping sound came again, and I tried to get up, but something on my arm prevented me from lifting it.

There was a needle to my arm. I followed the path to an

IV drip. My eyes were taking everything in, but my mind was still too hazy to piece it together.

I looked down at myself, and that's when reality hit me. I was on a bed, with a cream blanket draped over me. I was at a hospital, and I was fucked. I wondered if I could still run out or if it was too late.

With my free hand, I reached for the IV with the intent of pulling it out when something cold wrapped around my wrist. The feel of leather was all too familiar now that it caused shivers to break out on my skin. I looked down, and sure enough, there was a black gloved hand holding onto me.

Slowly I lifted my head, and the brightest thing in the room wasn't the light but the burning jade eyes that glared at me.

"Going somewhere, *pet?*" he rasped out.

The machine started to beep faster.

He looked past me, then at me, and smirked.

"Are you scared?" he said in a low tone as he bent down. "Or turned on?"

My chest still kept rising and falling.

"W-w-what do you want?"

He didn't know. Maybe I still had a chance to play this off and leave. He couldn't know that the moment he had been waiting for was finally here. If the events that had been unfolding weren't a testament to his patience, I didn't know what was. He had waited his time to get his revenge, and all of us who had betrayed him were ready to fall at his feet.

Mason rose to his full height, and those eyes pierced me. I felt small under his ministrations.

"I'm just wondering where the hell do you think you're going with my child."

The machine started to beep furiously.

It was too late. He already knew.

THIRTY-TWO

MASON

SOONER OR LATER, WE ALL HAD TO STOP RUNNING. THE FINAL nail on the Kings coffin came earlier today. I had been waiting outside of Kings' tower when Wilfred got arrested. I blended in with the crowd, so when our eyes met, I lifted my right hand and saluted him. I had been waiting to savor his glare, and it had been worth it.

That had just left Liam to be dealt with. And I'd like to think I knew him, so I was sure he would run. I thought I would savor my victory for longer, but all of that came crashing down when the search for Aspen had come to a halt. I didn't think I could be crippled by fear, but I couldn't think straight when they told me she was at a hospital.

I had been searching for her high and low, and I knew that sooner or later, she had to get a check-up, so I had Nate keep an eye out for me. I just never expected for us to end up back here so close to where it all began. Maybe it was a sign—a rebirth. Proof that life always came full circle.

The way she looked now, no one had pieced it together

just who she was. Sometimes I surprised myself with how prepared I was. Getting identification for her wasn't hard. It was the matter of others buying it, but the Aspen before me wasn't the same one from two months ago.

If anything, she reminded me of the one that had been mine. The one I only talked to at my house.

"What's wrong with her?" I asked the nurse.

She looked me up and down and then at Aspen. We were polar opposites, and I knew my appearance wasn't doing me any favors.

"My family didn't want us together," I told her as I put my hands in the pocket of my pants. "They wanted to pay her off, but she refused to take the money and ran."

Everyone loved a sob story. All those good intentions were turning back against you, keeping you from happiness. People loved martyrs.

The nurse still didn't look like she fully trusted me, but I was all Aspen had right now.

"She's dehydrated," she finally told me.

I kept my rage controlled.

"And my baby?"

"The fetus is fine. We set her up with an IV drip. Once she gets hydrated, she should regain her consciousness."

So after the nurse left, I waited. My hand trailed down her cheeks, touching her smooth skin.

She had lost weight. There was a sharpness to her face that I didn't like. I was getting desperate, waiting for her to regain her consciousness, all while I wanted to bend her over my knee for being fucking reckless.

The moment she woke up, I could tell by the change in her breathing pattern. That's how intently I was watching her. She hadn't noticed me, but I saw the panic on her face.

The machine monitoring her heart rate started to beat faster.

When I saw that she intended to pull the needle out, I knew she was trying to make a run for it. I stopped her before she could do it.

"Going somewhere, *pet?*" My voice came out hoarse. It had been so long since I spoke to her, and it felt like a lifetime ago.

The machine started to beep faster, and I looked at it and then her. She was scared of me—but then again, why wouldn't she be? I was curious to see how she would try and play her way out of this one.

"Are you scared?" I asked. "Or turned on?" I taunted. I was trying to figure out when we were going to start this little cat and mouse game we had been playing.

"W-w-what do you want?" she asked as her chest kept rising and falling.

I rose to my full height and looked down at her. I was beyond caring about the past at this moment. All those years, all that chasing, the games, the lies, and she still ended up carrying my child. I didn't give a fuck about any of it. She was coming with me. My biggest mistake had been giving her a choice, and she always chose wrong. So it was time to force her to kneel.

"I'm just wondering where the hell do you think you're going with my child?"

Being nice to Aspen wasn't going to get me anywhere except alone. So I just had to remind her who had the power here. She had lost it all, and if she wanted a family, she had to come home with me.

Her eyes widened.

"It's not yours," she rushed out.

I barked out a laugh, then my skin went hot, and the

only reason I didn't do something rash was because of where we were at. I leaned down so my face was all she could see.

"Don't say stupid shit, Aspen. Not when your pussy only knows the imprint of my dick."

She gasped.

"But if you need a reminder, I'll be happy to show you just how well your pussy sucks me in."

She avoided my gaze and looked across the room. Then I saw defeat all over her face. She wrapped her arms around her stomach, and the sight of her doing something so protective to a baby that was barely formed tugged at my heartstrings.

"P-p-please...don't take this baby away f-f-rom me," she begged me with tears in her eyes.

My hand reached for her face, and with my fingertips, I touched the moisture that had gathered in the corner of her eyes. I brought it to my lips, and it tasted salty.

"Why are you crying?" I whispered.

She was in hysterics now that I couldn't keep up with her.

"I'll give you anything else, but not my baby. Please don't take my baby away from me. There has to be something else you want."

I cocked my head, trying to understand what she meant. She kept going on, and I needed her to calm down before she got me kicked out of her room.

Gripping her chin, I forced her to look at me.

"Calm down," I said in a stern voice. "I won't be happy if the staff starts to ask questions."

In her little cunning mind, I could see the wheels turning. She didn't give up.

"It's in your best interest to stay on my good side," I

warned her as I gripped her harder. Once she calmed down and seemed to get the memo, I let her go.

By the time the doctor came back, Aspen was calm. You could see she had been crying, but no one said anything. Not when I kept kissing her hand. I could play the role of the loving boyfriend.

"Would it be possible to get an ultrasound? Things have been hectic, and we haven't had our first doctor's appointment." The lie flowed effortlessly.

Aspen clutched onto my hand tighter. I don't know if it was in comfort or a warning. Either way, she seemed to be appeased by the idea of the ultrasound.

We waited in silence as they came back.

Once they brought the ultrasound machine, she let go of my hand. I felt the loss but didn't comment on it. Instead, I watched as they bared her stomach and applied gel. I mean, I knew she was pregnant. That stick all but confirmed it. I had hoped for it when I came inside of her, but I didn't think it would happen. I did it as a fuck you to her, to Liam. But as soon as I heard the heartbeat, I felt like my knees got weak.

There was a life inside of her. One we had created in a fit full of rage, and I knew that I didn't want my child to come into this world that way. They gave us ultrasound pictures, and holding them made it more real.

We were left alone in the room. Aspen was holding onto the ultrasound pictures, marveling at them. Life wasn't fair. Love was a battlefield. And being weak for the ones you cared for got you killed.

I looked at Aspen, and for the first time tonight, she looked happy. Her fingertips traced every line on the picture, and her smile kept widening.

Too bad for her I wasn't a good man. I ripped the picture

from her fingertips, and she lost that shine she had managed to find.

"If you don't want to be ripped away from your baby, then you better do as I say."

THIRTY- THREE

I'd been foolish to think that I could outrun Mason. Our demons chased us, and Mason had always been a monster of my creation.

"If you don't want to be ripped away from your baby, then you better do as I say."

The long game he had been playing had paid off. He had me in the palm of his hands. When he took the ultrasound pictures, it had hurt, and at that moment, I had imagined what it would feel like to watch him walking, holding my child—our child.

As we walked out of that hospital—him ahead of me but still holding onto my hand, it finally sunk in that the baby inside of me was his as well.

He was gentle as he guided me out. Once we were outside the hospital, a car was waiting for us. He opened the door for me and waited as I seated myself. As soon as he got in, the air seemed to become thicker. Vivid images of what had happened the last time we had been in a confined space assaulted me. I looked away from him and out the window, but I could see his face reflected in the glass.

He was so handsome. His dark hair slicked back, his sharp features, but somehow, those green eyes added a softness that I wanted to dig deep and find. Then I got caught in my own gaze.

I was a peasant who tried playing queen.

"Where are we going?" I asked without turning to meet his stare, but I could feel him watching me.

"My home," he replied.

I felt something tingle in my stomach, and I put my hand to it. It was too early for any baby activity. I knew that, but something was blossoming inside of me.

"Are you okay?" Mason asked, concerned. "Is it the baby?"

I finally turned to look at him. Those green eyes that were always on guard showed fear.

"I'm okay," I whispered.

He looked like he wanted to say more but ultimately nodded.

The ride to his house was quiet. I sat there, a ball of anticipation, as we went back to the city. He kept tapping his hands on his knees, but I refused to believe Mason Stiltskin was nervous. It wasn't until we stopped for some food that he reached for his cigarettes, stepped out of the car and lit one up like he had been starved.

Before I knew it, I was smiling into my food. That feeling that I had felt earlier was back, but this time, a little bit stronger. He had held back because of me. But as soon as that thought came, it disappeared. Of course, this was his child too, and he wasn't about to put it in jeopardy.

He cracked his window open when he came back in and didn't come close to me. I leaned my head against the windowpane. I had eight months to figure out what would happen next, so I would just rest for now.

I had promised myself that I would fight for this baby, and I would. And if I had to fight dirty to be close to my child, I was prepared to do it.

I must have dozed off because I could feel a breeze on my face when I woke up. Two hands held me up bridal style. My head rested against something hard and defined yet somehow soft enough to be comfortable and made me not want to raise my head.

Still, I did it.

Mason's throat was all I could see. He seemed to notice that I was now awake because his gaze dropped down, and our gazes collided.

"Hi," I whispered.

It was so unlike me. It was soft, maybe even sweet like the old Aspen, the one that only knew him.

He didn't say anything, but I could tell he liked my greeting by the way he tightened his arms around me. I felt safe and protected, and I knew that as long as I carried his child, it would be that way. In his arms, I felt like I was floating.

Someone opened the front door for us, and we crossed the threshold. A silly part of me couldn't stop thinking about the fact that I got married but didn't get a chance to do it with my husband, and I was glad I was doing this now.

"Welcome back, Master Stiltskin," a familiar voice greeted.

I lifted my head and noticed the butler. Since my parents kept all the servants after the Stiltskin house burned down, it was one of the reasons I also didn't want to stay at that house. How could we become their masters when we were just like them? But now, here they were, back with their rightful owner.

"Bring me clothes and food to my room," he said as he kept on walking.

I bit my lip as I looked at his house. It was beautiful. It suited his tastes. Dark but elegant.

He had become a man, and I still felt like a child. I was supposed to be an adult, but I couldn't even take care of myself. How did I expect to take care of someone else?

The room we walked into was dark. There was a sliding window and a door that led to what I assumed was the master bathroom. A huge television adorned the wall across from the California king bed. The bedding was black, from the comforter to the pillows and everything in between.

Mason laid me on the bed, and without a word, he walked away.

The next few days had been much like they had been when I was with Erin. I was left alone, but there was an uneasy feeling within me, unlike last time. I told myself it was because I didn't know what Mason was up to. But each night that passed and I didn't see him, it felt like a lie.

My days were spent mainly in his room, and not because I wasn't allowed to leave it, I hadn't even tried. But how could I face all those people inside of this house? I was ashamed, and I wanted to do something that proved that I was not like my parents.

There was a knock at the door, and I sat up straighter. I bowed my head slightly and smiled. Out of everyone, I think the person who I was most embarrassed with was the cook. She had been teaching me to cook, so one day I could take over her duties, but life had changed so much since then. When she worked for my parents, I didn't even acknowledge her. Not because I was a pompous ass like them, but because I had been drowning in my own pain.

As always, she brought me more food than I could possibly eat. Soup and crackers, water with some juice, and as if that wasn't enough, a whole meal on the side.

"Please eat more, madam," she spoke for the first time, and her words weren't mean but concerned. I bit my lip and nodded.

"Where's Mas—Master?" I stopped myself from calling him by his name. I was no better than them, and if the staff that he had protected and brought back to his side didn't have formalities with him, then what gave me the right?

"He had some business to take care of, but he should be back by tomorrow."

She left without a word, and I felt more reassured. I managed to eat more than I had the other days. After the meal, I took a shower and watched a movie on his TV. I didn't remember falling asleep, but when I woke up, all the lights had been turned off, and there was a blanket over me.

I sat up, and right away, I knew I wasn't alone. I scanned the room and found Mason sitting in a chair across from me. The light outside the window illuminated him from the back. He looked like a god, what with the way he was casually leaned back with his legs spread wide and his arms resting on either side of the chair.

There wasn't fear; there was longing. I wanted to run to him, so I clutched the blanket harder to stop myself from doing so. Under the blanket, I crossed my legs because I felt a small jolt between them. I had never been a sexual person. I never had much interest in sex because no one caught my attention, and I had a lot to deal with, that getting laid was never a priority.

Somehow all that went out the window whenever

Mason was near. It was explosive the way we fought for dominance, and he got off on the fact that he made me submit.

"You're back." I broke the silence.

He didn't say a word, just stared at me. I couldn't see those eyes that caused so much havoc in my soul, but I could feel them.

"Is our baby the thing you love most in the world?" he asked in a husky voice.

My heart began to accelerate. I clutched onto the blanket like a lifeline.

"Answer me." He bent forward, resting his elbows on his knees.

"Yes," I whispered. I got closer to the edge of the bed and begged him, "Please, don't take this baby away from me."

He looked at me without saying anything, and with each passing second, my face grew hot. Fire was running through my veins. I was getting angry. I was determined to make him listen to me.

"You want my forgiveness?" he asked in a seductive tone.

The feeling I had between my legs intensified. I nodded and then removed the blanket, putting it aside.

My clothing wasn't revealing, but the way his gaze burned through me, it might as well have been—a silk camisole and matching short bottoms.

"Come here," he said as he leaned back once more and beckoned me forward with his index finger.

Slowly I got off the bed, and as soon as I took my first step, he stopped me.

"If you want forgiveness, pet, then you need to crawl."

He looked at my face, down my body, and then he lifted a brow to see what I would do.

I said I would play dirty too. I got down on my knees for him, and I wasn't disgusted or terrified. The feeling that coursed through me—I welcomed it.

THIRTY-FOUR

MASON

Leaving Aspen in my bed had been torture. She was near me, and we weren't fighting; she was just there finally at my mercy, and I was getting off on it. Seeing her cornered did shit to me. I liked when she begged me because, in the end, I couldn't help but give in and hand it to her, and I got off on that shit even more. I left her in my bed, and at the sight of her, a golden angel in all those dark sheets, I was tempted to blow the meeting I had and bury myself between her thighs. But I couldn't do it, not when she was still weak. So I walked out without another word.

I did the exchange, got my cash, and returned right away.

I had instructed the staff to feed her. To give her anything she asked for, but they told me she had not left the room at all. I was worried, but the moment I walked into my room, her sight hit me right in the gut. There was no trace of her in my house other than in here. All that gold hair in my bed fucked with me. I wanted to go and lie next to her, but I refrained.

The lights in my room were on, and the television I

never used was playing a movie, and there she was, sleeping, clutching onto her belly. Just looking at her like that had my dick hard as a rock. I turned off the lights so she could rest and put a blanket over her.

Instead of joining her, I pulled a chair and watched her. She was at peace, and I couldn't remember the last time she looked like this.

My dick was tenting my pants, and I imagined how it would feel to be buried in her mouth. As soon as the thought entered me, it fled. Usually, shit like this happened when Hilda's memory tormented me, but that hadn't been the case anymore. This time, all I could see was Aspen on her knees for that asshole.

I fisted my hands, reminding myself that I had to stay calm. Then what I had said to her in rage hit me, and my head snapped toward her. A smile spread across my lips. It was fucked up, but now that I knew what she feared, I would use it against her.

When she got up, I felt my blood rush to my dick. She was beautiful, and I was done for when she opened her mouth.

"You're back." Her voice was sleepy and hoarse. I wanted to hear that tone as I woke her up with my dick so deep inside her that the only reason she came awake was because she needed to moan.

"Is our baby the thing you love most in the world?" I asked, already turned the fuck on because I knew that what I wanted, and she wasn't going to refuse me. She said yes, and hearing that shit elated me because that baby was as much a part of me as it was hers.

"If you want forgiveness, pet, then you need to crawl," I told her as I spread my legs once more. The truth was my dick was trying to make a hole through my pants.

Slowly Aspen got to her knees, and my heart started to pump wildly. Once she was kneeling, she got on all fours and headed toward me. The closer she got, light from the window illuminated her golden hair, making her seem like an angel.

When she was right beneath me, she looked up at me with those damn whiskey eyes, and I was so fucking gone.

"Unzip my pants," I croaked.

She put her hands on my knees and lifted herself up. Once she was between my legs, she reached for my zipper and started to bring it down. My chest was rising and falling rapidly.

"Pull my dick out," I breathed.

She did as I asked.

She kept looking at me for directions, and I fucking liked that.

"Open your mouth, Aspen," I said as I brought my hand to her lips and rubbed my thumb over it.

She opened her mouth and sucked my thumb, her tongue swirling around it.

"How about I give you something else to suck on," I said as I removed my finger with an audible pop.

"Stick your tongue out," I commanded her, and she did as I asked her, pink tongue out, ready to have my dick rubbing against it.

I took my cock in my hands and slowly rubbed it up her tongue and into her mouth. I kept teasing her, and she kept drooling around my dick.

"Suck me off, Aspen," I hissed as I pushed myself into her mouth. I grabbed her head between my hands and thrust softly in and out.

"You're not stopping until my cum is dripping down your lips."

This seemed to turn her on. Her hands rested on my thighs, and the longer she blew me, I felt her nails digging into my thighs. I lifted my hips so she could go deeper. She gagged and looked up at me, her mouth stuffed with my dick. The image was so fucking sexy I did it again. Her eyes watered, but she bent and took me all the way back to her throat. The only reason she stopped was because she started to gag.

I grabbed her hair and pulled it so she would back off a bit.

"Ease into it, use your tongue," I said as I ran my hand through her hair.

She looked up at me as she deep-throated me once more. She sucked me, then brought my dick out and licked the tip. I groaned, and she did that again and again. My hips were bucking against her mouth, fucking her face. When she began to moan, I held onto her head and pumped my release into her mouth, not letting her come up for air.

Without giving it a second thought, I picked up Aspen from under her arms and sat her on my lap so she could straddle me.

"Open your mouth," I told her.

She did as she was told, and cum started to drip down. I used my left hand, stuck a finger in her mouth, and dragged out the cum, rubbing it against her lips and down her chin.

"You look so fucking beautiful right now," I whispered in awe.

Then I kissed her cheek. She looked at me with hooded eyes. I wrapped my right hand around her waist, then I used my left hand to touch her pussy through her shorts.

She was fucking soaked. I moved aside the silky material and used my index and forefinger to rub her clit. She threw her head back and moaned.

"You want your pussy played with?" I teased her.

Her answer was to grind her hips against my fingers.

I kissed the arch of her neck.

"Or do you want me to fuck it with my mouth?" I rubbed my piercings against her strumming artery.

"Mmhmm," she moaned, sounding so needy for me.

I smiled against her skin, and then bit it softly.

"Not today, baby," I told her, removing my fingers from her clit.

She watched me as I stuck them in my mouth.

"So fucking good," I whispered.

I got up and carried her to the bed, where I laid her down gently.

"That was for me," I told her. "Keep being a good girl, and I'll forgive you."

She huffed, and I bit my lip to stop myself from laughing. I needed to keep my resolve, at least for now.

"Night, Aspen," I said in a much gentler tone, and her face changed into a look I had never seen before, but one that I liked.

Before I could talk myself out of it, I bent and kissed her. She tasted as sweet as always, and like my release. She opened her mouth for me, and how could I resist. The moment my piercings rubbed against the roof of her mouth, she moaned against me.

"Please," she hissed.

I tried to pull back, but she grabbed my right hand and guided it down to her pussy.

"I need you," she moaned as she began to rub her pussy against the leather. "Only you."

Shit. I was weak where she was concerned.

I let her rub her pussy against my glove for a few more

seconds and watched the way she enjoyed it. I could tell she was getting close, so I removed my hand.

She glared at me.

I kissed the tip of her nose.

"Be a good girl for me today, and I'll give you the world tomorrow."

It wasn't a lie; that was a promise. I left her alone in that bed as I went to the bathroom. The next time I thought about her sucking dick, it would be her kneeling and crawling before me and no one else.

When I got out of my shower, she was already fast asleep again. I walked around to where she had curled herself up on the other side of the bed and kissed her forehead.

Then I walked out to my office where one of my men was ready with the report I had asked of him.

As I suspected, Liam was missing. The authorities were going to think he and Aspen made a run for it. I wanted that shit to stop. I wanted any connection she had to him gone.

Most of all, I wanted that asshole dead.

Now that his assets were frozen, he could only go so far, but one thing I was sure of was that he would be gunning for me.

Without bothering to look at the clock, I picked my phone and called Nate.

"You know what time it is?" he groaned.

"I want everyone gathered. Tell them I want to meet."

I hung up the phone before he could reply. It was time to put an end to all of this. I wasn't just thinking about myself anymore. I had people who depended on me. Most importantly, I had Aspen and my unborn child.

THRIRTY-FIVE

I was mad.

No, mad wasn't the right word.

I was frustrated.

Mason and I were playing a game unlike one we had ever played before. I'm not saying I didn't like it, but I just didn't know where I stood at the end of *this* game. He was more attainable than he had been all these years, but there was still a wall between us. Maybe the wall was me? Or the fact that we couldn't trust each other.

"Be a good girl today, and I'll give you the world tomorrow."

Those words still gave me shivers when I thought of them. Well, I had been a good girl for a couple of weeks, and I was about to go crazy with all this pent-up frustration. Sexual frustration, I might add.

He hadn't touched me since that night. Not that I was about to initiate it either, but things usually happened when we were together.

I huffed, annoyed.

Instead of contemplating this, I made my way out of the room. I've gone out more and more just walking around the house. My favorite place was his backyard. It was surrounded by trees and bushes, so no one could peek in here. And he had a hammock. I liked to swing on it so much I usually fell asleep there.

Slowly my body began to change. Not much, but my cheeks were rounder, and I finally understood what the pregnancy glow was all about.

Cravings have also been a new thing that I have been dealing with. Before, I had no time to think about them or pay them much attention since I was in survival mode. Now they came all the time, and usually, I could find what I needed in Mason's kitchen—except for today.

Shit.

I didn't want to ask him.

Most of the time, I felt him slide into the bed at night. He would wrap his arms around me, and I wouldn't protest because I was too tired. But every morning when I awoke, I still felt the loss of him.

This sucked. I needed a walk. Looking at my reflection, I cringed. I looked like a damn hobo, not that I went anywhere. Is that why Mason hadn't touched me anymore?

After my shower, I blow dried my hair, put on a cute black skirt that I found with the clothes that Mason had given me. And a cream blouse with a Peter Pan collar. There were also heels, and I admired them before putting them on.

When I was a little girl, I loved the shoes Mrs. Stiltskin wore. They were made for a princess, or so I thought. I used to carry guilt because of her death, but after discovering the reason behind her demise, that guilt disappeared.

Karma was one hell of a bitch.

Once dressed, I made my way toward the front door. I didn't even get one step out when a man I hadn't seen before stopped me. He wasn't one of the old servants, but I knew he was keeping an eye on me right away.

"I'm sorry, ma'am. But I can't let you go outside."

My throat constricted, and I nodded at him. So, after all, I had swapped one cage for another?

"Is there anything you need?" he then added.

I shook my head and turned around.

This was bullshit. I didn't even know why I was so mad, but Mason couldn't bother with me, yet he had people watching me? No one had ever tried to stop me from going anywhere inside the house. No room was off-limits.

To test this, I made my way to Mason's study. As I walked over there, I was expected to be stopped at any second.

When I finally made it to the doors to his office, I waited a second before I attempted to open them. I was preparing myself to be disappointed. My hand made contact with the gold knob, and when I pushed it and the door opened for me, I was surprised. I looked around and walked inside.

His office wasn't much to look at. Like everything, it was plain and simple. He had his desk, a small bar area, a computer.

This room smelled the most like him.

I went to his chair and just inhaled. It smelled like his aroma and nicotine, something I have missed smelling on him.

Just because I was already here, I started to fuck with the drawers, and to my surprise, they opened. Without thinking, I pulled a manila folder. It was a report filled with pictures of everyone in the Order. I looked at them with a gaping mouth as I read over the things these people had done.

When I came to the file on Erin's family, my stomach curled. Mason had pictures of her from after the fire. I knew her injury came from jumping off one of the balconies because she was trapped inside. I just didn't expect her face to have been so severely beaten. Along with those papers had been a report about her having vaginal tearing.

I wanted to throw up. I immediately searched for Jason's file. There were many things on him that showed a patterned behavior—him and Liam. Their parents spent more money covering up their shit than raising them.

There was a file on everyone, and then the one said, Miller. My heart felt funny as I opened that file. Pictures of my parents, even from way back when they were servants. The one that made me pause was one of two elderly couples. I touched the photo, and it was sad that this was as close as I had ever been to my grandparents. I don't know why, but I broke down into tears right there. Look at us now. We had no family. What a pair we were. He killed his parents, and I left mine to the wolves.

I had to be there for my child. I wanted my baby to know everything I didn't. I wanted my child to be loved like I hadn't. But the thing I wanted the most was for my child to have two loving parents.

I stayed in Mason's office for a bit longer because the smell comforted me. He had a pretty onyx letter opener in his office that I was playing with when the door busted open.

Mason was standing there, and he didn't look happy at all.

"What the hell are you doing in here?" he yelled, and I flinched.

I bristled at his tone. I gripped the opener in my hands and stood up. His eyes went from my face down to my body, and the way his mouth parted did funny things to me that I ignored for now.

He had made me crawl once but not anymore.

Feeling brave, I pointed the letter opener toward him.

"You can't do anything to me," I spat.

He calmly took a step inside.

"Is that so?"

I lifted my chin in defiance.

"I'm the mother of your child."

He gave me a wicked smile, and I saw a peek at those piercings that drove me wild every time they went near my body.

He started to walk toward me with one hand in his pocket while he raised the other one and pointed at me.

"Don't move," he demanded.

Yeah, you know what I didn't do? I didn't listen to him. I took a step back and started to walk in the opposite direction. The smile on Mason's lips grew bigger, and damn if it didn't change his whole face. It made me want to stand around and watch him.

He looked like a different person. Hard to believe that the Mason before me and the one I had betrayed were the same person.

"Let me go!" I screamed as he ran and wrapped his arms around me.

He dragged me back to his desk and sat me on top of it as he went and sat on the chair.

"Am I your prisoner?"

He leaned forward and began trailing his fingers on my bare legs.

"What are you wearing?" he countered.

"They were on the other side of your closet so I assumed they were for me, but maybe they belonged to whomever you spent—"

I gagged as he stuffed two fingers inside of me.

"Don't speak if you're only going to say nonsense, Aspen."

I could barely breathe, but I was okay with it because his comment filled me with joy.

"I wanted to go out, but they didn't let me."

"So you assumed I'm holding you here as a prisoner?"

I bit my lip and nodded.

"Did you perhaps stop and think that I was doing it for your safety?"

No, I didn't, but it was written on my face. The surprise.

"Liam is still out there, and we both know that if he gets his hands on you, he will kill you. So I'm just protecting you."

Because of the baby—of course.

"The door was open, so I didn't think I was intruding,"

He kept playing with my legs and nodded. "Just don't come in here again."

My eyes watered, and I blamed the hormones.

"What the fuck?" he whispered, and his hand cupped my cheek. "If you want to go out, I'll take you."

I shook my head. My cravings were now gone, so I didn't want anything anymore. I just wanted to leave.

"I don't want anything anymore." I sounded whiney and childish.

"Come on, let's go." He got up and started to pull me up too.

"Don't worry, I won't ever come in here again."

"What's your problem?" he said, frustrated.

I was being irrational, and I didn't want to say anything, but instead, I spoke, and maybe I should have kept my mouth shut.

I pulled up the letter opener, and I waved it at his face.

"Are you using this to cut yourself? Is this why you don't want me in here?

He let go of my hand and sat back on the chair.

"Are you fucking kidding me?"

Fear went through me. And I immediately felt guilty because I had insulted him.

"I'm sorry," I whispered.

"No, you're not," he said flatly. "How long have you wanted to ask that?"

For a long time, if I was being honest. I just didn't understand how tearing yourself over and over made you feel better.

"I don't understand how something that makes you feel pain gives you a release."

He looked up at me, and his face was so honest and sincere that I wanted to get on my knees and apologize to him.

"If I knew the answer to that question, Aspen, I would have left you alone a long time ago."

I gasped. I didn't know what he meant, but I knew this was as close as I would get as a confession from him.

"It smells like you in here," I told him, hoping that would make things better.

He reached for the letter opener and then tipped my chin down as he looked at me. "You stayed in here because you liked that it smelled like me?"

When he said it like that, it embarrassed me. My cheeks burned red.

"I smoke in here, Aspen."

"I know, I could smell it. It smells like you."

He grinned at me. "I've limited my smoking habits to this room. I don't want to harm you or the baby."

And my face was now beet-red. I really didn't know

anything about motherhood. I put my face in the palm of my hands and started to cry in embarrassment.

Mason pried my hands open. And he just looked at me confused.

"Hormones?" He cocked his head, and it was adorable.

He pulled open one of the drawers at the bottom that I hadn't opened, and he pulled out a book, and man, I never wanted to throw myself at a man before as much as I wanted to right now. He had been reading a pregnancy book.

"If you have cravings, tell me if something bothers you. This is not only your child but mine too."

His hand went to my midriff and I forgot how to breathe. This was the first time he had ever touched my stomach, and I felt an explosion of butterflies trying to break free. There was also a thumping between my legs that reminded me that I had been so horny.

I started to wiggle on the desk, and the room went electric.

"As for your other question," he went on, but I didn't know what he was talking about.

The tip of the letter opener scraped against my inner thigh. My chest rose and fell because it sent shivers up and down my body. Mason's other hand came to my waist and pulled me forward. He then opened my legs.

"I can fucking smell how turned on you are."

I bit my lip and didn't say a word.

"You've been a good girl, haven't you?" he asked as he stroked my cheek. I closed my eyes and leaned into him.

He did another swipe of the scalpel slowly and gently, this time a little higher. My legs opened up more and wider for him. Then he added pressure, and I could feel the warmth of my blood starting to trickle down. I looked down at the same time as my clit began to throb. It wasn't much, and it didn't hurt, but fuck did it feel good. Mason bent his head and then licked the spot he had cut. It hadn't been deep. There wouldn't be a scar.

"Sometimes, the only thing we have is pain, and we learn to find pleasure in that."

He was trying to explain a part of himself to me. I didn't have any words to say to him, so I stroked his head.

He kissed inside my thighs until he reached my center.

"If you want to come, you're going to have to fuck my face."

And so, I did. And then Mason took me out to get some food, and when I fell asleep on the way back home, he carried me to bed.

THIRTY-SIX

MASON

It had been four months, and there had been no word on Liam. I was getting annoyed at this point. If I wanted to draw him out, I had to do something to catch his attention.

Work had been busy. Mostly I had to reassure every-fucking-body that the Feds wouldn't be on our asses after what happened with the Kings. I knew my revenge could have ramifications on my business, but I still did it anyway.

By the time the day ended, I was so tired. Most of my work used to be done from home because I didn't care if one day shit got bad since it was just me. But now that I had Aspen and my unborn child to look after, I didn't want anything to harm them. The media was on a wild-goose chase for the Kings. Treating them like Bonnie and Clyde, and that shit pissed me off. Aspen wasn't Liam's; she might have been with him in name only, but her body had always been mine.

"Is he smiling?" I heard Erin whisper to Nate.

I looked up at both of them and glared.

"What are you guys doing here again? I asked since they kept coming to my warehouse.

"We are planning the meeting." Erin said it like it was apparent.

"Yeah, but why here?"

"Because everyone keeps trying to ask us questions about the Kings. As their closest friends, they think we know where they are, and it's annoying." Erin huffed like all of this should have been obvious.

"So, what are you going to do with Liam if you find him?" Nate asked in a casual tone.

"*When* I find him," I clarified.

I didn't tell them my answer, but they suspected it. I would kill him, and then I would let the world find him. Let the whole world know he had died. With the kind of enemies they made from that leakage, it would be chalked up to a retaliation attack.

"Tell them that I'm tired of waiting. If they don't want them to be my next target, they better show up to my house this Friday. If anyone is in contact with him, they will also sniff him out, and that way, we find out who is with us or against us."

"Have you told Aspen what's going on?" Nate asked.

"This doesn't concern her."

She was never supposed to be part of this world, and I wasn't going to let those people keep using her as a pawn for their sick games.

My child would be born soon, and I wanted all of this resolved before it entered this world.

"I'm going home," I told Nate. "My men can lock up."

And because I was in a good mood, I pulled out a set of keys and flung them at him. "If the media is bothering you both that much, use my safehouse."

Both of them just stared at me as I walked out. On the drive back home, I smoked two cigarettes to get me through the night. Until I was almost done with the second one, I realized that I no longer stopped and looked at the flames. I wouldn't say I moved on, but I wasn't being trapped by them anymore.

My dick was in a perpetual state of arousal, and it was by my own doing. I didn't even know why I wasn't fucking Aspen. She clearly wanted it. But every time I thought about our child and having them watch their parents interact, I didn't want our child to see the way I saw my parents growing up. It was cold, and my parents were more for show than for me. So I wanted to build a foundation so that when our child looked at us, all they could see were two people they were proud of.

Before I made it home, I stopped by the jeweler since the modifications I had asked to be made were finally done.

I was almost in the house when one of the maids called to tell me that Aspen had been craving Nachos. So I had my driver turn around and go in search of some.

When I was finally home, I ran straight to my room, but she wasn't there. I put the snacks on the middle of the bed and went to look out my window, and sure enough, Aspen was there lying down on the hammock.

She was talking. I could see her lips moving. I moved my angle to see who she was talking to, but no one was there. She held onto her stomach and smiled. I wondered what she told our child. Instead of joining her, I jumped in the shower so I could remove the stench of smoke off me.

The shower was cold in hopes that it could tame my dick. I refused to masturbate like a teenager.

Since Aspen was outside, I just wrapped a towel around my waist. In the harsh bright light of the bathroom, you could see my scars and burns clearly. Something she had only witnessed in the dark.

When I opened the door, something bumped into me, and all I saw was blonde hair everywhere.

"You're back." She looked up at me and beamed as her hands came to hold my sides.

"Back off," I told her in a voice much sterner than I had intended. "I'm trying to change," I said, trying to get away from her. Guess deep down, I was afraid she would be disgusted by me.

She flinched, and I felt like a dick.

I tried to move, but she didn't let me. She wasn't looking at my face but at my body. Her hands came to my stomach tracing the lines from my abs, and then they went to the side from where the burns started. She took hold of my burned hand and then traced her fingers up to where the scarring stopped.

I stopped breathing. The pads of her fingers were electrifying. I felt each and every movement she made.

"Your scars don't bother me," she said as she got up on her tiptoes. "They've made you who you are."

Yeah, fuck waiting. I took this girl in my arms, lifting her up. Her legs wrapped around my waist and her arms around my neck.

Things had changed between us. Not only today, but slowly that foundation I wanted to build had already been set.

I laid her on the bed as I hovered over her. My hands went to either side of her head.

"I've been a good girl," she hissed as I began to remove her pants.

I smirked at her. I kissed behind her knee and between her thighs. Then I licked between her legs because I loved how her pussy would beg me for more every time I used my piercings to tease her.

I lifted her shirt up and became dumbstruck. There was now a bump there that I had not seen before since she usually wore loose clothes.

I was finding it hard to breathe. I brought both my hands to her belly, and then I peppered kisses all around it. I never thought about having kids or even a family, but how could I not want to cherish the life I had created with the only person who has ever meant anything to me.

Maybe it was obsessive and unhealthy, but I didn't care. The feeling that flooded me was like a drug I wanted to have until the day I died.

I finished removing her shirt and then the towel I had on until we were finally skin to skin. We were no longer hiding our secrets in the dark. We had set our demons free, and they could bask in the light with us.

My mouth was greedy, kissing every inch of her skin. It had been so long. Her tits had gotten heavier and more sensitive. She almost came as I sucked them.

I kissed up her chest and her neck. Took my time on her throat. I wanted to mark her there so she'd remember just who owned her body when tomorrow came.

Her hands came to my back, gliding eagerly, waiting and anticipating what I would do to her.

I licked her earlobe, and she moaned. Then I tugged it down with my teeth. I put my mouth to the shell of her ear, so I could whisper.

"This is the last chance you're getting. You betray me again, and I'll fucking kill you."

She didn't push me away; instead, she opened her legs even wider so I could slide in.

"Ask me again what I want most in the world," she breathed as her hand came to my chest, trailing down to where my heart beat.

"What do you want most in the world?" I asked the question that she never had given me an answer to. I always knew she wanted her freedom, and my plan had been to give it to her as long as she lived that freedom with me.

When she said my child was the thing she loved the most in the world, my plan had been simple. If she wanted to be with her child, she had to stay by my side until the day we died.

"I want a family with you," she whispered.

I buried my head in the crook of her neck and inhaled her intoxicating scent.

Instead of shoving my dick deep inside of her, I did something I had never done before. I laid back and brought her on top of me.

"Then fuck me like you own me," I growled. "I want you to work yourself on my dick. I want to hear you moan because you love the way I feel inside of you."

One of her hands came to my shoulders, and slowly, she lifted herself up. Then she took the other one and guided my dick inside.

She felt better than I remembered. She was so fucking warm and wet I was fucking incinerating.

Her movements were timid and weren't going to get us anywhere. A reminder that she was only mine. I put my hands on her hips, and I guided her. Her head thrashed back as she found her rhythm. Her hips moved faster. My cock thrusted deep inside of her because I couldn't take it anymore.

From the way she looked on top of me, all that blonde hair spilling down past her tits to the bump in her belly, I was going to come just from the visual alone. When I couldn't take it anymore, I flipped her.

My hips started to pump into her furiously.

"Massee," she moaned. It had been so long since she called me that.

"Who owns this pussy?" I growled.

She mewled her response.

"Who owns this body?" I ground out as I held onto her hips and slammed in again and again.

Her eyes fluttered back, and she screamed, *"Youuu."*

My release was right after hers, and I thrust deeper to fill her with my cum.

"I fucking own you, Aspen."

THIRTY-SEVEN

I woke up to my heart racing. The first thing I did was reach for Mason, but he wasn't there. The second thing I did was run my hand down my belly because that always brought me comfort. Except when I touched it, it was flat.

When I tried to move, I couldn't do it. Something was holding me back. I brought one of my hands up, and I was rattled by how it looked. I was nothing more than skin and bones.

Footsteps echoed and they came closer. Instinct had me hurrying back. The door opened, and light flooded the room. A lone figure stood there.

"Hi, wifey," Liam said with a sick smile.

As he got closer, I began to feel cold. I wrapped my arms around myself and noticed that I was barely wearing anything. When I looked down at myself, I recognized my clothing. It's what I had been wearing under my dress the day of my wedding. Except for this time, there was blood everywhere.

"You didn't think you could escape from me?" He bent and stroked my cheek. And that's when I screamed because the happy ending I thought I achieved was just a dream.

"*Aspen!*"

"*Aspen!*"

"Dammit, pet, wake up."

I opened my eyes. This time, I was in my room. Fuck, it was just a dream. I put my hand to my chest and took deep breaths.

After a few calming breaths, I felt a hand rubbing my back soothingly. Without giving it a second thought, I wrapped my arms around Mason and began to cry.

"It's okay," he whispered as he hugged me closer. "I told you I would give you the world, and I will."

Maybe because my stomach was bigger now, and Liam had yet to be found. I knew that he was still holding a grudge against me, and I feared that the one who would pay would be my child.

Mason kept rubbing my back and reassuring me that it was all going to be okay. I fell asleep in his arms, believing in his words. By the time I woke up, it was already noon.

I made my way down to the kitchen because I was hungry. Day by day, I had gotten more comfortable in this house. I enjoyed doing tasks here and there, something Mason wasn't too happy about.

In the kitchen, attempting to cook is where Mason found me. I felt his silent presence at my back. Something I used to fear now gave me comfort.

"Hi, you're back." I smiled at him.

He walked up to me and wrapped his arms around my waist, holding onto my belly.

"The only good part about going out is coming back to hear you greeting me."

I rubbed his arms.

"Are you feeling better?" He gave me a questioning look.

I bit my lip and nodded.

"We're going to have guests tonight."

Confusion was written all over my face since this was the first I'd ever heard about it.

"Oh." I looked down at the floor.

"It's the Order. I've gathered all of them."

It seemed like a bad omen—the fact that I had this dream just as this meeting was set to happen. I was about to protest, but Mason caught my mouth with a kiss.

"If you want to be there with me, you can, but you don't have to. They've caused you so much pain already. They don't have to take anything more."

And what about him? He has been a victim of the same laws.

"I'll be there," I declared before I could second-guess my decision.

I wouldn't say I liked it, but I was done running away.

And I wanted to be there for him as well. So I took hold of his hand and told him again I would be there—even if I didn't want to. Because when everyone gathered, tragedies followed.

"About your parents," he went on and hugged me tighter.

"What about them?" I asked. "They were no parents to me."

His embrace was almost suffocating, but he gave me comfort in his own way.

Mason

Everything was set for today's meeting. I had guards on every entrance and hiding all around the house. I've been in my office getting the paperwork ready. I just needed to change into my suit. I was still hesitant with Aspen, but I knew that she was safe as long as I was there.

I went back to our room when it hit me that it was only natural for her to stay with me. I wanted her there because I didn't trust she wouldn't run away, but now, I didn't want her anywhere else. She belonged at my side.

"Are you ready?" I called out as I walked in.

She didn't answer me back, but the door to the walk-in closet opened, and I almost bit my tongue. She was in a tight black dress with a slit up to her thigh. Her belly stole the show in the best way possible.

Without another word, I walked up to my dresser where I had put the necklace that I had picked up from the jeweler's earlier this week. Next to it was a small black pouch with the rings I had taken off Aspen when she was unconscious at Erin's. I had plans for them. After securing them in the pocket of my suit, I made my way up to her. She was standing in the middle of the room, looking up at me.

I removed the hair from her shoulder.

"A long time ago, I told you this was important to me." I pulled out the diamond necklace so she could see it. "And you took care of it ever since."

I bent to kiss her throat. I could feel her breathing accelerating with each stroke of my tongue. She was very sensitive to my touch.

"This belonged to my birth mom. It's the only thing I had of hers...I want you to have it."

She held onto my arms.

"I'm sorry I sold it," she rushed out.

I chuckled. I kept an eye out on it since I burned that house down. She didn't need to know I gave it to her for that reason. I liked it when she felt indebted to me.

"It's okay, just don't take it off anymore," I said as I made my way behind her so I could put it on.

"It's shorter," she noted.

Once clipped, I kissed her nape.

"Every pet needs their collar," I teased.

She turned around so fast and aimed a lethal glare at me.

"It's chipped," I kept going. "Not because I don't trust you, but if anyone ever dares touch what's mine, I don't have to wonder where they took you."

Her hands slowly came to touch the diamonds. She had a pensive look on her face, but ultimately, she let it go.

"Why am I okay with you doing this?" she whispered to herself more than for me.

I pulled her into my arms and touched her belly.

"Because you know I fucking live for you, and the least you can do is be a good girl and ease my worries."

She bit her lip and gave me a slow nod. That wasn't good enough for me. I kissed her, and I was about to bend her over, but the knock at our door told us our guests had arrived.

I fixed my tie as Aspen and I waited for our guests to be seated. This was all a power play on my part.

There was no word from security, so all was safe—at least for now.

"You ready?" She looked up at me, and her eyes were shining with something that looked a lot like hope.

"Yeah, I'm finally ready."

She meant more than just now. I touched her cheek in reassurance. She looped her arm against mine, and hand in hand, we made our way down the stairs toward the dining room.

THIRTY-EIGHT

MASON

Everyone's head turned toward us as we walked hand in hand. Me—the monster they had created; and her—the pawn they had continued to toss around. Some gasped, others gave us dirty looks, but in the end, none of them mattered.

It was an impromptu Order meeting. Only the heads and successor of the family had been invited.

They were all gathered around the table. The only chair left to take was at the head. I led Aspen with me. I sat down and then brought her down to my lap. I didn't care if they thought it was low-class of me. I lifted my left hand and snapped my fingers. Food trays were set in front of everyone, and when they pulled back the metal cover, it revealed manila folders.

Everyone but Nate and Erin turned to look at me after they had seen the papers.

"This is bullshit!" Jason's father was the first to exclaim. He threw the file down, repulsed by what it suggested.

I had expected as much from him.

Then it was Rachel's turn. She huffed and got up. "You can't be fucking serious!"

Aspen was tense, and I knew why. I didn't tell her the specifics of our gathering, but still, she showed up to give me her support.

"I'm not saying you have to adhere to these rules, but I do think it's in everyone's best interest," I announced.

"And what interests are those? Fuck over all of us because of your little grudge?" someone else said.

I leaned back on my chair. My arm went around Aspen's waist in reassurance and to remind myself that the day I had always wished for was finally here.

"I think it's outdated that we have to keep a partnership that was forced upon us. We are so fucking tied to each other that one goes down and drags the rest of us with them." I went on even though I no longer had acquisitions with them.

I already knew who would protest and who would be relieved that this was suggested.

"You all sat back as the Kings took everything from my family and me, and none of you did a damn thing to stop it. But you all profited from the spike the sales brought." I said it casually like it no longer mattered because, in reality, it never really did.

"As of today, my family wants nothing to do with the Order," Erin spoke. "We are done living by the rules set up by people we didn't even know."

There was much arguing going on, and we had expected this.

"We all took a hit when King enterprises went down. And as agreed per our constitution, it's up to each other to get through these tough times." Nate opened his mouth, and he was furious. Some families had more power than others.

I had been one of them, and he was another, so were Erin's family and the Kings.

"You all were so up in Wilfred's ass that you lost all of your money with his bullshit. And now you want us to give you some of ours to repay your blind trust? Fuck that." He got up and threw a bunch of pictures down the table. "Why should we help you when you keep fucking betraying us?" Nate had had enough of them. All these years, he had felt the same as I did.

It was pictures of girls Jason had hurt. Erin had been one of them, but there had been no repercussions. He was a member much like Erin, and they told her to deal with it. There was no loyalty, just greed. And I believed that was not what our ancestors had wanted.

More arguing. I was mostly here to mediate and make sure things turned around the way we wanted. Dissolving the Order meant that we buried those fucking secrets. That everyone was on their own now, and maybe losing that security blanket scared them the most.

Once my guard gave me a signal, I spoke again.

"What I did with the Kings, I can do to any of you," I said calmly. "Why keep up with this facade. Half of you can barely stand each other. Just go your own fucking ways."

And then the real reason why we all had gathered showed up.

What sounded like a gun blasted in the front door.

Aspen screamed, and I immediately got up and shoved her behind me. Nate had done the same to Erin. But we had been prepared for this. Liam couldn't resist. And I knew this. He was a rabid animal backed into a corner, and I knew he would attack first.

The staff cleared out and people screamed, trying to get away from where he entered. He looked different. He no longer looked refined nor polished. His blond hair was greasy; he was sporting an unkempt beard. His clothes were all dirty and wrinkled. This is what happened when people who believed they were gods fell from grace. They didn't know how to live in hell. I just stood there and waited as one of the guards came in and took Aspen away from me. She screamed my name. This made Liam point the gun he had aimed toward me at her.

"Stupid bitch," he hissed. Then when he got a good look at her, his eyes widened. He gritted his teeth at the fact that she was pregnant, and there was no denying it had been conceived on her wedding day.

He had failed to rape her, and now she was with me, bearing my child. It was killing him to lose.

"Who told you we would be here?" I asked as I took a step forward.

He fired a shot, and I heard Aspen's scream above all, but he was so fucking livid he couldn't even aim straight.

His eyes slid to Rachel, and he didn't have to confirm what I already suspected. She was tied to him because of an emotional bond, while Jason's family was after the Kings because they gave them more power.

He pulled something from his back pocket, and my heart stopped for a second, fearing it would hurt Aspen. Screams echoed as he opened an emergency flare and threw it toward the curtain. They instantly caught fire, creating more chaos as people started to run out.

"We fucking made you, and now you want to turn your back on us?" he yelled manically toward the room. "How about we all just die here."

Even Rachel was screaming. She didn't think he would go this far. As for me, I stayed rooted in place, watching the windows begin to burn away.

Was this my karma?

Is this how I died?

I thought the flames no longer controlled me, but I was wrong.

Two arms wrapped around my waist, and even though they instantly calmed me, I felt a tendril of fear. I needed to get Aspen away from here, and that was what pulled me out of my haze. But before we could take another step, explosions were set off all around the house. They rattled everything. The windows shook, and the portraits clanged. Liam had set off a signal.

"We're all going to die here!" Liam screamed as he laughed. "If I'm fucked, so are you!"

The only thing I could trust was that the guards could take care of the outside. I just needed to get Liam neutralized on the inside. I moved so I could get Aspen to safety. I had her on edge, away from windows and oncoming blasts.

I expected Liam to show, but I didn't expect him to try and take us all out. That was a mistake on my part. I took everything away from him, so what did he have to live for?

"Stay here," I told Aspen in a calm voice as I kissed her lips. She tried to get me to stay, but I tuned her out. She was my priority, and life had no meaning if I couldn't keep her safe. And if I died here, well, she already had a piece of me.

"You...I'm going to start by killing you!" Liam screamed as he pointed the gun at me.

"And what are you going to do? Miss again?" My hands came up in mock surrender, but as long as he pointed it at me, I was fine. Everything I had was materialistic. It had no meaning if Aspen was gone.

The smell was getting stronger, and it brought back memories. But in comparison to what I had done, this was nothing. I had survived the flames licking me and trying to bring me down once. I could do it again, because now I had something to live for.

"Liam!" Rachel took a step forward. "Let me and my father go."

I curled my lip in disgust.

Liam laughed. "Why, so you can keep living your life like nothing ever happened to me?"

That's what everyone did when the Stiltskins fell from grace, so having the Kings dethrone wouldn't be any different.

"I can keep giving you money," she rushed out.

Liam was breathing heavily. She took a step forward, and that's when the gun went off again. Screams echoed. Rachel's father got up, but he was too late.

I used the opportunity to rush toward Liam. We both tumbled on the floor. He was weak compared to me. I took hold of the gun, and I cocked him in the head with it.

"Amateur," I joked as my forehead began to drip with sweat from the flames that were starting to spread.

"Fuck you!" he spat.

"Nah, but I did fuck your wife, which is a problem for me," I told him. Then I began to punch him until he lost consciousness. I could feel the flames get closer, but I ignored their call. The thing that gave me drive was the fact that I had to get Aspen out of here alive.

Nate came to my side a few seconds later.

"Looks like the back is clear. Come on, let's get out of here," he yelled as he went to the back and got Aspen.

When they were at my side, I hugged Aspen tightly.

"Go with Nate. I'll be right behind you," I told her as I kissed her forehead.

"No," she insisted, trying to come toward me, but I shook my head at Nate. He dragged her away, screaming.

I pulled Liam away from the fire that had spread to the front of the house. This felt like déjà vu, except I was trying to save a life the last time I did this.

A few seconds later, Liam woke up. The smoke was getting thicker. My only consolation was that I had enough time to get out from the back.

"Maybe this was destiny," I told him as his eyes opened. I pulled him up by his shirt and pushed him against the wall. "According to our records, this was a long time coming, don't you think?"

The Kings came from a bastard lineage from King James. At the same time, my family Rumpelstiltskin had done everything to get them into power, only to be betrayed in the end. All of this was supposedly water under the bridge when we came to America.

Our past didn't define us, and I was done letting mine define me. As I sat there, I looked back on my life. Everything I went through, I wouldn't change it for anything. Sure, at times, it fucking sucked, but I had everything I ever dreamed of and more.

Everything before that fire felt like it was in another life. I knew this would too. I had to endure the proximity of the fire for a bit longer. He wanted death by fire, then who was I to deny him a dying wish?

"You touched what was mine, and now you're going to die," I said calmly as I brought my hand up and punched his face. Not hard enough for him to lose consciousness again.

Liam tried to move, but my grip on him was too strong. Either way, he had nowhere to go.

"Does this feel good?" I taunted him. "You used to love doing this to me."

I let him go, and his body dropped to the floor. As soon as he was down, I kicked his stomach. Then I grabbed him and dragged him back. Since the flames had begun to spread faster, I couldn't afford to go farther than this point. Not if I wanted him to burn down with this house.

"These don't mean a thing," I said. I pulled out Aspen's wedding rings. I smiled when I saw the size of the diamond ring. His statement was going to work in my favor. "You might have married her, but she's always been mine."

"Fuck...you..." he managed to wheeze out.

It didn't faze me. I walked up to him and then I took his chin in my hand. His hands came up, trying to block me. I grabbed one hand and twisted until I heard his wrist break. He hissed, and I did the same to the other hand. Liam was wailing, and it was music to my ears.

"See you in hell," I said as I forced his mouth open. He fought it, but I was the one in power. I was holding onto the rings between my middle and pointer fingers. I pushed my fingers down his throat, and when I was deep enough, I let the rings go. He gagged around my mouth, but I kept pushing, knowing the leather was suffocating him. His body trashed and moved, and his eyes started to water the deeper I pushed my fingers inside.

I coughed as the smoke had surrounded us now.

Shortly, his face started to change color. It went from purple to almost blue. My fingers felt every constriction from his throat as his body tried to push me away. Right now, his body was rushed with adrenaline from all places. I went a little deeper, and his throat tightened around my fingers. I felt his jaw open to an unnatural width.

"And now, she's nothing to you at all," I hissed before I took off, running away from the hell that was unleashed.

AND THEY LIVED HAPPILY EVER AFTER

Aspen

How did life get like this? One moment, I was miserable hating everything about it. Hating myself and my decisions, but in the end, they led me to where I was today. Actions had consequences, and I had paid for mine. And what came afterward—pure fucking bliss.

Living a good life didn't require riches, big houses, fancy cars—I had all that, and I hated it. I went from a prisoner to living in a gilded cage. And the man who set me free, he wasn't a good man, but he was good to me.

Most importantly, he was a good father.

A chunky hand pulled at my hair, and I laughed.

We were sitting outside as the ocean breeze hit our skin. This was paradise. We left America and decided we wanted to settle elsewhere. Neither of us had ties, and the two friends we had...well, they could come to visit whenever they wanted.

I hoisted my baby on my hip and made my way to the

water. We both loved to watch the waves. They were wild and untamed—they were free.

Once upon a time, I would have been envious, but I now understood the madness that came with living life your own way.

"Morning." I waved as some of the locals passed us by.

If they thought it was weird that me and my family had come to live here, they didn't show it. They accepted us as a part of their community. Although most people were scared of Mason. When it came to his family, he was very overprotective.

My eyes found the sea again, and I felt some sadness about all the things I lost and missed out on, but I had decided I wasn't going to let it bother me. I never heard from my parents, and it was better that way. Whatever happened to them was of their own doing. They were alive, and that was more than some people had.

As for Liam, I was sure he was dead. I didn't ask Mason any questions after he came back. All I know is that night, he fucked me with intense satisfaction that only came with knowing that there was nothing left of the man you hated.

My marriage was a sham, and I just pretended like it never happened. I wasn't religious, I didn't like the people who had gathered around me at the wedding. It was just another event that I was forced to take part in.

"Come on, baby. Daddy is going to get home soon," I cooed to my child.

We turned around to head back to the house. It was so freeing and liberating to be able to go out just to feel the sun on our faces. Knowing that nothing would harm us—and all because the man I loved made it that way.

Mason

They say killing stains your soul, but it had let mine soar. Death never took from me, but instead, it gave me its blessing. Maybe, one day, I'll have to pay back for what I had done, but for now, I was more than okay with the life I had.

After the meeting, we moved houses. Neither Aspen nor I had anything holding us back from living in our paradise. I could do business from almost anywhere. And since I wanted my daughter to live a good life, I was a silent partner in one of Nate's businesses.

The house I now called home wasn't even a house, more like a luxurious cottage, but it was more than enough for the three of us. There were no drivers, no maids; just us together, living our life our way.

We had been enslaved to our worlds for so long it felt good to be finally free. I opened the door to our home and walked in, putting the groceries on the table.

There was light everywhere inside of this house. Toys were scattered in the living room. Mismatched plates in the cabinets. There were a few dirty dishes in the sink. And I couldn't help but smile that this was home.

It was chaotic, but it was real.

"I'm home," I called out.

Those words had a different meaning now than they did when I was young. Back then my house wasn't a home. I walked into the nursery room, and no one was in there.

I made my way to the master bedroom, and sure enough, my girls were there. I leaned against the door frame and took my fill of their profiles. They seemed so calm and serene as they slept. Aspen's blonde hair was all over the pillows, while my little Macy's black head of hair peeked through.

Living in a tropical area would have been a bitch if I still used my glove like a crutch to hide from the world. People sometimes stared, but I didn't pay any mind to it. I didn't really care for anything else unless it was Aspen or my child.

The diamond necklace I gave Aspen was always on her neck. A testament to her love for me or my obsession for her. It didn't matter. If the GPS bothered her, she didn't say anything. She was mine, and she was never going to go anywhere without me knowing exactly where she was.

My daughter started to cry, and I got closer because I thought it was cute as hell when she pouted. I picked her up before Aspen could. She opened her eyes and brought her hand to her chest in surprise.

"You could have woken me up," she scolded me.

"I didn't want to wake you," I said as I put Macy over my shoulder and rubbed her back. She was a chubby baby, that sometimes, I fought hard not to pinch her cheeks because I was scared I would bruise her.

"What did you bring? You took so long."

Since my daughter wasn't going back to sleep and started to slobber on my shirt, I turned her around to face me.

Jet back hair and whiskey eyes. She was going to cause me a lot of trouble. I knew it. Good thing Daddy could kill anyone who got close enough to hurt her.

"What's that smirk for?" Aspen questioned as her eyes narrowed on me.

I shrugged. "Just thinking on how I'm going to kill anyone wh—"

"Mase!" she yelled at me. "Death is not the answer to everything."

"You're saying you didn't want to see your funeral on TV?" I raised a brow at her.

Aspen King was no more. She was pronounced dead a few months after her husband was found murdered. I made her a widow, and then I killed off the version of her I didn't like. It seemed like a win-win for everyone.

"You have issues," she said as she got up.

Before she could take another step, I curled my free hand around her waist and brought her toward me.

"Yeah," I whispered. "And you get off on each and every one of them and beg for more."

She shivered but otherwise rolled her eyes. I kissed the crook of her neck and then tugged at her necklace with my teeth.

"I'm thinking of updating your collar, *pet*," I teased her.

She took Macy away from me.

"Come on, let's feed you before Mama kills your daddy."

I stood in our room and watched them walk away. This was the life. Simple, but never dull.

When I made it to the kitchen, they were already seated. I watched as Aspen did with our daughter all the things we wished our parents would have done with us. We didn't know anything about being parents. We never loved ours growing up, but maybe learning all the things that shouldn't be done allowed us to do things right.

I walked to the space between them and kneeled. Aspen looked at me cautiously, and as for my daughter, she threw part of her food at me. Ignoring that without a word, I took hold of Aspen's left hand and slid a diamond ring on it.

It was small and not massive like the last one she wore. This was for us. Neither one of us was religious. Even though she married that asshole, we forgot it happened.

He choked on those rings, and nothing had ever given me more satisfaction.

Aspen froze; she looked at the ring on her finger and then at my face.

"Is this because the guy at the market was hitting on me?" She tried to play it off, but I could tell by the look on her face she liked it a lot.

I brought her palms to my face and kissed them.

"No, this is because I want everyone to know that someone already owns you."

She rolled her eyes.

"Our new identities already say we are married, Mr. Stilts."

I grinned at her sass. My last name didn't mean much. It wasn't even the one our ancestors had before they came to America. They shortened it to become modernized; I just did the same to start my life over again.

"Mason..." Aspen said as she held onto my hand and then touched our daughter with her other hand. I raised a brow for her to continue. "I love you too."

The smirk I had earlier was wiped out.

So, this was love?

Betrayals.

Lies.

Deceptions.

A lonely road you had to travel alone.

But if done right, it was worth more than all the gold in the world.

"Yeah..." I said in a husky voice. "I love you."

THANK YOU

Thank you for reading Gilded Cage!

I hope you enjoyed this twisted fairytale, but even if you didn't reviews are always very appreciated!

Thank you again for taking the time to read Aspen & Mason's story.

If you want to read more about the Twisted Tales Collection you can get all the information here

https://campsite.bio/twistedtales2

ACKNOWLEDGMENTS

Thank you to AJ Wolf for putting together this fantastic anthology! You rock.

Cassie Chapman and Nikita, who pushed me in our daily sprints—this book wouldn't have been done on time without you.

Jenny, Kristen, and Sue thank you sooooooo much for betaing this baby. I know it was rough, but you guys braved through it and really made this story shine. You guys are my dream team.

To Ashley Estep—my momager, my codependency person, the most amazing PA, I love you. You listened to me bitch and moan about these two for almost a year, thank you for always taking my calls. I promise to always be there when a bat sneaks into your house.

To my mother, who has been helping me with my demanding little spawn so I could meet my deadline—you are the best mom ever.

Zainab, you know I love you; thank you for always making room for the disaster that I am. I promise I will have my shit together by 2025! And Jennifer Mirabelli, who proof-read last minute, you are a gem!!

And to Becca, who always is there to remind me that there is always time, and even when there isn't, it takes away the stress. My wifey, co-write author, and soulmate.

Lastly, to all my wonderful readers. Thank you for reading my books.

Xo
Claudia.

ABOUT THE AUTHOR

Claudia lives in the Chicagoland suburbs. When she's not busy chasing after her adorable little spawn, she's fighting with the characters inside her head.

Claudia writes both sweet and dark romances that will give you all the feels. Her other talents include binge-watching shows on Netflix and eating all kinds of chips.

Want to know more?
    Stay up to date on Facebook
    Join her reader Group: Claudia's Coffee Shop
    Instagram account: @C.Lymari